Meet Me on Mistletoe Lane

Also by Cassie Miller

Meet Me Under the Lights

Meet Me on Mistletoe Lane

BY CASSIE MILLER

VIKING

VIKING
An imprint of Penguin Random House LLC
1745 Broadway, New York, NY 10019
penguinrandomhouse.com

Edited by Dana Leydig
Text set in Perpetua MT Pro

Library of Congress Cataloging-in-Publication Data is available.

First published in the United States of America by Viking, 2026

Manufactured in the United States of America
BVG

ISBN 9798217320356
1st Printing

The authorized representative in the EU for product safety and compliance is Penguin Random House Ireland, Morrison Chambers, 32 Nassau Street, Dublin D02 YH68, Ireland, https://eu-contact.penguin.ie.

For David: my husband, my best friend, and my biggest support. Thank you for watching so many Hallmark Christmas movies with me for the sake of "research."

"Christmas isn't just a day. It's a frame of mind."

—*Miracle on 34th Street*

Chapter One

"When I grow up and get married, I'm living alone."

—HOME ALONE

Thank God for Christmas movies.

Beautiful, cheesy, blissfully predictable Christmas movies.

There was no better fix for holiday burnout, or, in my case, day-to-day burnout.

Most of my friends were lucky if they got to see their relatives once a year, but when your entire family lived in the same town like mine did, it became, well, *a lot*.

It wasn't that our Mancini family gatherings had gotten more outlandish—although Uncle Rick's attempt at spatchcocking the turkey this year and Nona screaming "You're murdering it!" will definitely go down as one of the funniest moments I had ever witnessed.

It was more that I couldn't bounce back from it as quickly as I used to.

I didn't stand and sneer at them Grinch-style, but I did relate to his feelings about the constant noise of it all.

At least he had a literal mountain cave retreat.

Me?

I had an oversize beanbag and cheap noise-canceling Bluetooth headphones.

Had my phone buzzed a few times since I started *Meet Me in St. Louis* an hour and a half ago?

Yep.

Would I answer those messages right now?

Nope.

The only thing that mattered was me and my girl Esther wondering if she should allow John to kiss her.

Sadly, not as relatable for me as the Grinch's sensory disorder.

I didn't earn the nickname "Steadfast G" by spending my time thinking about my next kiss (not that I've ever had anyone really pursue me anyway). It's hard to think about kissing when your family watches your every move and keeps you busy twenty-four seven.

And now that we were officially entering the Christmas season?

Forget about it.

Mistletoe never mattered to the Mancinis—except when Nona was on a mission to hook up my mom with someone in town. But when it came to relationships, my mother and I were definitely two pine cones from the same tree. Don't date anyone in Mullings Creek unless you want the *entire* family involved.

My phone buzzed again, and this time I allowed myself to look down at the screen.

Two missed texts from Jo. One from Sam. One from my cousin Nico. A calendar reminder alert, and a Gmail notification from the Adventure Italy Academy.

The Adventure Italy Academy?!

I sat up quickly, hit pause on my laptop, and then took in a deep breath through my nose, filling my belly the way my little brother Leo taught me, before exhaling through my mouth.

I had applied to the Adventure Italy Academy months ago on a whim, thinking it would be the perfect way to end my senior year of high school. I could immerse myself in the language while visiting all the places Nona and Papa—before he passed—spoke about. And I'd be doing it alone.

No Aunt Helen breathing down my neck, analyzing every color I wore.

No Nona telling me to "eat more" even though I always ate all day every day.

No cousins shouting "proteggi la tua signora!" across our yard from their bedroom windows next door.

Which was totally unnecessary.

No need to "protect my ladyhood" or any other part of me when my dating experience is literally in the negative.

Nope. Just me and Italy.

I would take pictures of anything and everything and then write it all down. My stories would be so front-page newsworthy that Sarah Lawrence would, of course, put me on the staff of *The Phoenix* as a freshman because Steadfast G had become Globetrotter G.

"But first you actually have to get in, Gianna," I said to myself as I remembered I hadn't yet opened the email burning a hole in my inbox.

My fingers hovered over the screen.

I had successfully distracted myself from obsessing over the program for weeks, but now that the answer was finally here, I couldn't bring myself to read it.

Just breathe . . .

I took in another deep breath and released it as I swiped open the alert. No sooner had I read the opening lines of "Congratulations, Gianna Mancini! You have been chosen to study abroad in Italy's . . ." than I leaped out of my beanbag and screamed.

I GOT IN!

I GOT IN?

Oh my God, I can't believe I got in!

I mean, yeah, a small, foolish part of me had *hoped* I would, but come on.

Their acceptance rate made Harvard's look easy.

My head spun with possibilities. In just over a month, I would be on the other side of the Atlantic, taking classes like Ancient Cultures while being a stone's throw away from some of the oldest ruins and landmarks in the world. My notebooks would be filled cover to cover with my adventures, stories so vivid that it'd be like the reader was right there, floating along with me on the Tiber.

I wanted to open my door and shout the news to my mom the way Scrooge shouted "Merry Christmas!" after his visits with three spirits, and I almost did until I remembered Mom wasn't here. She was already in her studio above The Market, working on her new holiday pieces that would be displayed in a couple of days. Everyone else in town was probably there or nearby, too, doing the same thing they did every year the Saturday after Thanksgiving: blasting Christmas music, debating about their window displays and whether or not they needed more twinkle lights (please . . . why would you *not* want more twinkle lights?), and then ultimately asking me for my opinion.

Oh crap. My calendar alert!

I snatched my phone off the floor.

How is it already 11:45?

Nona and the others were expecting me two hours ago to help them get things ready.

I started to FaceTime Mom about the news and let her know I was on the way, and then I stopped. News this big needed to be delivered in person, especially when it was Mom who encouraged me to apply to begin with.

So, ten minutes later, I said goodbye to Esther and John, promising to finish their story after dinner tonight, before I dashed out the door and all but fell onto my bike. Within seconds, I wished I had remembered my earmuffs and a pair of gloves, but I was too late to pedal back home for either. At least my puffy vest would keep part of me warm for the quick ride into town, and the sprawling quiet streets and their charming homes didn't hurt the eyes much either.

Mullings Creek looked like something straight out of a Hallmark movie: a mix of alpine-style cabins and cozy brick bungalows with Victorian-pitched roofs framed by tall trees and pristine fences.

The off-key bells of the local clock tower chimed the hour, and I cursed under my breath.

Nico and Marco would definitely hold this against me. My cousins, who also happened to be twins, loved keeping tallies of my "faults," so they could bring them up in an attempt to distract Nona whenever she started prying into their personal lives. It rarely worked, though.

That woman was as dedicated to meddling as Buddy the Elf was to spreading Christmas cheer.

When I turned onto Mistletoe Lane—our town's Main Street, renamed decades ago when a write-up in the *Post* called Mullings Creek "*the* place to visit if you want the real Christmas experience"—the first request for help arrived. Eve, owner of Eve's Drop, the best and only coffee shop in town, was once again arguing with the owner of the Wanderin' Eats Diner, Phineas, about the proper placement for her light-up snowman.

Every Tudor-style store had one that they adorned with something that represented their brand. Eve's snowman held a to-go coffee cup with her logo on it. Phineas's had a bib with the diner's slogan of GREAT FOOD, GOOD MOOD.

"Gianna! Thank God you're here." Eve adjusted her reindeer antler headband over her short caramel-colored hair before blowing the bangs off her forehead. A light sheen of sweat glistened on her brown skin. "Phineas *Krampus* believes my snowman will block the flow of traffic if I put him to the right of my entrance instead of the left—"

"Everyone puts their snowman on the left and the Holt poinsettias on the right!" Phineas yelled from across the street. His long curly hair was tucked underneath his worn blue baseball cap. If Luke Danes from *Gilmore Girls* had a twin brother, it would be Phineas.

He threw his hands in the air and said, "She knows that but *claims* she's trying to 'shake things up' this year," startling the Salvation Army Santa ringing his bell two stores down.

"What's wrong with shaking things up?" Eve asked, stepping into the street.

Phineas mimicked her, hopping over the curb, leaving his snowman behind. "If it ain't broke, don't fix it, *Evelyn*."

"The only one who calls me Evelyn is my mother, Phineas, and need I remind you that if I so much as whisper to her about you stealing my pie recipe for your diner that she will tell *your* mother?"

Oh snap.

I thought that pie tasted familiar.

"I never stole your recipe." Phineas shoved his hands into his jean pockets. "I may have been . . . inspired by it, though."

Eve pinched the skin above her nose. "Look, I don't enjoy making pies anyway, so why don't I send people your way if they ask for it, and you send them my way for breakfast pastries?"

"That's . . . not a bad idea," Phineas mumbled before going back toward his snowman and propping him to the left of his door.

"Can you believe that guy?" Eve sighed and picked up her snowman and set him to the right, twisting him until he was facing forward. "I mean, to think that moving a snowman to the other side of a door would throw off the whole town's display when we have bigger things to worry about now . . ."

Bigger things?

Like what, keeping Nico away from the eggnog?

I mean, sure, we don't want a repeat of the disastrous ending to last year's Eggnog Chug, but hopefully, he's learned his lesson?

Eve stopped speaking and took a step back, cocking her head to one side and then the other while pursing her lips. "Well, fudge. It does look better on the left."

I laughed and looked over my shoulder at Phineas, who was pretending not to watch her with great interest but doing a horrible job of it. "Will you move it back?" I asked.

"Eventually," she replied, winking. "But I'll let him sweat about it for a few hours. By the way, *love* your earrings. Dana's?" She reached out to touch one of the silver chords with colored gems that looked like a strand of Christmas lights.

"Yep! She made them for me as a thank-you for folding those brochures for Creek Gems." I grabbed my bike and threw my leg over it. "I gotta go find Mom before helping the rest of the fam, so I'll catch you later, okay?"

"Okay, sweetie." Eve took out her phone and began scrolling. "I still can't believe it. I mean, I always assumed he'd outlive us all, but—"

"I gotta go!" I cut her off and sped away.

The last thing I needed to do was stick around for Eve's latest round of gossip.

Besides, whatever she was talking about would catch up with me eventually. Secrets never stayed secret for long in a small town like ours.

Sadly, I only made it a block before I had to help Hal and his son hang the big "Mullings Creek Holly Days" banner across the street near the town square. Normally, the mayor would be here barking out orders about the big Christmas tree and the fence of candy canes that would surround it, but there was no tree, no candy canes, and no mayor to be seen.

Weird.

Mayor Moore was the most punctual person I knew.

After giving the banner the "official Gianna seal of approval,"

I pedaled toward The Market, a big barn-shaped structure with a dark green roof and matching green shutters. My best friend Sam—a paperback book sticking out of his back pocket, as usual—stood near the entrance, one hand holding a cookie, the other steadying a ladder. His friend Isaiah stood several rungs up where he looped lights around the old sign, his sweater rolled up to his elbows of his dark brown arms.

"Fair warning, Mancini," Sam said to me as I propped my bike against the closest light pole. "Marco and Nico are already in there complaining about your being late."

"Tell me something I don't know, Holt," I replied, bumping his shoulder—technically his arm, since he'd decided to grow a foot in the last few months—as I brushed by him.

"Pine trees are one of the oldest living organisms," he said matter-of-factly.

"Already knew that."

"Well did you know that they have male and female—"

"Cones?" I spun around. "Yep. You told me."

Isaiah chuckled from above.

Sam made a face and took a bite of his cookie, spilling a few crumbs on his signature maroon flannel shirt that must've shrunk, because I didn't remember Sam having such a broad chest the last time I saw him. Not that I ogled my best friend's chest or anything.

Okay, maybe sometimes.

Truthfully, part of me might've always had a small crush on him.

At six feet tall, with fiery red hair, and always in jeans and a button-up, Sam was the textbook definition of an eighteen-year-old lumberjack.

He swiped his hand over his shirt. "Glad to see someone actually hears me around here, then."

"Oh we all *hear* you, Sam. We just don't always *listen*." I stuck out my tongue and darted inside, laughing at the sound of what was likely the last piece of his cookie hitting the doorframe behind me.

The Market looked exactly as I predicted it would: organized Christmas chaos. Sam's parents stood on the stage rotating the new trees from their farm so the best side was facing forward, while several townspeople attempted to untangle their white lights. Others were already behind their stands, setting up their merchandise and weekend sales signs. A few waved at me as I passed by, but their smiles seemed forced, almost sad.

Which was strange.

Shouldn't they be happier about the start of our busiest and most successful season of the year?

Marco and Nico stood near the center of the room underneath the big mason-jar chandelier, yelling at their mom, my Aunt Helen, to get off the ladder and "let someone younger hang the garland this year."

That someone would likely be me, as it had been for the last few years, even though they all knew I hated the unsteady wobbliness of ladders.

A blur of green charged me from the side, and I grunted as the gangly legs of my brother Leo wrapped around my mine. "Where have you been?" he asked, out of breath. "Everyone's—"

"Looking for me?" I tousled his dark brown wavy hair that matched my own. "Yeah, I know."

"No, Gianna, not that."

I carefully peeled him off me and crouched down, laughing at the smear of chocolate around his mouth. "Were you in Ms. Louisa Mae's chocolate-covered pretzels again? You know they make you crash hard."

"I only had a few." He smiled mischievously, his blue eyes bright.

"Well, don't eat anymore. Mom will freak." I stood and motioned toward the stairs. "Is she up there?"

Leo nodded, wiping his mouth with his sleeve and then frowning at the stain. "Aren't we going to, you know, talk about it?"

Talk about what, my trip to Italy in less than two months? "The only thing I need to talk about right now is something with Mom, bud. I'll catch you later." I patted his head one last time before running over to the stairs, ignoring my cousins who called out to me as I passed them.

"But, Gianna!" Leo's voice carried over the chatter and sleigh bells being taken out for the tree decorations.

"Not now, Leo!" I yelled back, skipping the first couple of stairs to go up to Mom's studio. She and I had so much planning to do, and I hadn't even started a packing list yet because I didn't want to get my hopes up. What was the temperature in Italy like this time of year, anyway?

"You can't go up there!" his voice screamed, making me stop mid-step.

I sighed and braced myself against the railing, already draped with fresh greens. "Okay, I give up. Why can't I go up there?"

Marco, wearing his favorite hockey jersey that was ripped in three places, scooped Leo up and put him on his broad shoulders like he weighed nothing. "Because your mom, my mom, Nona, the mayor, and a bunch of other people are up there having a meeting about . . ." He paused, then whispered, "Mr. Paxton."

Mr. Paxton?

Why were they meeting about the owner of The Market?

I adjusted the spacing of the decorations as I descended the stairs and then snapped my fingers. "He forgot to turn off the sink and flooded the back kitchen again, didn't he?" I laughed and snorted once before I realized no one else was laughing.

In fact, everyone had stopped what they were doing to stare at me.

Even the Christmas music on the old record player had started skipping.

What the heck was going on?

"You mean you haven't heard?" Marco said, stepping around a few open boxes on the old wood floor.

"Heard what?" I asked, semi-regretting that I didn't stick around for a cup of coffee and Eve's gossip.

"Mr. Paxton died, G." Marco lowered Leo to the ground before leaning in closer to me, his tight curls bouncing as he did. "He was . . . killed."

I gasped, putting my hands in front of my mouth. "*Killed?* By what? Or who?"

I mean, sure, I had always wished for something scandalous or exciting to happen here that I could write about, but this? Mr. Paxton? I'd never wish for something like that.

And then Marco rubbed the back of his neck and whispered three words that changed my town forever: "A runaway piano."

Chapter Two

"How could it get any worse? Take a look around you, Ellen! We're at the threshold of hell!"

—NATIONAL LAMPOON'S CHRISTMAS VACATION

You know that scene in *Home Alone* where Kevin's family is scrambling, panicked, through the airport? Or the one where he uses aftershave and slaps his hands on his cheeks and screams?

Yeah.

Hold my cocoa, Kevin.

Marco's words quickly launched everyone into a frenzy as if they had forgotten about Mr. Paxton's death and all suddenly remembered. Sam's mom dropped a box of ornaments on the stage, and the ones that didn't break rolled away onto the floor like they were attempting to flee the scene. Aunt Helen reached too far to her left and was airborne, screaming, for a moment before she grabbed the garland on the chandelier and then dropped into Nico's large, outstretched arms. And my only female cousin, Bianca, tripped over a messy pile of Christmas lights, making her toss an entire stack of used books into the air, which then landed on her splayed-out body.

Thankfully, they were small mass-market editions.

Leo cupped his hands over his ears and immediately sat down before drawing his knees up to his chest.

Sam appeared out of nowhere and crouched down next to him, using his finger to slowly write numbers on his back—a grounding technique we all used to help Leo when his sensory disorder overwhelmed him. "G, where do you keep his headphones?" Sam asked.

"I've got a pair under Mom's table display over there." I jumped off the last two stairs and sprinted across the floor. Within seconds I gently positioned Leo's blue noise-canceling headphones over his ears and sat down next to him.

Instinctively, I placed my hand on Leo's back near Sam's, our fingers touching as we both did four-count breaths in and out until Leo joined us and took over.

"Well, that was . . . unexpected," Sam whispered over Leo's head.

"Everyone crashing out, or Leo?" I whispered back.

"Um, yes." He smiled, and his freckles crinkled around his nose. "Want me to take him outside to cool off a bit?" He pulled out his book. "I can introduce him to *The Swiss Family Robinson*."

I nodded. "Thank you. I'll—"

"G, do something!" Nico called out from the other side of the room.

Ugh. Why does it always have to be me?

I took a quick survey of the room, which still looked like a Christmas war zone, as Sam stood and helped Leo up before offering me his hand to do the same. I stretched onto my tiptoes to ruffle Sam's red floppy hair like I always did, but he surprised me by catching my wrist. His brown eyes twinkled mischievously as he smirked.

My eyes trailed slowly over his face.

His bright, windburned cheeks.

And lips clearly chapped from the cold and sun . . .

"Gianna!" Nico called for me again.

Sam and I jumped apart, severing whatever strange new energy had just settled between us.

Strange . . . but interesting.

By the time I reached the microphone, Mr. and Mrs. Holt had stepped off the stage and were chasing the escaped ornaments around the floor. Aunt Helen was sitting on the bottom rung of the ladder, sipping a cup of water as Marco berated her about being reckless, and Nico had all but unburied Bianca from the pile of books.

The rest of the room was still shouting and throwing their hands up the way my family did when they spoke. Nona liked to tease that we Mancinis helped everyone in Mullings Creek find their inner Italian.

I tapped the mic, but it didn't work, so I tried clapping my hands a few times the way my dad used to in his classroom.

Still chaos.

I cupped my hands around my mouth, and shouted, "Hey!"

No change.

Well, at least Leo won't be bothered by this. I put my two pointer fingers in my mouth and let out an ear-piercing whistle. The room froze and turned to stare at me again.

Oh, shoot.

Now what?

Giving a pep talk to the town after finding out one of its oldest members was run down by a piano was not on my to-do list today.

"Hey, everyone." I cleared my throat. "I . . . um, well, I know we're all a bit upset right now about the timing of this—"

"Upset?" Phineas shouted from the doorway. "Upset? Holly Days starts next week."

"She knows that." Eve pushed by him, entering The Market. "Everyone knows that, Phineas. Christmas is always our busiest time of year."

"But we've already bought the prizes for the games and booked a band for the Mistletoe Masquerade!" Dana added from her booth near the Holts'. "We can't get that money back."

"Why would we need to get that money back?" I asked, putting my hand above my eyes so I could see everyone better under the lights.

"This place literally hosts most of the events in town. We can't have Holly Days if we don't have The Market, G," Marco said. "And we don't have a Market without Mr. Paxton."

"Whoa, wait a minute," I replied, but the room had already started buzzing with noise again. Within seconds, the volume rose with "what-ifs" from every corner of the place.

"What about the Reindeer Games—"

"Movie Night in The Market—"

"I can't open my own store to sell this stuff—"

The door to Mom's studio on the second floor opened and a bunch of people filed out, hurrying down the stairs with my mom, who had more paint on her hands than on her apron. Nona, Mom, and Sam's Gram joined me on the stage.

Mom hugged me from behind. "Hey, sweetie. Sorry I didn't see you this morning before coming here. Any word yet on Italy?"

Ha.

I *would* receive word about something I had been obsessing over for months on the same day the literal floor of our town was being ripped out from under us.

"No," I lied to her. "Nothing yet."

Now was definitely not the time.

Nona's whistle pierced the air, making everyone stop the way mine had.

She stepped forward, her braided silver bun sparkling like tinsel under the spotlights, and propped both of her hands on her hips. She called it her "non scherzare" or "don't mess with me" stance. Nona may have only been five feet two and barely over one hundred pounds, but the woman always commanded the attention of a room simply by walking into it.

Goals.

She flipped a switch on the microphone, easily turning it on.

Well, now I feel like an idiot.

"Everyone needs to settle down," she said. "I know the . . . passing of Mr. Paxton is unexpected and, well, terrible."

"Heartbreaking," Sam's Gram added.

"Sì, heartbreaking," Nona said while nodding in agreement. "But Arthur Paxton was a smart man. He wouldn't want to leave this place"—she paused and motioned to the room—"or any of us in any distress over the future of our businesses. So you see it is va bene. Okay. Right, Mayor?"

Mayor David Moore, who looked suspiciously like he was on his way out of the side exit, froze and whirled around. "Of course!" he said, his voice cracking. "I'm sure it'll all be okay. I just need to, um, run to Town Hall to check on the status of some of his affairs, and then, I'll, uh . . ."

"Send us a message?" Sam's Gram finished for him.

"Yes!" Mayor Moore clapped his hands. "A message. I'll do that. Soon." And with that, he disappeared through the door, the echo of it slamming shut bouncing around the room.

Um, if the mayor literally runs away from the problem, it doesn't seem to me like "it'll all be okay . . ."

"All right, so let's all get back to work. We have lots to do!" Nona added before turning toward the rest of us on the stage.

"A runaway piano," Gram mumbled, rubbing her forehead.

"How awful." Her eyes looked more shaded and tired than usual.

"How exactly *does* a piano run away?" I asked.

"The wheels were not locked, apparently." Nona adjusted one of the pins in her silver hair and shook her head. "That moving company better be held responsible."

"Agreed, Silvia—" Gram started coughing and pulled a lacy handkerchief out of her embroidered cardigan pocket. Nona stepped around me and placed a hand tenderly on her best friend's shoulder as her coughing fit subsided.

"Let's get you home and out of the cold, Suzie," she said to Gram, who nodded in agreement.

The two of them looped arms, the way they always did, before walking slowly down the stairs of the stage, Gram's long skirt billowing around her ankles as Nona's bracelets jingled against her wrists.

Later that evening, Mom brought me a mug of tea where I sat on the front porch steps. The night was still and quiet except for the occasional breeze that wove through bare trees lining our short driveway.

"Your dad used to love these kinds of temps," Mom said as she draped a quilt over both of our shoulders.

I smiled over the tiny pinch I felt in my heart every time I thought of him. "'Cool enough for a fire but not too cold to sit outside for a bit.' He loved to say that." I took a sip of my tea and immediately felt better. Mom always knew the perfect portion of honey and lemon to add to chamomile.

"I went by the cemetery early this morning." She pulled the quilt tighter around us. "Someone had placed a white poinsettia by his stone. It looked lovely."

Sam.

His family grew the most beautiful poinsettias. It seemed like everyone took turns replacing the flowers on Dad's grave since his funeral years ago. Even the high school where he had taught for over twenty years regularly donated plants from their greenhouse.

Dad had been that kind of teacher—the one everyone thought of as their own parent—so much in fact, that his nickname "Pop" was etched as part of his name on his marble headstone.

"I miss him, especially around Christmas." I rested my head on her shoulder and inhaled her familiar scent of oil paint and eucalyptus.

"Me too." She leaned her head on mine, wisps of her graying hair brushing my forehead. "He'd be proud of you and Leo. You two are so smart and strong."

Strength.

Something told me I'd need a lot of it in the coming weeks.

"Mom?" I said.

She turned her face so her lips brushed my hair. "Yeah?"

I swallowed over a lump in my throat. "I got in. To Adventure Italy . . . I got in."

Mom jumped back, making the quilt fall from her shoulder. "Oh my gosh, Gianna!" She wrapped her arms around me and squeezed me tightly. "I knew you could do it. I knew you'd get in! What a wonderful early Christmas present!" She kissed both of my cheeks.

I looked down at my tea. "Is it, though?"

Mom touched my cheek. "What do you mean?"

The wind moved the chimes on our porch into their low bell tones and rattled some of the icicle lights against the gutter.

"How can I think about leaving after . . ." I paused and sniffed, my eyes now burning. "After everything that happened with Mr. Paxton? What's going to happen to everyone if I just disappear, and we lose The Market—"

"Gianna." Mom laid her hand on mine. "That's not for you to worry about."

I wiped my eyes. "What kind of person just runs off to Italy while half the people in her hometown, including some of her own family, could lose everything? Who's going to make sure things don't fall apart?"

"No one has lost anything yet. And besides, this town was taking care of itself long before you started offering to help everyone." Mom scooted in closer and wrapped herself in the quilt again. "It's officially Christmas season, honey. Know what that means?"

The absolute worst time for this kind of thing to happen?

"It's the best time of year to have hope and take big risks." She nudged me.

I took another sip of my tea before setting it down and resting my head on Mom's shoulder again.

I wanted to believe her.

To celebrate this big win for me.

But for the first time in my life, I wasn't so sure that Christmas could fix all of my problems.

Chapter Three

"Am I just eating because I'm bored?"

—HOW THE GRINCH STOLE CHRISTMAS

Everyone moved slowly Monday morning after the unexpected passing of Mr. Paxton. I always assumed he had family out of town or that maybe he visited for the holidays, but apparently, Arthur Paxton had been completely alone. Never married. No siblings. And both parents had already passed.

My family was often the definition of suffocating, but I couldn't imagine not having them.

Who had he opened presents with on Christmas Day?

Who had called him for his birthday?

Would I be lonely like that when I was overseas for a few months?

And what would everyone think of me if I just up and left?

"G?" My best friend Jo tapped my desk with her pencil during second period. She wore one of her many Christmas bandannas—this one was red with green and white snowflakes—tied over her honey-blond hair, which spilled into the hood of her *Stranger Things* sweatshirt. "You okay? Seemed like we lost you for a sec there."

I pinched the bridge of my nose before forcing a smile. "Yeah, I'm good. Just . . . a lot on my mind."

"Same." Jo leaned back in her chair and sighed. "My dads were saying that Mr. Paxton owed a lot in taxes on The Market, and they didn't know how that would be handled now that he's . . ."

Gone.

I opened my latest article about the new food company our school had outsourced to. The quality of the food wasn't bad, but their servings were half of what we used to get, and at double the cost. I'd probably get an earful from our assistant principal, who was our school paper's sponsor, but news was news.

"How's your column coming on last week's game?" I asked her.

"Almost done," she said. "I'll be happy when their season is over. Basketball is *so* not my sport. Can't wait to write about soccer in a few months."

I chuckled. "Easy to write about a sport you kick ass in."

She smiled. "Precisely."

When the bell rang a few minutes later, we packed up and walked toward the front of the school to meet up with Sam before heading toward Government.

"Are you coming over to Nona's later for Mr. Paxton's reception?" I asked her. "Mom can give you a ride if you need one.

She said she'd be coming straight from the studio. Apparently, she's got a painting to finish while she waits for some new pieces firing in her kiln."

"Cool. I'll text my dads." She stopped and refilled her water bottle at the fountain. "Do we have to dress, like, nice for something like this?"

"I don't think so." I adjusted my book bag strap on my shoulder and waved to Sam, who stood chatting with Isaiah at the end of the hallway. "Nona just said 'come hungry.' "

Jo scoffed. "As if that would stop her from shoving food down my throat." She held her hands up the way Nona did and spoke with an over-the-top Italian accent. "Buon Dio, Josephine Collins! You are-ah so thin that Marco could-ah pick you up with-ah one finger."

I threw my hands up and added, "Stai scherzadno! Are you kidding me?"

Isaiah raised his eyebrows. "Something wrong?"

"Just doing our best Nona." I pulled out a nut-free granola bar from the side pocket of my book bag and opened it, offering Sam half before he could ask.

"Grazie," he replied with a far better accent than Jo. "Did you guys do the homework?"

Jo and I stopped short. "Homework?" we asked.

He winked and ran a hand through his floppy hair.

"Hilarious." I smacked his arm.

Whoa.

Did the Holt family buy him a gym membership or something?

"Gianna." Sam snapped his fingers in front of my face. "Can I have my arm back, please?"

My hand was still gripping the spot below his shoulder. *Oops*. I let go. "Sorry. All yours."

Isaiah made a face, but before I could decipher its meaning, sleigh bells suddenly sounded behind us, and the boys pulled Jo and me out of the way of an oncoming caravan of students wearing Santa hats. Each of them carried fliers, probably for the upcoming Mistletoe Masquerade Ball.

"Oh man." Sam sighed. "I forgot that the Santagrams will start tomorrow."

Santagrams were the way people in Mullings Creek High asked each other to the ball. Starting the first day of December, anyone could interrupt a class (as long as there wasn't a test in progress) with a gram. Theater kids did the best ones with the most festive costumes, but most students held up signs with corny Christmas rhymes or riddles during lunch or in between classes.

Since none of us ever had a serious relationship—outside of Jo's four-month stint with Douchebag Darren—she, Sam, Isaiah, and I would usually skip the ball and watch Christmas movies at someone's house instead.

"Maybe since we're seniors, we should go this year?" Jo offered as we entered Mr. Bennington's classroom. We all grabbed a folded-up piece of paper from his fishbowl; each had a short current event and a reflective question that we were supposed to "think about" before class began so we could have a discussion after the tardy bell rang.

"I mean, other than the ball and prom, that's it, right?" Jo continued.

I froze.

Prom.

I completely forgot that I'd be missing my senior prom by going overseas next semester. Not that I was a big dance person. I didn't go to my junior prom last year, but still.

I swallowed hard. "Yeah, maybe we should."

Isaiah settled in his seat up front as we three moved closer to the back.

"Like as a group thing?" Sam lifted his eyes off his Chromebook and settled them on me. "Or with a date?"

Hold up.

Did he just say *with a date*?

Like a *date* date?

Where we'd get each other corsages and pose awkwardly in front of our families?

Oh, sweet Jesus, my family would go full-on Whoville for that.

Aunt Sofia would 100 percent have a photo booth set up at the B&B for us.

Uncle Gabe and Uncle Leo would undoubtedly act out scenes from *The Godfather.*

And Marco and Nico?

Forget about it.

But despite all that, the idea of walking down my stairs in a gorgeous dress and then opening the door to a smiling Sam did sound a bit exciting.

Jo cleared her throat and looked at the two of us, biting back a smile. "I guess we should just wait and see how the season unfolds."

Sam and I both broke eye contact at the same time, but my head still spun dizzily with questions until I remembered I hadn't yet told either of them about my acceptance into the Adventure Italy Academy.

Four-thousand-plus miles was a long way away.

Sure, Jo and I would have college together, but what about Sam?

He was staying here in Mullings Creek after graduation.

We had been friends for over a decade, but was that really enough to carry us through a semester abroad *and* me leaving for college soon after?

Later that evening, most of the town showed up with food at Nona's. I loved her brick house. In some ways it felt more like home than mine. It was small, but it never seemed that way. Walking through her front door gave the impression of going back in time, especially during the holidays.

Her entryway was a short hallway that had a long coatrack against the wall where my Papa's old jackets still hung. I used to love disappearing behind them during hide-and-seek with my cousins. Even after he passed, they still smelled like him: cinnamon and tobacco. Her scratched oak floors creaked in every room, especially near the doorways, and the braided rug near her wood-burning fireplace still had singe marks from an incident years ago involving the twins and a flaming marshmallow Leo had named Toastie.

The kitchen always smelled like homemade pasta sauce and meatballs, the pink-tiled bathrooms with her fluffy towels like her fabric softener, and the living room like old books and, during this time of year, fresh pine from her Christmas tree.

Mom and my dad and his siblings tried to get Nona to "update the place" more than once, but she and Papa always waved them away. They said every scratch, burn, and creak was a memory they didn't want to forget, a lesson they had learned.

And oh boy, had our town learned some lessons over at Nona's, too.

Like how you always took off your shoes in the front hallway unless you wanted to dust all the creepy antique dolls in the basement.

Or if you wanted Chianti during the winter, you'd find it outside her kitchen door because "the winter air is the best way to chill a bottle."

Or how you should never challenge Marco to a Ping-Pong match unless you were Jo.

And how you shouldn't waste your time asking for one of

Nona's recipes because she didn't have any, and the ones she did were more like "guidelines."

Tonight, we had set up multiple card tables for the food, and folding chairs in her office off the kitchen and in the living room for additional seating. Thirty or so different conversations were happening simultaneously, some about the holidays and upcoming events in town, but most were about Mr. Paxton and the future of The Market. Leo stood in the center of it all, yapping it up with the adults as if he were one of them.

My little brother didn't like loud, unexpected noises, but he did love chatting with adults—especially more than with kids his own age. He just didn't get their sense of humor, and his big heart was never keen on the way his classmates liked to tease each other. Leo played it off like it was no big deal, but a part of me always worried about him finding "his person" before I left for college.

Or now, before I ran away to another country.

Sam and I sat in front of the living room fireplace, eating our third helping of my Uncle Rick's famous cannoli. I was just adding a few more to-dos in the notes app on my phone when Jo came in with a plate piled high with meatballs.

"I don't know how you guys do it," she said to me as she sat down on the braided rug and crossed her legs.

"Do what?" I asked, mouth full of the whipped ricotta cheese mixture and chocolate chips.

God, these taste like heaven.

"Pay attention to anything when there's like a million conversations going on at once." She popped a meatball into her mouth and sighed happily.

Sam stole one off her plate before she could swat his hand away, and then said, "Just think like an oscillating fan, Jo."

"A what?" she asked.

"An oscillating fan." He set down his now-empty dessert plate. "You just kinda scan the room like this." He paused and turned his head slowly to the left. "And then swing it right back. You know, like a fan."

Jo tried it and stopped midway. "Doesn't that hurt your neck after a while?"

"Yep," I chimed in. "Dad used to say it was the reason most Italians, at least in his family, had arthritis in their necks. Too much back-and-forth movement to keep up."

"That checks out." Jo rubbed hers and stared at her plate. "Why am I even eating? I'm not hungry."

Literally, the story of my whole life.

Sam reached for it. "I'll take it."

Jo moved the plate away. "I never said I *wouldn't* eat it. Just that I forget I should fast before coming here."

She turned to me and paused mid-bite. "Is it true that your Aunt Sofia had an uncle whose hair turned white overnight?"

"Yep," I said, picking at one of the stains on the rug. "But it didn't happen because he ate tainted scallops, like she claims.

He probably had an autoimmune disorder. Or at least, that's what Leo says." Leo loved going on deep dives with research when the inexplicable happened.

"Interesting." Jo ate her last two meatballs and then stood. "I'm going to go eavesdrop on Mayor Moore. He's on his third cup of Eve's spiked eggnog, so he should start spilling some tea about The Market. Be right back."

Sam yawned and stretched his legs in front of him. "Mom and Dad were talking today about opening up a farm stand on our property to sell plants and herbs."

"Instead of The Market?" I set my empty plate down. "Why?"

"Well, if The Market closes or gets turned into something else, they'll need to sell their stuff somewhere—"

"But you guys live at the edge of town." I turned to face him. "We wouldn't see each other—" I stopped and forced a cough at my slipup. "I mean, Nona wouldn't get to see Gram as much."

Smooth, G.

The corner of his mouth pulled up ever so slightly. "I said the same thing to them," he added quickly, rubbing his chin. "But I don't know what other options we have if it closes."

"*If.*" I nudged him. "We can stay positive." *For now.*

"I'll try." He smiled and then clapped. "You wanna go get a couple bottles of water or something?"

"Sure."

He stood first and then held out his hand to pull me up, but

I must've kept my legs crossed for too long because one of my feet had fallen asleep. No sooner had I stood than I stumbled into him.

"Whoa, easy there, Mouse." His hands quickly found my waist to steady me. "Did you sneak some of Eve's eggnog, too?" The corner of his mouth inched up in a smirk.

"No. My foot fell asleep." I tried putting weight on it but only felt thousands of pinpricks. "And 'Mouse'? Seriously? I *have* grown since fifth grade, Sam."

He took a step back, motioning from the top of my head to his chest. "Not much."

When I tried to smack him, my silver claddagh ring flew off my finger and landed on the floor beneath Nona's small ceramic Christmas tree. The ring was a gift from Sam's Gram from a few Christmases ago and had always been a little big, despite my attempts at wrapping thread around it.

Sam walked across the room and brought it back for me. "Right hand?"

I nodded and held out my hand, thinking he would just drop the ring into it.

But he didn't.

His callused fingers were normally rough and dry from years of working on his family farm, but right now, as he slid the ring back onto my finger, they felt soft, gentle.

I knew these hands, every scar and freckle on them.

So why was his touch now sending zips of electricity through my wrist, numbing it the same way my sleepy foot felt just a moment ago?

"Heart out, right?" he asked, his voice rough as he let go.

"Right." I flexed my hand at my side, but the humming feeling didn't go away.

Heart out.

Because I was definitely not in a relationship.

And I definitely hadn't thought about starting one with my best friend, who was still standing far too close to me.

Just a momentary lapse of judgment from too many rom-com holiday movies.

And stupid Santagrams.

Sam opened his mouth to say something, but then Jo ran into the room with a half-eaten slice of Italian bread in her hands. "Guys, guys! You will never guess what I just heard by the eggnog."

Chapter Four

"You smell like beef and cheese. You don't smell like Santa."

—ELF

"How could he not have a will?" Sam asked the next day for the hundredth time since Jo dropped the bomb after eavesdropping at Nona's. He laid his tray onto the round table in the cafeteria and sat across from me, rolling up the sleeves of his green sweater before he pulled his latest book—*Fahrenheit 451*—out of his back pocket.

"Well, I mean, he was pretty old and alone. Maybe he just didn't think about leaving anything to anyone." I reached across the table and snagged the tomatoes out of Sam's salad at the same time that he grabbed the carrots out of mine, and tried not to think about how good he looked in that sweater.

To be fair, most guys looked hot in cable-knit.

Which was entirely unfair, considering they already held the monopoly on flannel and hoodies, too.

"Are you going to eat all of that?" Jo pointed to his tray, which was covered with mashed potatoes, steak, gravy, three rolls, and a side salad.

"It's steak and gravy day," he said matter-of-factly before adding ranch to his salad and closing the box to mix it up. "But seriously, Paxton owned a place half the people in town rented for their small businesses. He didn't think to make a plan?"

I sighed and started picking pieces off my roll, suddenly not very hungry. "I dunno. But we can't do anything about it now."

"Except worry about a hoity-toity lawyer from the city coming in to sell it off in pieces," he said before shoveling in a heaping forkful of potatoes.

Jo snorted. "'Hoity-toity'? What are you, seventy years old, Sam?"

He rolled his eyes. "Whatever. I just have a bad feeling about this. Like . . . everything's about to change."

Ha. Understatement of the year.

"Is that really such a bad thing?" Jo leaned back in her chair. "Maybe this big-city lawyer will bring a little life back to this town. Switch things up a bit."

"What needs to be switched?" I asked.

Isaiah sat down at our table with his tray. "And what do you mean *life*? Town's doing fine." He swatted at Sam's hand, which was reaching to take a roll.

Jo started counting on her fingers as she listed things. "The clock tower's been broken for years. Phineas never changes his menu at the diner. The 'new books' display at the library is about three years old, and most of the Holly Days stuff is the stuff we do every single Christmas."

"What's wrong with what we do for Christmas?" I asked. I loved the Holly Days traditions and how they hadn't changed in over a decade.

Just like Christmas movies, it didn't matter that you knew what was coming.

You always watched them because the familiar brought you joy.

True, we hadn't drawn as big of a crowd the last couple of seasons, but Nona said that most people just preferred to shop online rather than with small businesses in person. It was probably happening in other small towns, too.

Right?

"Nothing is wrong with Christmas in Mullings Creek," Jo said, patting my arm. "I'm just saying maybe this is the year we do things a little . . . differently."

"It would definitely look and feel *different* without The Market at the center of it all," Isaiah said between bites of mashed potatoes. "I don't see a Trader Joe's or Starbucks fitting in here, do you?"

No, not at all.

That scene from *A Charlie Brown Christmas* about his own dog going "commercial" flashed in my head, and my heart felt a pang of sadness.

We stayed quiet for a moment before Sam spoke up. "I can't speak to what will take the place of The Market, but my dad did let slip who's taking Mr. Paxton's job as Santa." Sam set his fork down and took a swig of his milk. "Hal volunteered to do it."

"Hal?" I accidentally yelled, making a few tables in the cafeteria look our way. I lowered my voice to an almost whisper. "He can't be Santa. He smells like . . . like rust and stale bread and WD-40!"

They all laughed before Jo spoke. "He does not, G. And anyway, he doesn't have to *smell* like Mr. Paxton did to be Santa."

Yeah, but it wouldn't hurt. Since Mr. Paxton smelled like peppermint year-round.

The bell rang for lunch to end, and we all stood and moved toward the exit.

"Like I said"—Sam banged his tray against the trash can before setting it on the counter to be cleaned—"I've got a bad feeling about all of this."

Much as I hate to admit it, you and me both.

Later, during study hall—my last period of the day—I ran errands for the main office, one of which led me to the Shop classroom, delivering mail to Mr. Hernandez. Sam waved me over to his table as he switched off his sander and lifted his goggles onto his hair.

"What do you think of this plant stand?" he asked me as he held up a beautiful corner stand with six rounded tiers.

"I love it." I ran my hand over the smooth finish. "Is this for your parents?"

"Kind of." He took off his gloves and set the stand onto the floor in between us. "I was thinking of making a few pieces for my parents to sell during the springtime. Mr. Hernandez said he'd order some wicker strips, so I could learn how to make some baskets as well. Maybe some small pieces of furniture."

"That's a great idea!"

"Thanks." He rubbed the back of his neck. "Just trying to figure out the best way I can help them."

"You already help them out plenty." Sam helped everyone, in fact.

I may have been "Steadfast G," but Sam seemed to know what people needed even before they knew it themselves, and if you made a big deal about it, he'd just brush it off. He was as eager to please as a golden retriever but ten times quieter about it.

I reached across the stand to wipe sawdust off his shoulder and immediately drew my hand back because the same zippy feeling happened again.

What the heck was wrong with me?

He lifted the plant stand back onto the table. "I just hope it's enough."

"It is." I shook my hand at my side but the feeling lingered. "You can only do so much, Sam."

"Ha. Look who's talking." He grinned.

"I'm just usually in the right place at the right time."

"*Or* they wait until you're around to ask you for help. Like Eve did this morning with her plumbing issue."

How did he hear about that? "I was there with Uncle Gabe and Hal when they installed that sink!"

"So why didn't she call them?" He crossed his arms over his chest.

"Because . . ." *Did his forearms always do that when he rolled his sleeves up?* I blinked fast. "Because . . . she knew I was coming in for my Tuesday morning peppermint latte. Okay. *Okay*, she waited for me."

He smiled like he'd won whatever standoff we were in before the classroom door flew open. In skipped a group of basketball players dressed in their jerseys, elf shoes, and those little elf hats with the fake pointy ears.

"Oh great, another one," Sam mumbled, running his hand down the side of his face. "I just don't understand it."

"The big gestures?" I asked.

"Big gestures I get." He pulled the goggles off his head. "But the whole making-a-fool-of-yourself-in-public thing? I don't know. It's like if you don't go big *and* it's not caught on someone's phone, then it never happened. Why can't it just be about the two people involved and not about the number of likes, y'know?"

Fair. But in all honesty, I didn't really mind these kinds of things. Watching someone go all out to profess their feelings to someone they cared about, while making it Christmassy? That was some Hallmark aura.

And I was a sucker for a big romantic gesture.

Unless my cousins were nearby.

Then I'd rather eat gum off a subway pole.

After the elfish basketball guys sang a rendition of "Jingle Bells" with a horribly rhymed Masquerade Ball proposal thrown in, a very red-faced May shouted, "Yes!" The entire room erupted into cheers until Mr. Hernandez shooed the elves away.

Sam leaned against the table. "So, ironically, I've been thinking about the Mistletoe Masquerade."

"I thought you didn't dance?" *At least that's what you've always told me.*

And Nona, anytime she's tried pushing us together at parties.

"I dance."

I made a face.

"Just haven't found the right partner, I guess," he added in almost a whisper.

Oh.

My heartbeat thrummed faster like it did when I had one of Eve's espressos. "What about the mistletoe?"

His eyes snapped up to mine. "What about it?"

"I mean . . . you hate it, right? You really want to go to an event named after a plant you despise?"

"I don't *despise* it; I just don't think an invasive species should get all the glory at Christmas. It should belong to—"

"Douglas firs." I had heard this speech from him at least a dozen times over the years.

"Exactly." He beamed and then cleared his throat. "But I do

feel like maybe Jo has a good point about us being seniors and how it's our last one—"

"Well, that's not entirely true." I stuck my hand, which still felt a bit tingly, into the back pocket of my jeans. "The ball is open to everyone in town, since it's held at The Market."

"Yeah, but who knows if it'll still happen after this year." He sighed. "Everything seems so up in the air right now."

In so many more ways than you could possibly know, Sam.

I still hadn't told him or Jo about the Adventure Italy Academy. Technically, I hadn't even confirmed with the travel group that I would be going. It just didn't feel right to say anything. Not yet.

"So . . ." I swallowed, trying to process what my best friend might actually be proposing. "You're telling me you *want* to go to the ball now?" I asked him.

He dropped his gaze to his boots. "I mean, only if you . . . erm, you guys planned on going. Or something."

I had only ever seen Sam in jeans, except for the occasional "nice outfit" for holiday church services. The thought of him wearing dress pants and a tie made my stomach do unexpected flip-flops.

Wait.

What was I doing?

Sam was my best friend. I wasn't supposed to think those kinds of things or feel all those fizzy bubbles around him. If he and I changed, if we both took that leap, it could totally ruin the friendship.

Could I really take that risk? What if it didn't work out?

Would we be able to go back to being just friends?

Or worse: What if one of us could but the other couldn't?

The thought of not having Sam in my life filled me with such a hollow, cold emptiness that it made it hard to breathe.

Slow down, G.

He probably didn't even think of me that way.

He had mentioned both me and Jo when he spoke about the dance, so clearly it would be a group thing.

Right?

A text alert chimed all around us in the shop. Normally, no one would take out their phone to check a message during class since the state banned cell phone use in schools, but if we all got a message at the same time, then it must've come from the same place.

The Mullings Creek Remind App.

And sure enough, the notification on my lock screen proved me right.

Emergency Meeting at Town Hall Tonight. 7 PM.

Chapter Five

"Faith is believing in things when common sense tells you not to."

—MIRACLE ON 34TH STREET

Tourists often said that Mullings Creek felt like a trip back in time to when things were "slower" and "more meaningful." That our small town was like something out of a movie, especially during the winter holiday season. Maybe it was our wreaths and garlands on every light pole, or the white twinkle lights draped over two dozen bare crepe myrtles lining both sides of the street, or the warm Christmas displays unique to each shop in their front windows. Whatever the reason, we knew how to really shine during the month of December.

But the one place that didn't have the same coziness was always Town Hall. Yes, it had wreaths on its two wooden front doors, and sure, the poinsettias from Sam's family looked great lining the walk up to those doors, but inside, it felt like a scary doctor's office.

Bare.

Cold.

Sterile.

Definitely not the place I wanted to be to hear the fate of my favorite place in town.

By the time Mom, Leo, and I showed up, most of the metal folding chairs in the assembly hall were filled.

"Gianna! Alice! Over here!" My Aunt Helen stood on a chair and waved her arms wildly above her head. "We saved you seats!"

"My God, woman! Do you have a death wish?" Her husband—my Uncle Rick—tugged on her arm. "Stop standing on things!"

Aunt Helen frowned at him and then stepped down as we reached the front row where, sure enough, three open seats sat between Nona and my Aunt Sofia. Sam and his family waved from the row behind mine, Sam high-fiving Leo as he passed him before going back to reading.

Nona placed her hand on mine and squeezed it as I sat down. "Ciao, cara," she said to me before leaning forward and adding "Ciao, cuoricciolo" to Leo.

Nona had been calling me "my dear" and Leo "little heart" for as long as I could remember. I kissed her warm cheek and smiled at the familiar scent of her Neutrogena face wash. "Buonasera, Nona."

She tipped her head to the side. "Your Italiano has gotten much better, Gianna. Have you been practicing?"

I held up my thumb and pointer finger with just a bit of space in between them. "Un po'," I admitted. Sadly, my streak in Duolingo ended about a week ago when I passed out after my tryptophan overdose on Thanksgiving.

I pulled out my phone and typed a quick text to Sam.

Me: I visited Dad today.

Me: The poinsettia is beautiful. Thank you.

The conversation bubble immediately popped up, and a second later, his reply came.

Sam: Of course.

Sam: Did you bring him a cannoli?

I grinned as I typed my reply.

Me: Of course. 😊

The back doors of the hall slammed open, making all of us jump, as Eve and Phineas barged in mid-argument. From what I could make out, she was accusing him of stealing a package of sugar off her front stoop, and he told her to check the cameras, to which she reminded him she never needed till now. They separated into opposite rows off the main aisle, but not before she smacked him with her mail.

I took out my favorite pen and notepad, flipping to an empty page to jot down the highlights from the meeting for next week's school paper. Mr. Clark had asked that I try for an interview with Mayor Moore as well, but that would be tricky. His assistant had always been notoriously difficult to pin down.

"Those two desperately need baciare," Nona said to my cousin Bianca on the other side of her.

"You still think they're into each other?" Bianca took out one of her earbuds and pushed her dark bangs away from her eyes to get a better look as I took a swig of water from my tumbler.

"Assolutamente." Nona turned forward again. "All that arguing is just passion in a different form. Kissing would do them both a lot of good." She smacked my arm and lowered her voice. "Like you and Sam, eh, cara?"

I accidentally inhaled my water, which made me me cough several times.

Leo jumped out of his seat shouting, "Oh no, was it nuts?!"

This naturally made my entire family, and Sam's, and the two rows behind them, look around as if the lethal nut in question had an accomplice who was attempting to flee the scene.

"My Great-Aunt Elena once gifted nuts to a crow." Aunt Sofia stayed seated and looked forward while speaking to no one—a common habit. "Days later, he returned, bringing back only the cashews. Another time, he brought her a button when she'd lost one. She called him Aldo for his wisdom."

Bianca stared at her, mouth open. "Mom, that cannot be true."

I held up my hand and shook my head as the coughing

subsided. "It's okay, guys. I just breathed my water instead of drinking it," I said with a wheezy voice.

Leo put a hand on his chest and exhaled loudly. "Thank goodness. I really didn't want to stab you."

I laughed, which only made my throat hurt worse. "I've got a neffy on me, bud. No needles today."

Being the only one in the family with a severe food allergy was not my favorite thing. True, my family had gotten really good about keeping peanuts and tree nuts away over the last several years after some close calls and hospital trips, but I still felt like a burden every time I double-checked recipes brought to family gatherings. They all said they "didn't mind" my questions, or how I'd sometimes wash a serving spoon or knife just in case, but their tone didn't always convey the same message.

The side door to the hall opened, and Mayor Moore entered the room, looking paler than the Ghost of Christmas Past. He gave a feeble smile to the town before stepping onto the podium at the front of the room.

I spun the claddagh ring on my finger, and not one chair squeaked or moved as he opened a green folder and took out a single sheet of white paper.

"Good evening," he said before clearing his throat. "Thank you for coming here tonight on such short notice. I know this has not been an easy few days for any of us—"

"You can say that again!" someone shouted from the back of the room.

"I know this has not been an easy few days for any of us," Sam whispered behind me, making me cover up my laugh with my hand.

"But I appreciate your patience as the council and I sifted through, well, a lot of paperwork and made some calls to the local probate court," Mayor Moore added.

Whispers drifted around the room until the mayor continued. "As many of you know, Mr. Paxton did not have any family." The mayor paused and looked at the crowd, which had turned silent again. "He also, unfortunately, did not create a will."

The room erupted in shouts and jeers.

Clearly, most of the room didn't have a professional, eavesdropping bestie like Jo to deliver the deets ahead of time.

Mayor Moore raised both hands and waited till everyone quieted down again before he continued. "Be that as it may, the court has informed me that they appointed an administrator to Mr. Paxton's estate. This person should arrive in Mullings Creek in a few days to see the property and let us know of a timeline involving its appraisal and next steps."

"Next steps?" I whispered to Nona.

She frowned. "Probably selling it off in pieces, like fancy lawyers always do."

Selling it in pieces?

To whom?

Isaiah's comment from lunch about things looking and feeling different floated to the surface, making every part of my body go cold. The Market was the nucleus of our town. It had been for decades. Tearing it down and replacing it with some tacky, cheesy chain store would completely ruin the charm of Mullings Creek.

I flipped my notebook closed and shoved it back into my crossbody bag.

Screw writing an article about "embracing the winter winds of change." Mr. Clark would have to pick another senior to write *that* piece. I was not the kind of girl to "embrace" something with more red flags than a new underground power line.

Mayor Moore held up a hand again. "I know you're all scared about what this may mean for the future of The Market. But don't worry yourselves—"

"Yet," Bianca mumbled before putting her earbuds back in.

"This is the time of year when it's important that we keep the faith, right?" The mayor paused like he had hoped someone would jump up with a resounding "Yes!" But the room had returned to its stony silence. "The best thing we can all do in the meantime is make sure our Market and the surrounding stores look their best. After all, Holly Days begins this weekend—our best time of year! I can't wait to see what wonderful things our town turns up this Christmas season." And with that, he put his paper back in his folder, stepped down from the podium, and walked out of the room.

"We are so screwed," Marco said, crossing his arms in front of his chest as he slumped in his seat.

Jo hit him on the back of the head. "Must you always be so negative?"

Marco smirked but kept facing forward. "I wouldn't be, if you would reply to my texts more often."

Not the best time to flirt, bud.

Jo rolled her eyes and sat back, but not before I caught the way her cheeks flushed.

Nico ruffled Marco's curls, which he knew he hated. "You gotta keep the faith, brother! I'm with the mayor on this one."

But Marco just scowled, and said, "You keep the faith. I'll be realistic."

"I'm with Marco. This is the beginning of the end," Sam said later as he, Jo, and I sat with our backs against one of the railings of the clock tower. Technically, no one was allowed up here, but my older cousin Francis "forgot" he still had a key from when he worked for the local Parks and Rec before college. No one had ratted us out yet, so we kept coming when we needed to get away without actually leaving town.

Besides the Fourth of July fireworks, the view of the town from up here during Christmastime was unmatched.

"I still think you're looking at it through the wrong lens," Jo said as she passed Sam the open bag of chips. "Maybe this administrator will sell it to someone who can bring in even more businesses, and that will only help our sales, right?"

"Wrong." Sam passed me the bag of chips. "What always happens if someone puts a Starbucks or a chain restaurant in a small town, Jo? Those places will put the smaller ones out of business."

"Or . . ." Jo drummed her hands on the railing. "It could be sold off to someone here in town—someone who would look out for us—"

"And then eventually the rest will be replaced with other chain stores and soon Mullings Creek will be invaded like Fairfax or Manassas," Sam continued, unfazed by Jo's optimism.

"Fairfax and Manassas are almost an hour away," I said before popping a couple of chips in my mouth and instantly regretting it. They turned to flavorless sandpaper, and I had to force them down.

"And a decade ago they looked a lot smaller, too," Sam added, taking the bag back.

The clock chimed horribly off cue above us, and none of us spoke until it finished its warped version of "Westminster."

"Well, you'll have plenty to write about now," Jo said, turning to me.

"Yeah, but this was *not* the kind of article I wanted to write before Christmas," I mumbled.

My phone buzzed with a text message from Mom, who sent me a selfie with a pair of large sunglasses resting on her nose.

Mom: I forgot all about these!

Mom: But you should totally borrow them for Italy! ♥

I sighed and stole a quick glance at my two best friends. *Guess it's now or never.* "So, um, speaking of writing articles about better things . . . it turns out I'll be able to do that a lot next semester when . . ." *Deep breath, G.* "I'm overseas."

"Shut up." Jo startled, slapping my shoulder. "You got in?"

I smiled and refused to look at Sam, who I could feel staring at me. "I got in."

"Oh my God!" Jo screamed, and threw her arms around me, knocking her steel tumbler over with a loud clang. "Congratulations! When do you leave?"

"The week after New Year's."

"What an amazing Christmas gift, right, Sam?" Jo reached around me and smacked his leg.

The neon OPEN sign at Between the Pages Bookstore blinked out, and a moment later, its owner, Ann, stepped outside and locked the door before disappearing around the corner.

I finally willed myself to look at Sam and immediately wished I hadn't. His eyes were so empty and dark, and even his freckles looked grayer in the moonlight, almost sad. "You're really going?"

I nodded. "I'd like to, yeah."

"But that's just over a month away. What about . . ." He ran a hand through his hair. "What about everything that happens this year, like, like prom and graduation and—"

"I'd be back in time for graduation," I said.

"Yeah, but then you and Jo are leaving for college right after that, and . . . there's just"—he sighed—"so little time left now, G."

"I know." Guilt knotted itself in my stomach.

But . . . don't you want this for me?

Next to my mom and Nona, Sam had always been the one to push me to go after my dreams. He was the one to stay up late with me for weeks, pretending to be a Sarah Lawrence rep in mock interviews.

He even printed their logo and safety-pinned it to his shirt during them to "make it more believable."

I reached out to put my hand on his, but he scooted out of reach, the inches between us now feeling like miles.

I forced a small smile and pretended that my eyes were tearing up from the cold and nothing else. "It's kinda like what you said to me earlier, Sam. Right? Maybe since we're seniors and so many things are up in the air, we should finally go to the Mistletoe Masquerade?"

Together?

But he shrugged and looked away.

"This is my chance. My chance to finally figure out who I can be without my family breathing down my neck. To finally find something worth writing about."

"Change *can be* a good thing, Sam," Jo chimed in.

"It's so easy for you two to speak about change . . ." Sam

stood and flicked chip crumbs off his jeans before tucking his book back into his pocket. "When neither of you will be around to see its aftermath."

And without another word, he crossed the balcony and disappeared through the old door, his boots echoing down the spiral staircase.

Chapter Six

"You surprised?"

—NATIONAL LAMPOON'S CHRISTMAS VACATION

Saturday morning blew in faster than the winter storm in *Rudolph the Red-Nosed Reindeer*, and everyone in Mullings Creek was acting like the elves when they believed Christmas was canceled.

Full-blown Christmas-panic mode.

And I was being pulled in about eighty different directions because of it. My checklist for today had already doubled since last night, and it was barely eight a.m.

So much for writing that article on the disappearance of snow days thanks to virtual learning.

Maybe Mr. Clark would give me an extension?

Aunt Sofia panic-texted while Leo and I shared a sudoku puzzle over our cereal and cinnamon toast.

Auntie Sof: I CAN'T FIND THE FABRIC SOFTENER!!!

Auntie Sof: DO YOU REMEMBER IF IT WAS INCLUDED IN MY INSTACART?!

I sighed and showed the text to Leo, who laughed and went back to penciling in another number. "Does she ever *not* use all caps when she texts?" he asked.

"Not really." I typed a quick response.

Me: It was. I think I saw it under the sink the last time I was there.

A moment later, she replied with a "thank you" GIF and asked if I could pick up her order of pastries and bagels from Eve on my way into town.

Ugh. Going back to my aunt's B&B after heading into town was completely out of the way, but family was family.

Me: Sure. ❤

Before I grabbed the order for Aunt Sofia, I had to swing by the Wanderin' Eats Diner. No sooner had I turned off Cherry Street than Phineas ran out the front entrance, hat askew and apron untied. "Gianna! Thanks for fitting me in." He stopped next to my bike and braced himself on the handles while he took several gulps of the cold morning air. "I need your opinion on my new menus."

Oh! "Trying out some new recipes?" I couldn't remember the last time Phineas had changed his menu. Something like that could definitely bring in more customers and stronger reviews. And both of those things would show that big-city lawyer that maybe a small town like ours didn't need something fancy and new in place of The Market, right?

But Phineas frowned, and said, "No. Of course not. Food's great. Why change it?" He held up his phone and zoomed in on the top of the menu. "I changed the border and even added one of those nifty QR codes so customers can go right to my blog about all the travelin' I did."

Hmm.

Not as exciting as a new menu, but at least he's trying?

I tested the QR code and handed Phineas's phone back to him. "The link works, but maybe you should think about syncing it to the menu instead. That way, when you do update your menu someday—*soon, I hope*—you won't have to worry about reprinting it with each new change."

He adjusted his hat. "So, hold off on the adventures bit?"

"You already have clippings and photos posted all around your diner." And over every booth and on the bar and even in the bathrooms. "I think you're good."

God love the man, but I didn't think people came to his diner to relive his adventures.

"Brilliant! I'm on it!" He hurried away, almost slipping on a small patch of ice before turning around with a "Thank you!"

Hal waved from his front window display, which had had a serious glow-up since earlier in the week. Normally, he'd build some kind of Christmas tree made of tools and gadgets, but this year he added a sleigh trimmed in twinkle lights and stuffed with discounted items.

Ann from the Between the Pages Bookstore had also tweaked her typical book-tree window display by adding a family of book-snowmen with their pages facing out. She tipped one of their top hats as I parked outside of Eve's Drop and then stepped around another small patch of ice.

I need to text Jo about salting that.

The bell rang when I pushed open the door, revealing a frantic Eve hurrying around with a cloth and spray bottle.

"Oh! You're here!" She stopped and propped herself against the counter. "Thank God."

"I need your help" in three . . . two . . .

"I need your help, G." She tossed me the rag and pointed toward the front three tables. "Could you get those for me? I have to check the scones . . ." She patted her apron pockets as if the scones would be there instead of the oven.

"Actually, I'm here for Aunt Sof—"

"Be right back!" Eve disappeared into the kitchen, the door flapping back and forth twice before going still.

I checked the time. Jo should've been here by now to work her shift. Maybe she got stopped on the way in, too?

Oh well. I had a few minutes to spare for Eve before my aunt's nerves got the best of her.

I picked up the spray bottle from the counter and went to

work on the last few tables, moving the tiny snowmen and tea lights to the chairs so I could wipe the entire surface.

But then Eve cursed from the kitchen and stormed back into the café. "I burned them!" She ripped off her apron and threw it. "I *never* burn my scones! Oh God, do you think it's an omen? It must be an omen. I'll go grab some sage from Ann. She's always good for sage."

"Whoa, hold on." I grabbed Eve's arm as she tried to rush past me. "It's not an omen, Eve. You're just stressed out. Lots of people mess up when they're stressed."

Eve groaned and sank into a nearby chair, putting her head in her hands.

"But you're not like most people." I sat down opposite her and laid my hand on her knee to give her the same pep talk I usually did when she had a meltdown like this. "You're Eve freakin' Edwards."

She lifted her head and sniffed.

"And you are a boss in that kitchen," I added.

"I am?" she asked.

I nodded. "So, I want you to go back in there, tell that oven who's boss, and make another batch of scones." I moved my hand to her shoulder. "But first, I need you to bring me Aunt Sofia's order, or she may kill me."

Eve laughed and wiped her eyes. "You got it, kiddo."

She picked up her apron and stomped her way back into the kitchen, returning a moment later with a box that smelled like raspberries, chocolate, and brown butter. "All nut-free too, honey, in case you wanted to sneak one before handing them off." Eve winked.

"You're the best!" I took the box and turned to leave. Sam had said change was a bad thing, but not all change was bad. After my first anaphylactic reaction to nuts over a decade ago, Eve and Phineas did some homework and realized several families in town also had nut and other major food allergies. Within a couple of months, the kitchens at the diner and café soon had dedicated work-spaces and equipment that were allergy-safe. How many chain-store bakeries and diners would also do the same?

My phone buzzed in my pocket just as I stepped through Eve's door.

Probably Aunt Sofia wondering if I fell in a manhole, or Nico wondering when I'd swing by the florist.

I carefully balanced the box of treats in one hand and tried to reach into my side pocket. My phone wouldn't budge.

Come on you piece of . . .

I stepped forward while finally yanking the darn thing free, but my left foot slid out from under me, bringing me crashing down onto the icy sidewalk with a loud, ripping tear.

The pastries were unscathed, thank God.

But then I leaned forward, wincing, and reached under my butt. The fabric of my jeans flapped open. I fell back and pulled my scarf over my face.

Well, that's just fan freaking—

"Ouch," someone said above me. "You look like those *Peanuts* kids after Snoopy threw them loose on the rink."

"'Everything I do turns into a disaster,'" I mumbled.

"Here." A gloved hand gently pulled the scarf away, appearing in front of my face. "Up you go, Charlie Brown."

A stranger who references Christmas movies? I suppose I can trust that.

I grabbed the warm glove, letting it lift me to my feet before finally getting a good look at my rescuer. He was tall, maybe even a tad taller than Sam, with fair skin and dirty-blond hair cut close above his ears. His striking blue eyes crinkled on the sides as he smiled.

Whoa.

A hot stranger who references Christmas movies?

Maybe I hit my head harder than my butt?

"So did you damage the goods?" he asked.

My entire body flushed with heat. "Er . . . excuse me?"

"The goods." He chuckled and pointed to the ground where the box from Eve's still sat. "Did they survive?"

"Oh." I bent down to grab them.

And quickly realized that this guy just got a full view of my underwear.

Red-and-green-polka-dotted.

I jumped back and angled the open part of my pants away from him. "They're good. I think."

"You, however, look like you're in a hurry." He pulled his

green sweater over his head, which lifted the white T-shirt underneath it up high enough for me to see a smidgen of a very hard, very toned stomach.

Hello there.

"Why don't you borrow this?" He stepped forward and swiftly reached one of the arms of his sweater around me before looping it into a loose knot over the bottom of my jacket.

He smelled like some kind of spicy, expensive cologne and stood close enough that I could make out a tiny scar near his chin in the shape of a half-moon.

"Won't you be cold?" I asked him as goose bumps dotted his bare arms.

"My jacket is in the car around the corner." He pointed to the box. "Do you need a hand?"

"No, thank you. I've got a basket on my bike." I nodded toward down the street where the Christmas music had already started playing. "So, are you here for The Market?"

He looked behind him. "Yeah, you could say that."

"Cool." I swallowed. "I, um, I have to go deliver this to my aunt, but can I leave this sweater somewhere so you don't forget it?"

"Don't worry." He smiled. "I'm sure I'll run into you again."

My ears prickled underneath my earmuffs. "Oh, okay. It was nice to meet you, er . . ."

"James." He stuck out his hand.

"Gianna," I said, shaking it.

"Be careful out there, Gianna." He gave a small salute before he disappeared into Eve's café.

Thirty minutes and one run-in-with-a-cranky-aunt later, I made my way back onto Mistletoe Lane, my eyes darting everywhere for any more unexpected ice patches as I parked outside of The Market. Fresh Christmas wreaths with bright red bows hung on the two open barn-style doors. Potted poinsettias covered the tops of the barrels that framed the entrance along with two new large trees with silver and gold ornaments.

Trees that perfect must've come from the Holts.

Inside, white lights ran across every exposed beam in the ceiling, and the garland Aunt Helen had attempted to wrap around the mason-jar chandelier a week ago now hung perfectly from it. Bing Crosby crooned from the nearby record player, and for just a moment, it felt like it always did this time of year.

Magical.

Sandy, an old American bulldog who technically didn't belong to anyone but nevertheless made herself at home at The Market, trotted inside carrying a small square frame in her mouth.

"Come here, girl," I said, crouching down. She walked right up to me and cocked her head as if to question why I summoned her. "Whatcha got there?"

Sandy gently dropped the frame to the floor. I patted the

cluster of spots on her back before picking up the frame and wiping away the grime on the glass. It was an older picture of my Papa and Sam's grandpa, arms around each other's shoulders, both beaming with pride, as Sam's grandpa held up a large fish.

"I love that picture," Sam said, suddenly appearing at my side with two travel mugs of something steaming hot. "Gram used to have one just like it near her piano . . ."

It had only been five years, but it still felt like yesterday. Gram had said their husbands passed on the same day because they hated competing with each other. Nona believed it was because they didn't want either of their wives to be a third wheel.

Whatever the reason, that kind of friendship was precious and rare.

I should know, because I felt the same way about the boy in front of me.

And yet I still couldn't stop Taylor Swift's "Ruin the Friendship" from playing through my head.

"Do you want to keep it?" I stood and held out the picture for Sam.

He shook his head. "Let's just add it to her pile of other stuff."

Sandy had been presenting everyone in Mullings Creek with random items from the town and its history for years. We all assumed they held some cosmic purpose we didn't yet understand, so we chose to keep all of them in an old chest near her doggy bed at the back of The Market.

I placed the frame next to Sandy and rubbed her cold fur before she picked it up again and ambled away.

Sam held out one of the cups. "I got your favorite: cocoa with a shot of peppermint and a dash of cinnamon on the whipped cream."

I took the cup and breathed in the familiar scent. "Thanks."

"Sure."

We both drummed our fingers on our cups for a moment before speaking at the same time.

"I'm sorry—"

"I'm sorry." I laughed.

"You have nothing to be sorry about." Sam stepped closer to me. "I was the jerk who completely ruined your good news about Italy. And it *is* good news, G. I'm so excited for you."

He smiled, but I knew that smile.

It was the same one he gave his parents when they forced him to accept a mayoral award for "Spirit of Mullings Creek" a couple of years ago after he spent weeks building new benches in the park. The same one reserved for any foolish adult who argued with him about pine trees, despite knowing a thousand times more on the subject.

And seeing Sam fake smile about my news gave me a pang of sadness deep inside.

"I know it's not how you envisioned our senior year going, but I promise to make up for it with the best holiday season ever. Okay?" I touched his arm, and that new warm, fizzy feeling wound around my hand and wrist.

"Gianna!" Leo squealed, startling me. My little brother leaped onto my waist, wrapping his legs tightly around my own as Sam and I walked toward the stage where a crowd was gathering.

"Have you seen the lawyer?" he asked, his voice muffled in my jacket.

"Not yet," I said, looking to the left and right as I passed the Whispering Wicks Candles, Cozy Covers, and Glass Works stands.

"New sweater?" Sam asked, touching one of the sleeves tied around my waist.

I pulled the fabric down a bit more. "Something like that."

Sam hung back to talk to Isaiah and his dad, Pastor Aaron, as Leo and I kept moving forward. "So where is he?"

Leo dropped his feet but took my pinkie finger with his, our secret handshake. "There," he said, pointing with his free hand toward the stage. "Marco said he brought his son, too."

I followed his gaze, and my stomach bottomed out.

Talking intently to Mayor Moore was a tall man who definitely looked the part of a fancy lawyer, stern-faced and dressed in a designer suit, shiny shoes, and long dress coat.

And standing next to him was none other than James, the hot guy who saw my festive underwear less than an hour ago.

"*Son of a nutcracker.*"

Chapter Seven

"You, I can tell, are a leading lady, but for some reason, you're behaving like the best friend."

—THE HOLIDAY

The microphone at center stage made a screeching sound of feedback as Mayor Moore cleared his throat. "Happy Holly Days, everyone!" Those people in the room who weren't already moving toward the stage stopped what they were doing to lock in.

"I'd like to introduce you to Travis Bailey, the lawyer appointed by the court to oversee Mr. Paxton's affairs, specifically our Market. Mr. Bailey's father was Mr. Paxton's lawyer for many years before he passed, isn't that right?" Mayor Moore gestured to the imposing figure beside him, who gave all of us the smallest of nods. "And this is his son, James," Mayor Moore added.

James beamed and waved. "Hi there!" he called warmly.

How in the world were those two related? It was like looking at the real-life version of Scrooge and his jolly nephew.

Except I didn't recall anyone in that story almost flashing said nephew.

Mayor Moore smiled at James and then turned back to us. "I was just suggesting our guests—"

"Trespassers!" Nico and Marco coughed into their fists loudly.

Mayor Moore shot a quick warning glare at my cousins—*ha, as if that would ever stop them*—before he continued. "Our *guests* should take a tour of the town before Travis assesses the property." Mayor Moore put a hand above his eyes and scanned the crowd. "Ah! Phineas! You know so much about our town, how about guiding our new friends—"

"How about her?" James interrupted, pointing, shockingly enough, at me.

Wait.

Seriously?

The entire room spun around, my name floating through the air in whispers.

"Me?" I asked, my voice cracking.

Nice one, G.

"Yes, you." James grinned. "I bet Gianna knows everything there is to know about this town."

I mean, yes, but–

"How does he know your name?" Sam whispered to me.

"Long story," I whispered back as James and his father stepped off the stage and made their way toward us.

"I like long stories . . ." Sam's voice turned cautious, guarded, as he stood up straighter.

"Dad, Gianna. Gianna, Dad." James motioned between us.

Mr. Bailey stuck out his hand. "Nice to meet you, Ms. . . ."

"Mancini. Gianna Mancini, uh, sir." I shook his hand and shivered. Definitely a different kind of hand than his son's, but I pressed on. "I'm more than happy to show you around town—"

"As am I," Sam stepped forward, offering his hand as well. "Sam Holt. My family owns the Christmas tree farm and greenhouses here in Mullings Creek."

"Ah, a farmer." Mr. Bailey shook Sam's hand quickly. "That's a pretty thankless job, or so I've heard."

Sam's smile vanished faster than fresh gingerbread in the same room as my brother. "My family always says that farmers are like teachers: We don't do what we do for praise. We do it because we love giving to our communities."

My dad used to say the same thing. I felt instantly taller listening to Sam and fought the urge to put an encouraging hand on his back.

"We actually have a lot of support here," I added. "So much, in fact, that lots of families travel from over an hour away just to get their tree from our farm. Isn't that right, Sam?"

He gave a short nod.

Leo appeared out of nowhere, a skill he inherited from Nona. "The Holts have three different species of pine trees on their farm, too!"

I patted his unruly hair and smiled.

"Is that so?" Mr. Bailey put both of his hands behind his back and then his eyes dropped to the green sweater around my waist.

Uh-oh.

"James, isn't that—"

"My sweater?" James stepped forward. "Yes, it is."

Sam bristled.

Mr. Bailey raised an eyebrow. "Care to explain why Ms. Mancini is wearing it around her waist?"

"No, I do not." James smiled with all teeth.

And neither do I, thank you.

But my brother hated unanswered questions. Before I could stop him, he lifted the sweater and gasped. "Oh, G. You ripped your pants?"

Diversion. Need a diversion stat.

Fire alarm?

It does smell a bit like smoke in here.

Most certainly from the countless people who came from homes with wood-burning fireplaces, but what the Baileys didn't know wouldn't kill them.

I laughed awkwardly. "Yeah, buddy, I sure did. But enough of that. Let's go ahead and start this tour, shall we?"

"Here." Sam unzipped his jacket and shrugged out of it before holding it out to me. "Why don't you use this instead so *James* can have his sweater back?"

"It's no problem." James pushed Sam's jacket back. "Green goes with her eyes better."

Where the heck even are the fire alarms?

"Wow, Sam." Leo patted his arm tenderly. "You look like I do when Mom makes me stop playing *Zelda*."

James chuckled, which only made Sam's face flush redder.

Thankfully, Mr. Bailey stepped in. "Please, lead the way, Ms. Mancini, so we can see more of this . . . charming town." His voice dripped with sarcasm.

By the time we made it outside of The Market, everyone had their businesses up and running pretty smoothly. Since I was volunteered for this lovely assignment with zero prep time, I made up my route on the spot, picking out places I felt sure would win over Mr. Bailey at first glance.

Eve's Drop was first on my list because everyone knew caffeine and pastries were the way to anyone's heart, even one as small as Mr. Grinch's. The warm smells of hazelnut and nutmeg wafted out into the street as we neared the front entrance, which had an additional poinsettia opposite the snowman. I elbowed Sam and gave him a secret thumbs-up, but he gave his typical "no big deal" shrug before he opened the door for our guests.

Jazzy Christmas music played over Bluetooth speakers, and most of the tables were occupied with familiar faces and a few tourists. The display case was full of fresh savory and sweet options, like her spinach and sausage quiche bites, bacon and egg pockets, cinnamon streusel muffins, and (unburned) white chocolate and raspberry snowmen-shaped scones. The Baileys moved to the side, where Mr. Bailey took a phone call as James read the menu aloud, occasionally tapping his dad's shoulder to try to get his attention.

Jo waved Sam and me over from behind the counter. "Hey, guys! Did you come in to escape the cold claws of the new Scrooge in town?"

My chest tightened. "Shh, Jo. Not now—"

"I heard he makes Krampus look like Cindy Lou Who." She laughed, oblivious to Sam and me jerking our heads to the left.

"I've never been a fan of that myth, actually." Mr. Bailey pocketed his phone and joined us at the register.

Maybe the fire alarm would go off in here?

Eve already burned something once today. She could totally do it again.

"A bit dark, even for someone with cold claws like myself," Mr. Bailey added, adjusting his tie.

Jo's face turned ashen, and her green eyes stopped blinking.

"Jo, this is Mr. Bailey. The lawyer appointed to Mr. Paxton's estate," Sam said slowly.

"And I'm James, a junior from East Ember Academy, son of Krampus, and heir to cynicism and contempt." James smiled and stuck his hand forward.

I cackled before I could cover it up.

"Honestly, James," Mr. Bailey muttered, shaking his head. "I'll take a coffee. Black, please."

"Like his soul," James whispered, making Jo and me giggle. "And I'll have . . ." He had raised his voice and was looking at the chalkboard menu behind the counter. "The gingerbread latte, please. And a muffin."

"Liquid sugar," Mr. Bailey mumbled.

"'Tis the season!"

Sam chortled this time, surprisingly, before I spoke up. "Jo makes those." I pointed to the oversize muffins in the display case. "And the breakfast pockets and quiche. She's going to culinary school next year. We'll be in New York City together, actually."

"For real?" James asked, leaning an elbow on the counter as Jo handed Mr. Bailey his coffee and then went to work on James's latte. "Culinary school must be intense. I mean, based on what I've seen on *The Bear.* Do you want to be a pastry chef or like an executive—"

"James," Mr. Bailey hissed. "Let the girl do her job so we can be on our way, please."

James immediately deflated.

Geez.

What was so wrong with James showing interest in Jo's dreams?

We waited in awkward silence for the next two minutes, while Jo finished ringing up their order, before continuing the tour.

Both Baileys stayed quiet as I showed them the sheriff's office, explaining its distinction as a historic landmark, as it had been here since the Civil War, and then the Mullings Creek Library, pointing to the brickwork from the original one that burned down in the 1980s. But James finally perked up outside of

Chordcrafters Music Shop. "Whoa, check out the vinyl!" He pressed his face and hands against the glass like a little kid. "And that seven-string guitar! Oh man, they've even got a jazz box!" He turned around and quickly frowned at his dad, who was busy swiping away on his phone. "Dad, remember Granddad's jazz box?"

But Mr. Bailey ignored the question, tapping his screen a few more times before he looked up. "We should be going, yes? We're due back at The Market in a few minutes."

Sam's face turned stony as James immediately shrunk down like a child who got slapped on the wrist when reaching for a treat.

What the heck was wrong with Mr. Scrooge?

I'd give anything to be able to talk to my dad again.

Sam cleared his throat and motioned to the side. "Why don't we head on over to The Market then, sir."

"Gladly," Mr. Bailey said, tapping his phone a few more times as he stepped off the curb. But the moment he did, an undeniable wet squelch sounded, followed by the distinct smell of poop.

"Bleh!" Mr. Bailey shouted, spinning around while looking at the bottom of his now poo-covered loafers. "What kind of a dog left *this*?"

"That would be Sheriff Kingston's horse, Shadowfax," Sam said matter-of-factly.

"Good name," James added, smirking.

Sam looked at him in surprise. "Excellent name."

The rest of the afternoon hurried by in a blur of tourists shopping the opening-weekend Holly Days sales. Sam spent most of his day on the farm, helping his parents with the holiday rush and making deliveries around town. I hurried from booth to booth inside The Market, making sure everyone had what they needed while Nona followed closely behind, shoving different foods in my face till I conceded and ate a sub with her famous olive pesto.

Mom sold several pieces of pottery and even a painting while taking orders for three custom holiday signs. She always played the modest card, but I loved seeing her work get the recognition it deserved. Designs by Alice had received several write-ups in local and state newspapers and magazines over the years, yet despite her consistent sales and success, Mom never talked about taking her business outside of Mullings Creek.

"I give to the town that gave me everything" was her motto.

But part of me always wondered if she ever dreamed of a different life and new places like I did.

The Glass Works stand was, without a doubt, the busiest, due to their gorgeous handblown ornaments. Several families came here every year for a new ornament to add to their growing collections.

By the time the sun set and the crowds fizzled out, everyone looked plumb exhausted. Dana stepped away from her gems booth and switched off the Bluetooth speaker before placing a jazzy instrumental Christmas vinyl onto the record player—a tradition after a Saturday rush. Eve and Jo came by as usual with muffins and pitchers of hot cider, and everyone sat on the edge of the stage or near it to mingle and unwind.

If only it could be this calm all the time.

And then on cue, Mayor Moore, Mr. Bailey, and James entered again. A few of us hopped off the stage, but Mr. Bailey held up his hands. "Please, don't move on our part. I just wanted to come back by here to tell you that I enjoyed seeing your town today."

"Well, that was unexpected," Jo whispered to me.

"I can see that you all take great pride in what you do here, and I too want to make sure that this establishment is left in the best of hands . . ."

"Spoke too soon," Jo mumbled.

"Since my father and Mr. Paxton did things . . . differently . . . and neither believed in digitizing records, Mr. Paxton fell woefully behind on payments. So, the court has decided that we should sell this property to pay off those back taxes. We feel confident that a new owner with fresh ideas will be just what Mullings Creek needs." Mr. Bailey clasped his hands in front of him, oblivious to the jaws dropping around him.

New owner?

Fresh ideas?

Jo's optimistic point of view melted faster than ice on salt and was replaced with something more ominous.

"I will be staying here with my son till the end of December to handle Mr. Paxton's affairs. Enjoy the rest of your evening." Mr. Bailey then turned on his heel and disappeared into the night with James, frowning, following behind.

No one moved.

The clock tower chimed the hour.

A truck blasting "Jingle Bell Rock" drove by.

Till finally, Marco spoke first. "One month?" He jumped off the stage, mouth still full of muffin. "Did that guy literally just ruin our Christmas by putting a death warrant on The Market?"

The room started buzzing with panicked voices.

Thirty days till everything changed for Mullings Creek.

And barely two weeks after that, I'd be leaving them all alone to deal with it?

I don't think so, Scrooge.

"No," I said, louder than I meant to, silencing the chatter. I handed Jo my cider and faced my town and my family. "He gave us a timeline for saving it."

Chapter Eight

"This is my house. I have to defend it."

—HOME ALONE

The next day, Mom asked me to drop off some Linzer tarts to the Baileys, who were now staying at Aunt Sofia's B&B. Nona had apparently asked her to do it first, but she was in the middle of a commissioned piece she didn't want to stop working on quite yet. When Mom had her "creative head" on, she was a force to be reckoned with, skipping meals and sleep until she was "done." I knew better than to ask her to hit pause.

So, after our traditional Sunday brunch at Aunt Helen's, I swung by Nona's for the cookies before taking the long walk to the B&B. Riding my bike would've saved me several minutes, but I loved walking toward Aunt Sofia's this time of year. The sun burned deep orange on the treetops, making their long shadows stretch across the sidewalks and streets.

Hal and his son Darryl were busy hanging new wreaths over their storefront windows as Sandy sat nearby with a candy-cane-shaped toy in her mouth, supervising. Mr. Phillips waved to me as he flipped over his sign to CLOSED at Chordcrafters, and a block down, Ann rolled her garland-covered carts of discounted books back inside while her Bengal cat Scout wove in between her ankles. Most of them would meet up for a cup of coffee to unwind at Eve's before heading home, and then wake up and do the same thing the next day.

Once upon a time, I thought a life like that would be boring in its predictability, but after Mr. Bailey came to town and ripped the sleds out from under us, sending us spiraling down a hill toward a finish line we couldn't see, predictability was all anyone could cling to.

Like me and my Christmas movies.

As I rounded the corner of Mistletoe Lane and Elm Street, Aunt Sofia's sweet soprano drifted down the walk. In a wide-legged green jumpsuit with a ruffled red-and-gold-plaid top, she rocked back and forth in one of her old porch chairs, crocheting something and singing "That's Christmas to Me."

I smiled and lifted my hand to brush one of the white Christmas ball lights hanging from a tall oak in the front yard.

"Gianna!" Aunt Sofia waved before setting down her hook and yarn to hurry down the front steps. "How was brunch? I hated missing it."

"It was good until Marco accused Nico of using his toothpaste again—"

"Oh boy . . ."

"And then Nico accidentally let slip that he uses Marco's towel, too, because his was always 'so much softer.'" I shook my head and cringed. "Marco almost gagged, and then the two of them started throwing food until Aunt Helen made them take it outside. They're probably still out there rolling around in the dead leaves."

Aunt Sofia put her arm around me. "To this day I don't know how my sister-in-law didn't need therapy while raising her three boys."

Same.

As we walked up the steps to the front door of the B&B, I pointed to the red yarn on the rocking chair. "What are you working on?"

"Oh!" She held up something resembling a wonky beanie with weird vine-like things coming out. "It's a new hat for Sandy, since she ate my last one. Isn't it cute?" She flicked the vines. "I made antlers!"

God bless that poor dog.

I gave her my best fake smile. "I'm sure Sandy will love it."

For about two seconds.

She opened the front door. "Did I ever tell you about the time we went skinny-dipping with Bruce Springsteen in Goose Creek back in eighty-one?"

I stopped. "You knew Bruce Springsteen? Like, the musician?"

"No, silly. The captain of the Mullings Creek High mathletes." Aunt Sofia laughed and waved a hand at me. "But he and everyone else knew to swim in that creek on account of the eels. Good for the skin. Everyone knows that, Gianna."

"Right." *How silly of me to forget.*

I stepped inside the B&B and sighed, immediately feeling my body relax in the heat coming from the parlor room fireplace and the familiar ticking of Nona's old grandfather clock.

"The Baileys are in the North Pole, third-floor suite," Aunt Sofia said before stepping back outside to finish her crochet.

Each room on the main and second floors were decorated in different Christmas themes like White Christmas, Cozy Cabin Christmas, Blue Christmas, and even Gingerbread House. But the third floor was always my favorite because of the North Pole theme. Two reindeer statues with faux fur and real pine wreaths flanked either side of the door that led upstairs to the grand suite, which took over the entire floor.

I knocked and waited a moment, but no one answered, so I opened the door and started ascending the twinkle-lit stairs, each one adorned with a different wooden toy.

"It's Gianna Mancini," I announced as I climbed. "I come bearing gifts!" At the top of the stairs, I patted the head of Hermes, a very old rocking horse that had once belonged to my dad, before rounding the corner. "Who wants cook— Oh my gosh!" I froze and put my hand over my eyes.

Because standing just a few feet away was James.

Shirtless.

Dripping wet.

And wearing only a red towel around his waist with the quote WHY IS THE CARPET ALL WET, TODD?

I peeked through my fingers to see if he had moved at all.

Nope.

Still there.

And half naked.

He smirked as he rubbed a second, green towel with the matching quote I DON'T KNOW, MARGO! over his blond hair. "Did someone say cookies?" he asked.

My heartbeat raced as I tried to look around the room but kept getting distracted by the broad chest assaulting my eyes. "Yes, um"—*Wow, that is one toned stomach*—"I'll just set them . . ." I darted behind the closest Christmas tree and stuck my arm out, the bag with the box of cookies dangling from it. "Here."

James laughed and stayed on the opposite side of the tree as he took the bag from my fingers. "They smell amazing." The bag crinkled. "Is that raspberry?"

"And lemon," I added, adjusting a Santa ornament in front of my face, because what else was there to do except stare at his naked chest?

Which had the slightest bit of hair swirling around his nip—

Oh my GOD, Gianna, do NOT stare at those.

I started as a bedroom door opened behind me with a loud creak.

"James, can you call down to Sofia and double-check that there is, in fact, a router somewhere in this old house? The Wi-Fi keeps dropping, and I got kicked out of a very important Zoom. Oh." Mr. Bailey, still dressed in a suit, stopped short.

"Ms. Mancini, I'm sorry I didn't hear you come in. James!" He grabbed a shirt hanging over a chair and threw it at his son. "For God's sake, put something on, will you? She doesn't need to see that."

Oh yes, she does . . .

"There's a router," I blurted. *Think about computers, G. Boring, cold, non-sexy computers.* "It's just not a great one. The Wi-Fi is stronger in some other places in town, though," I said, stepping away from the tree now that James was fully clothed.

"Delightful," Mr. Bailey muttered before taking a long look around the main living area. "James, when I told you to unpack your suitcases, I meant to put the items *away*. You're seventeen years old, for Christ's sake. When will you ever—"

"Gianna brought cookies!" James held up the bag like a peace offering.

"We already had dessert—"

"And there are lemon ones."

"Lemon?" Mr. Bailey's eyes widened. "I love lemon. Do they by chance have powdered—"

"Sugar?" I added. "Yep. A Linzer torte without powdered sugar would be criminal."

"Quite right, Ms. Mancini." Mr. Bailey walked over to the old desk facing one of the twinkle-lit dormer windows and placed his laptop down before grabbing a small notepad and pen.

"Would you mind writing down some of those places with the good Wi-Fi? I have several important meetings I can't miss."

Meetings about The Market?

I paused before I began writing.

Maybe I should put down the worst places to go instead?

No. Then he'd have an even worse opinion about our town. You gotta win him over, G. Not drive him away.

"Sorry about that," James said, rubbing the towel over his hair. "My dad lives by lists."

"It's okay. I do, too," I said.

"Huh." He cocked his head. "I took you more for the spontaneous type."

"Ha. Yeah, no. That'd be my cousins." I wrote down Eve's Drop, Wanderin' Eats Diner, and Between the Pages Bookstore, and then glanced behind Mr. Bailey to the TV in his bedroom.

"Are you watching *Holiday Inn*?" I asked him.

"Oh, um, yes." Mr. Bailey turned around and scratched the back of his head. "Not as popular as *White Christmas*, but—"

"It's a great movie," I said, smiling. "I love the Christmas scenes, but my favorite number is when Fred Astaire dances with firecrackers—"

"During the Fourth of July!" James interrupted. "That's our favorite part, too."

"Did you know that scene was added after they filmed the movie?" Mr. Bailey asked me.

I nodded. "Because they wanted a patriotic scene, since they were filming when Pearl Harbor was attacked, right?"

"That's right." Mr. Bailey smiled and took a lemon Linzer torte out of the bag. "Impressive that you know that, Ms. Mancini."

I shrugged. "I watch a lot of movies, especially ones with a Christmas theme, even when it's not that time of year."

"Doesn't that get tiresome?" Mr. Bailey asked me as he took a bite of the cookie.

"No." I shifted on my feet. "I read that rewatching your favorite movies or shows helps reduce stress and regulate your emotions."

James grabbed another cookie. "Maybe you should look into that, then, Pops."

Definitely couldn't hurt.

I gave Mr. Bailey the piece of paper with my notes before I headed back toward the door. "You guys have a nice night."

"Feel free to drop by anytime." James winked and saluted me with his cookie.

My ears burned. "I'll definitely call first next time."

My feet had just reached the bottom step of the suite when James called down to me. "You can keep my sweater! It really is a good color on you."

I looked down and cursed under my breath.

How had I worn this thing all day and not remembered it wasn't even mine?

I turned around to take it off and chuck it at him, but my

jeans pocket caught on the doorknob and threw me off-balance, right into one of the reindeer. Dasher and I went down hard. One of his antlers broke off, and I got a face full of Christmas wreath.

Fabulous.

"You good there, Charlie Brown?" James asked, amusement in his voice.

"Yep." I pushed off the reindeer and jumped up, spitting out a pine needle before pulling the sweater over my head and draping it over Dasher. "Never better."

Later that evening, Leo, Sam, and I fixed ourselves ice cream bowls covered in everything from Twizzlers to gummy bears to M&M's before we settled into the old sofa in the den for our annual viewing of what was my dad's favorite holiday movie: *Home Alone*. Our cabin was one of the smallest on the block, but every room had something that represented one of us. Leo's action figures and framed puzzles took over the den; Mom's unsold artwork and sculptures lined the living room, breakfast nook, and kitchen; and the framed maps Dad and I had used to chart our future adventures climbed the stairs, eventually connecting with my room. With three different Christmas trees, a candy cane village, and plenty of candles, some would call it "cluttered."

But I called it cozy.

"Is your mom working late?" Sam asked me, pulling a

familiar, worn book out of his back pocket and placing it on the table, as we settled into the sofa and turned on the TV.

"*Fellowship* again? Really?" I took a gummy bear off his ice cream before he could stop me.

"It's Christmas." He snatched one off mine. "Tradition. You know that."

"Isn't that, like, a really old copy?" I asked. "Shouldn't you keep that locked in a special case or something?"

He held it up and sniffed it, smiling. "And miss this smell? I don't think so."

Far be it from me to get between a man and his books. "Mom said she 'couldn't stop' yet," I told him, explaining her absence. Which I got. Sometimes when I was writing, I'd get in this rhythm and the last thing I wanted to do was stop.

But Leo had hoped she'd be here for this movie.

So had I, honestly.

Leo hurried in last with several Oreo cookies forming a pyramid on the top of his already smothered ice cream and squeezed himself between Sam and me. I hit play and smiled at the familiar opening credits and one of my favorite John Williams pieces.

I pulled out my phone to check my notes, but Sam cleared his throat, and then whispered, "It can wait, G."

I mean, yes, it can, but that just means more piled onto tomorrow.

I added another quick note and then held up my phone over

Leo's head to show Sam how I was putting it on Do Not Disturb.

As usual, Leo whisper-narrated a good portion of the movie and added his own commentary like our dad had always done. "Salt actually wouldn't turn the bodies into mummies," he said while carefully placing an equal ratio of gummy bear to M&M on his spoon. "It would make them dissolve."

"Leo!" I looked at him incredulously. "Where did you hear that?"

"Aunt Sofia told me that was how she got rid of warts . . . by rubbing salt on them until they melted off." He cleaned off the spoon and then held it up as he spoke. "Do you think if I did that to my freckles on my nose, they would disappear?"

"No," Sam and I said in unison.

"Why would you want to get rid of your freckles?" Sam asked, pointing to his own that outlined his cheekbones and speckled his nose. "Freckles are awesome."

"Trent said they made my face look dirty." Leo dropped his head, and I immediately pulled out my phone to start a group text with Marco and Nico to figure out where this punk lived.

Those two spent way too much time rewatching *The Godfather*, but sometimes it came in handy.

"Trent's a moron." Sam draped an arm around Leo's shoulder. "He's obviously jealous of your freckles. Lots of people are jealous of mine."

Leo looked up at Sam. "They are?"

"Yep. And my red hair." He grinned and bopped Leo's nose before going back to watching the movie.

My throat grew thick seeing the two of them. They laughed at the same scenes, and Sam always joined in with Leo's quoting of most of Kevin's dialogue.

What would happen next semester with me gone?

Mom worked later and later these days, so who would be with Leo?

Would he just stay at Nona's most nights or would she come here? And what if this Trent kid or someone else kept picking on him? Should I just ask Sam to watch over him for me?

Let's be honest, Marco and Nico would definitely go overboard if they got involved.

I tried to enjoy my favorite scenes, like when Kevin goes grocery shopping, but all I could think about was the boy sitting next to me and how small and vulnerable he looked.

How could I ever leave you, Leo?

An hour later, Sam tapped my shoulder, smiling, and nodded to Leo, who had apparently passed out, head drooped against Sam's arm. Leo's ice cream bowl was licked clean, and it wobbled with his heavy breathing on the gingerbread blanket covering his lap.

I picked up the bowl and placed it with mine on the decoupage end table before carefully peeling off the blanket. Sam inched away far enough to turn his body, and in one smooth motion, he stood and lifted Leo, carrying him slowly out of the den while I walked ahead, making sure no bright lights were left on.

Sam carried him all the way up the stairs without straining once and held on to him as I took off his elf slippers and pulled back the quilt and sheet of his bed. Sam laid him down and pulled the covers up to his chin before tucking them in snuggly at his sides the way he liked it. My heart squeezed.

I wouldn't have to ask Sam to look after Leo.

Sam looking after Leo was as second nature to him as Sam looking after me.

He backed away from Leo's bed, and after I closed his door most of the way, we crept back down the hallway, avoiding the squeaky spot near the top right of the stairs as we headed back to the den.

"Something about the booby-trapping of the house always tires him out," Sam said, chuckling under his breath as we cleared the bowls and brought them to the kitchen.

"I know." I ran water into each of them. "I always feel bad because he gets so excited about Kevin's big plan drawn out on paper, but he never actually *sees* how it works. Guess it's for the best, though. We'd have to skip the scene with the tarantula on the guy's face."

"True." Sam wandered over to our fridge, covered with family Polaroids. "You know at the beginning when Kevin's family is running throughout the house and the fake cop is all irritated?" He brought a hand up and righted a photo that was crooked. "Is that how it feels to have that much family around you all the time?"

"Sometimes, yeah." I dried my hands on one of the snowman towels hanging on the oven before joining him. "You don't realize how that noise becomes a part of you, part of your routine, till you're alone for a bit. Don't get me wrong, the quiet is great, but it does get old after a while."

"That is something I do get." His voice sounded smaller, almost distant.

I turned to him.

Sam didn't have extended family anywhere nearby, and something always got in the way when what little family he did have planned to visit.

But he seemed so happy here working with his parents, helping the town.

It never occurred to me that someone like him, someone surrounded by a sea of people, could, in fact, be lonely.

Sam fixed another photo, one of me sitting on my dad's lap while he read the paper, and then wordlessly went back into the den. I followed him, but before I could ask more about what he'd said in the kitchen, he motioned to the movie still on pause. "Did you . . . did you want to finish it?"

Had it always been this dark in here?

My mouth had suddenly gone dry, but I swallowed anyway. "S-sure."

Why are you stuttering?

This is Sam. Your best friend.

In your den.

Where you've hung out with him a million-plus times.

But the kaleidoscope that was my stomach said something different when we settled next to each other on the couch, and Sam threw the banket over both of our legs. One of my socked feet touched his as he hit play, and I didn't move it.

And neither did he.

Okay, so our feet are touching.

Totally normal for friends sharing a blanket.

In a dimly lit, Christmas-cozy room.

"I always feel bad that he never got to eat that mac 'n' cheese." Sam's voice was low and soft. "Such a travesty."

"Truly regrettable." I pulled a pillow onto my lap and rested my arm on it just as Sam put his arm on his lap. Our elbows touched, and neither of us moved them.

Okay, so your elbows and feet are touching.

This is fine.

That buzzing feeling racing through your body is from all the sugar you just ate.

Nothing more.

But my brain continued to work overtime till the cozy warmth of the room made me a bit dizzy, my eyes heavy.

Maybe if I closed them for just a moment, this would all work itself out . . .

"Gianna." A voice near my cheek.

The familiar smell of pine trees and Ivory soap.

I opened my eyes, and my breath caught in my throat.

Sam's face, all aglow from the multicolored twinkle lights of the nearby tree, hovered inches away from mine. "You fell asleep, Mouse," he whispered.

I blinked a few times. "I'm not a mouse."

The corner of his mouth quirked up. "True, you don't have cheese on you, but you do have some pine needles here." He paused and gently pulled a needle nestled near my temple and held it up. "Where'd this come from?"

I plucked it from his fingers and stretched, dropping it on his fluffy red hair, smiling. "Dasher's wreath."

He chuckled. "You are something else, you know that?" Before I could process it, Sam tucked a piece of hair behind my ear, his hand lingering a moment before falling back to the blanket. His chocolate-brown eyes searched my face, finally settling on my lips.

And I think I stopped breathing.

What is going on here?

This was Sam.

My Sam.

My best friend.

Yet I couldn't stop staring at his lips either.

What would it feel like if we just . . .

I inched closer.

Wait. Did he inch closer?

Our eyes met.

I slowly tilted my head. Permission. A plea.

His fingertips once more hovered a whisper away from my cheek.

And then he stopped.

"I . . ." He drew his hand back to look at his wrist only to realize his watch was on his other one. "I should go. It's getting late. Chance of ice tonight, too."

"Ice?" I asked.

I thought the forecast said clear skies tonight.

He stood, knocking the remote to the floor. "Um, yeah. Ice. Don't want to drive with that."

Right.

Of course.

I sat up and smoothed out my hair, looking anywhere but his face as I stood and folded the blanket. "No, you definitely don't want to, um, slip." I forced a laugh, but it didn't lighten the awkwardness that had settled over us. "Thanks for hanging with me and Leo. He . . . he really cares about you, you know."

I stood there, hoping he read the subtext.

Sam gave a quick nod and went to work finding his coat and hat. Once he had both, he turned to go but stopped at the doorway and looked back at me. Maybe I was imagining it, but his eyes looked almost sad.

"Goodnight, G," he said before stepping out of the den.

The front door opened and closed.

Goodnight, Sam.

I fell back onto the couch and tried not to think about the way his fingers had lingered on my cheek.

Or the way he had stared at my lips.

Because in the end, he was still just Sam.

And I was just Gianna.

His best friend.

Nothing more.

Chapter Nine

"Personally, I think I have too much bloom. Maybe that's the trouble with me."

—MEET ME IN ST. LOUIS

"Walk me through it again," Jo asked for the hundredth time since I told her about the "almost-kiss" between Sam and me last night. From the moment I had walked into AP Lit at the beginning of the day, she had known something was up.

Apparently, I had a "glow"—whatever that meant.

I sighed and rolled a piece of tape for the back of one of the many Holly Days posters we were hanging around the school during study hall. "Okay, so after we tucked Leo into bed—"

"Adorable, by the way . . ."

"We cleaned up the ice cream bowls and then went back into the den, and he kinda stood there all shifty on his feet until he asked if I wanted to finish the movie." I pressed the poster against the wall and then adjusted it so it was straight.

"Right, *he* asked *you*, got it." Jo unrolled another poster as we walked closer to the cafeteria. "And then you got cozy on the couch and your feet touched."

I nodded and peeled off another piece of tape and handed it to her. "And then I guess I fell asleep, because the next thing I knew he was waking me up and his face was like"—I paused and stepped closer to her—"this far away from mine, Jo. And it was all blurry with color from the Christmas lights, too."

"Straight out of a movie." She took the tape from me and placed it on the back of the poster before sticking her finger out for another piece. "And then he pulled a pine needle from your hair, right?"

"And tucked my hair behind my ear like this." I mimicked the motion before giving her two more pieces of tape. "And then it was like we were both, I dunno, frozen in this moment. Like everything slowed down. And I moved, or maybe he did? I'm honestly not sure, but suddenly his hand was about to touch my cheek when he, like, woke up."

Jo shook her head. "And made a dumb excuse about ice—"

"Well, I mean, he wasn't wrong, apparently there *was* a chance—"

"And just up and left."

I ripped a final piece of tape for the poster. "You saw him today. Like, it was definitely weird, right?"

"Totally." She pressed the poster against the wall and stepped back. "The tension between you two was so thick, it would've given my Miyabi knife a run for its money."

"Ugh." I slumped against the wall. "What should I do?"

"Honestly?" She leaned against the wall next to me. "Just let it play out. See what happens. Just remember that when it *does* happen, I called it first."

"*When?*"

Or if?

Sure, for years, Jo had created all kinds of ridiculous "shipping" name combos like Team SamGi or Team Samanna—my personal favorite—but would Sam ever want to risk our friendship over it?

Would I?

The bell rang for the end of the day, bringing dozens of students into the hallways. We walked back toward the library where we had placed our jackets and book bags.

"I remember it like it was yesterday," Jo said, holding her hand in front of her face like she was taking us through a flashback together.

"Please don't bring up fourth grade again," I said as we wove around people going in the opposite direction. *I never even wanted to be in that play, but Aunt Helen signed me up before I could back out.*

"You were the best Dorothy I had ever seen!"

I laughed. "I could never do her skip down the yellow brick road without tripping."

"Girl, Sam didn't care about your skip." She grinned as she opened the library door for me. "All I know is, I've never seen anyone look at you the way he did when you clicked your heels and chanted, 'There's no place like home.' He's been down bad for you ever since."

Then why didn't he kiss me last night?

After school, I hung up a few more posters around Mistletoe Lane before stopping at The Market where Christmas jazz played over the speakers. Scott was busy showing some tourists the newest scents he'd created for his candles, and Mom hurried over to tell me she had sold three pieces today!

Guess all her late nights were finally paying off.

After mingling with everyone for a bit longer and complimenting all their updates and changes, I picked up a loaf of Italian bread from Bake My Day for our pasta tonight and left The Market to head home.

Only to once again run right into James and his father—phone glued to his ear.

"Gianna!" James beamed and took out one of his AirPods. "Running errands?"

"Kinda," I said, lifting the bread. "I was on my way home but swung by The Market to check in with everyone—"

"So, this really *is* one of those places where everyone knows everyone, huh?" His head tipped to the side. "Does that get, I dunno, kinda old after a while?"

I frowned.

"Not really." Sure, I got tired of my family poking their noses in my business, but this guy barely knew them, knew *us*.

"Plus, when you know the right people, they set things aside for you before they sell out." I held up the paper bag of bread.

"Is it any good?" James asked, stepping closer to peek inside.

I opened the bag and pulled off a small piece of the end, offering it to him. "You tell me."

James popped the piece into his mouth, and his eyes rolled back. "Oh my God, Dad. You *have* to try this." He tapped his dad on the shoulder, but Mr. Bailey held up a finger as he finished whatever he was doing before he turned around. "Sorry, what was that?"

"The bread," James said, pointing to my bag. "It reminds me of that one place we used to go to in the city. Remember the funny cat that sat in the window?"

"Yes, yes, great window, son." Mr. Bailey held up his phone and turned different directions. "Where did you say there was good Wi-Fi, Gianna?"

Pretty sure I wrote that down for you already.

Not that you pay much attention to anyone other than yourself.

"Eve's Drop, sir." I pointed to the café a block away. "And while you're there, ask Jo for a couple of the hazelnut biscotti and a cup of the organic dark roast. The beans are locally roasted. Best around."

Mr. Bailey gave the smallest of nods and smiles. "I will do that. Thank you."

"What's that you have there?" James pointed to the posters I still held.

"Oh, these are for all the events coming up for Holly Days." I opened one to show them both. "You haven't experienced Christmas till you've celebrated it in Mullings Creek."

James's and Mr. Bailey's eyes scanned over the events.

"Who designed these? They're pretty impressive," Mr. Bailey said.

"That'd be me." I shrugged. "It's not hard. I just used Canva."

"I use Canva for all my stuff, too," James added.

"James here is vice president of the honor society and co-captain of the chess club and varsity soccer." Mr. Bailey patted his son's back.

"And I wear a T-shirt listing all of my accomplishments every Friday," James deadpanned.

"There's nothing wrong with keeping busy. It's an admirable trait, son." Mr. Bailey tapped a few things on his phone, missing the way James scowled at him before turning his attention back to the poster.

"Ringing Rudloph!" James tapped the image. "Hey, remember when we won that goldfish at the Goshen County Fair ring toss?"

Mr. Bailey rubbed his cleanly shaved jawline. "You named the fish Cyclops because it had one golden spot above its eyes. The rest of him was white."

James looked away wistfully. "He was a good fish."

Mr. Bailey smiled at his son, and then, as if to catch himself in the act, went back to looking at the flier more seriously. "So, they're called 'Reindeer Games'? Don't tell me you guys fly here, too?"

"No," I replied. "But my Aunt Sofia swears she did once, after drinking four pints of green beer at the St. Paddy's Day parade."

Mr. Bailey laughed a rich, hearty laugh, loud enough to make several people on the street stop and stare. "Four pints . . . That would make anyone think of flying, I imagine." He wiped his eyes as he walked away toward Eve's, but James lingered behind.

"I haven't heard him laugh like that in years, and *I'm* supposed to be the funny one," he said to me, voice low.

"Or maybe you're not as funny as you think," I said, grinning.

He made a sound like I hit him and pressed a hand against his chest. "Shots fired by the Italian. I'm impressed." His eyes crinkled in the corners as he walked away. "I meant what I said earlier, by the way." He whirled around and walked backward. "You could've kept my sweater."

"It wasn't my color," I called back, my heartbeat quickening.

"Gasp!" he yelled back before turning around and hurrying into Eve's.

"You *do* look better in red than green, dear," a voice said from above, making me cry out and leap off the curb.

Aunt Helen sat on the roof of The Market just outside of Mom's open studio window with a half-eaten apple in her hand.

Nico and Marco would flip if they found out she climbed up there again.

Last July on Amelia Earhart's birthday, the window jammed shut, and the fire department had to come rescue her.

"Why must you always go up so high?" I asked her, squinting against the sun reflecting off the small stained glass window hanging.

She took a bite of her apple and chewed with a pensive expression before saying simply, "Perspective."

That night, Jo and I sat in the den with *The Family Stone* on TV and a plate of cookies between us. Our Chromebooks were open to give the appearance of studying for our upcoming Pre-Calc final exam, but in reality, Jo scoured Google Maps and added more restaurants for me to visit in Rome based off her favorite TikTok accounts, and I worked on new signage for the pastries she'd sell at the upcoming Reindeer Games.

Nona entered, carrying two mugs of hot tea, and placed them down on the coffee table in front of us. "Decaf for you both, although with all that sugar . . ." She pointed to the heaping pile of cookies. "I guess you'll be up late anyway."

"Sleep is for the weak, Nona," Jo said, lifting her cup. "But thank you for the tea."

"Prego," Nona replied, stealing a cookie. "Tell your fathers I am still waiting for them to call me back about my loan question."

"Loan?" I asked, placing my Chromebook to the side so I could grab my cup of tea. "Why do you need a loan?"

"I don't. Just had some questions about it." She peered over Jo's Chromebook. "Ah, helping Gianna plan for her big trip?"

"Of course." Jo turned the device so she could see the screen better. "Focusing on the food first."

"Buono, good, good," Nona said before sitting on the arm of the couch. "Cara, we haven't even celebrated yet with the family. When can we throw you a party? I'll do all the cooking. You could use some more food. You're so skinny . . ." She pinched my arm.

"I eat all time, Nona." I rubbed the spot she pinched. "And I don't need a party. It's not a big deal—"

"Ridicola!" she shouted, standing. "It *is* a big deal. I will start planning." She walked out of the room, mumbling under her breath while clasping the locket around her neck.

"She still talks to your Papa with that?" Jo asked, nodding after Nona.

"Yep." I took a sip of my tea before grabbing another cookie.

About two months after Papa passed away, Nona began talking to her locket with his and my dad's pictures as if Papa would respond. Sometimes, she'd hold it up to her ear and pretend that he did. It'd worried my mom and me for a little while, but it helped her cope.

Why get in the way of that?

Mom's car rolled onto the gravel driveway, and the engine cut promptly. Not a minute went by before the front door slammed open.

"Mother!" Mom yelled into the house. "I need to speak with you now."

Oh boy.

I know that tone.

Jo and I looked at each other for a beat before leaping off the couch and shuffling up next to the doorframe to eavesdrop.

"Is everything okay, Alice?" Nona asked calmly as she walked toward my mother from the kitchen.

"No, it's not," Mom snapped. "These were dropped off today *from Albert.*"

Ew.

Albert used his shirt collars to wipe his mouth.

I peeked around the corner. Mom held up a bouquet of white roses in front of Nona's face.

"He said they were delivered to his shop by mistake and had *my name* on them," Mom added, flustered.

Nona held up her hands, feigning innocence. "And what would I have to do with that?"

"They were dropped off to him by Nico, Mom." My mom tapped her foot on the floor. "Nico has been delivering flowers for Bud and Bloom for years. He wouldn't mess up." She pointed at her mom. "Unless he was told to."

Nona smelled the roses before turning around and walking back to the kitchen. "Put those in water. They're already drying out."

"Stop trying to set me up with single men in town!" Mom shouted at Nona's back. "Albert isn't even my type!"

Thank God.

Nona stopped and spoke over her shoulder. "You will never know what kind of 'type' you have until you start putting yourself out there, darling."

She had a point.

Mom growled and kicked off her shoes before stomping toward the den, where Jo and I quickly jumped back into our spots as if we had been there the entire time.

"Are those Befanini?" she asked, out of breath, pointing to the plate of cookies on the table.

I held up the plate. "Nona put a bit of orange in them this time."

Mom grabbed a couple and then plopped onto the couch next to me. "She bakes so we forget her meddling, but it never works." She sighed as she took her first bite. "Damn, these are good."

I bit back a smile.

Point Nona.

Mom gestured to Jo's computer. "So can this trip to Italy come with a plus-one?"

Chapter Ten

"I find most people, they don't know what's in their own hearts, let alone anyone else's."

—NOELLE

After another school day filled with adorable but slightly annoying Santagrams, and Jo trying—and miserably failing—not to be obvious with her delight about Sam and me, Nona asked me to walk her to one of the Holt greenhouses, where she was supposed to meet up with Gram and help her repot some poinsettias.

Because, sure, why not?

Being around Nona and Gram after wanting to kiss Sam wouldn't be awkward at all.

I'd just psych myself up once we got there. Maybe rehearse a couple casual conversation starters in my head so they wouldn't get suspicious if Sam showed up?

But no sooner had we entered Greenhouse Number Two than Gram did as well, on the other end. With Sam in tow.

"Silvia!" Gram waved. "You're early!"

Nona waved back and then motioned to me. "I was just telling Gianna how I missed you, Suzie."

You literally saw her this morning for coffee.

We all stopped in the center of the greenhouse, surrounded by rows upon rows of beautiful red and white poinsettias.

"Well then, why don't we let these youngsters get to work while we go catch up at the house with a cup of tea?" Gram wove her arm through Nona's, and without another word, the two of them disappeared back through the door we'd come in, the plastic tarp flapping shut behind them.

My God.

Those women really can't help themselves, can they?

Sam cleared his throat. "You'd think by now they'd come up with other ideas instead of just putting us in the same place at the same time."

"I know, right?" I took off my gloves and shoved them into my coat pockets. "Two smart women like that could definitely come up with something better, like signing us up to donate blood, knowing we're both squeamish around it and would need extra time next to each other in the recovery room with our juice boxes."

"That is . . . oddly specific, G." He fought a smile.

I shifted awkwardly in my red booties and shrugged. "I'm a writer." *Who may have had that thought once or twice when the Red Cross came to town.*

Sam chuckled as he rubbed the back of his neck. His jawline had the slightest shadow of stubble, something new he had started this fall.

I tried to ignore how much I liked it. "So, let's just get to work then," I said before turning on the Bluetooth speaker in the greenhouse and hitting play on one of my many Christmas playlists.

"I'll grab what we need." Sam began rolling up his flannel sleeves—*because apparently, the universe loved to torture me*—and walked away toward an empty potting bench where the family kept an assortment of trowels, gloves, and containers of liquid fertilizer.

Nothing like the fumes of plant food to really set the mood.

I took off my coat and earmuffs, tossing them to an empty pallet, and pulled a hair tie off my wrist. As I finished weaving my hair into a loose braid and securing the end with the tie, I turned around and caught Sam standing there with some gloves and trowels staring at me.

"You good?" I asked.

He blinked several times and cleared his throat. "Yeah . . . yep. H-here." He held out the gloves and a trowel.

"Thanks." I quickly tucked any loose strands behind my ears as Sam turned around, squatting to lift a large bag of new potting soil. My cheeks warmed at the sight of his tight jeans—

Gah.

Get a grip!

I cleared my throat and met him at a bench where several poinsettias sat next to a set of larger, empty pots.

We worked silently and methodically, scooping new soil into empty pots, before carefully shaking out each poinsettia from its current pot and placing it into its new one. The Christmas music of Leslie Odom Jr., one of my favorite singers, floated around us before Sam finally spoke. "Mom said she left a message at the B&B for the Baileys to come tour our tree farm earlier today, but Mr. Bailey never responded."

Ugh.

How would he ever see the magic of our town if he never got away from his work?

"I ran into them yesterday afternoon," I said while gently picking up a poinsettia and placing it into its new home. "Mr. Bailey was on a hunt for good Wi-Fi."

Sam chuckled. "Good luck finding it here."

"I know, right?" I smiled. "He did seem intrigued by the Reindeer Games, though. So maybe he'll come around?"

"Yeah, maybe." Sam scooped more dirt out of the bag and dropped it into the new pot around the poinsettia before pressing his gloved fingers around the soil to help anchor the poinsettia into place.

I loved watching him work—his quiet confidence that said "I could do this in my sleep."

"How do you know they're ready to be repotted?" I asked him.

"Usually, you can see it with the way the leaves droop, but I go by touch." He finished up with the one he was working on and then faced me. "Take off your gloves."

I did so, and he tossed his to the side as well.

"Now carefully run your fingers over the leaves just there." He pointed to the plant closest to me.

I touched the leaves, running my fingers down toward their tips, and he laughed.

"It's not a dog, Gianna." He crossed the space and stood behind me. "Like this."

His fingers gently wrapped around mine, guiding them forward toward the leaf where he pressed my thumb under it and my pointer and middle finger above it.

The humid greenhouse air suddenly charged with energy, and a delicious shiver zipped through me.

"Do you feel that?" he asked, his voice now husky.

Uh, yeah. I feel it.

"The way the leaves are dry, thin?"

Oh right. Leaves. Plants.

We're talking about plants.

I nodded.

"Sometimes, it's more about intuition than anything else." He slowly let go of my hand. "You know what I mean?"

Honestly?

No.

My intuition had been dead wrong lately.

Or . . . has it?

I turned around, facing him, and tried to slow my racing heart. "I feel like we need a concrete plan or something."

"For the poinsettias?"

"No, um, The Market." I stepped back a bit and braced myself against the bench.

This is good.

Benches are good.

Distance is good.

"Right. The Market." Sam stepped back too and then crossed his arms. "So, you want a plan to, what, win them over with Christmas magic?"

"Exactly," I replied. "But Mr. Bailey is so consumed with his work . . . I don't know how we'll get him away from it."

"Maybe you should ask *James*," Sam said, turning back to the plants, and the air immediately changed between us.

I was about to ask him what he meant by that when a scratching sound made us both glance toward the door. Sandy sat there expectantly with something hanging from her mouth.

I opened the door to let her in. She dropped an old, laminated baseball card at my feet and gave a short bark. "Hey, I recognize this card," I said, picking it up. "This is Don Mattingly's rookie card. Hal had one like this in his shop. Belonged to his dad, I think." I scratched Sandy's head. "Where did you find this, girl?"

"Where does she find anything?" Sam asked, giving her a treat from the jar his family kept in the corner.

Sandy gobbled down the treat and then gave us a happy

"thank you" bark before turning around and waiting at the door to be let out. The sun had started to sink below the tree line, long rays of deep orange and red melting behind blankets of gray clouds in the distance.

"I should go," I said, letting the door close behind me as I grabbed my stuff. "I promised Leo we'd make biscuits to go with the Crock-Pot stew tonight."

"Do you guys need a hand?" Sam asked.

I so wanted to say yes.

Normally, I would have.

But Sam's new back-and-forth moods were making me dizzier than watching Marco and Jo play Ping-Pong.

"Thanks, but we got it." I slid my earmuffs down over my ears.

"Okay." Sam kicked a few pieces of loose gravel and then turned back to the poinsettias. "See you tomorrow then."

"See ya." I turned to go, but Sam called to me as I opened the door.

"Don't worry about getting Mr. Bailey on board with Christmas here," he said as he grabbed a pair of pruning shears from the workbench. "You're like the Queen of Christmas, G. I'm sure you'll think of something."

I sure hope so.

The streetlights blinked on as I walked home from the greenhouse, and the smells of wood-burning fireplaces drifted in the air, carried through the trees by the crisp wind. The glow of the lit trees and wreaths hanging from every light pole on Mistletoe Lane greeted me with a welcoming smile.

What kind of person chooses to stay inside when they have all this beauty surrounding them?

Was it just work that kept Mr. Bailey from giving our town a shot, or was it something else?

We may not have been as fancy as a big city, but we were special in our own way.

Like the almost rhythmic flapping sound the Holly Days banner made when the wind moved it, and how that sound softened when its edges were covered with freshly fallen snow. Or how everyone—except Eve and Phineas, of course—seemed to go out of their way to be a little kinder and gentler in the weeks leading up to and after Christmas.

Grace was not the exception but the expectation in Mullings Creek during the holidays, and as our wonky clock tower chimed the hour, I found myself stopping outside of The Market to make a wish.

Please don't let any of this change.

The strumming of a guitar sounded up ahead from inside Chordcrafters.

Levi is playing again?

He hadn't played in ages, so I snuck closer to listen in, only it wasn't Levi who was playing.

It was James.

He sat facing the front window, eyes closed in concentration as he strummed the opening chords to "I'll Be Home for Christmas." His fingers moved as if they had a mind of their own.

It was wrong to watch him, to listen to something that was so clearly meant to be a private moment, but my feet were rooted to that cold sidewalk.

And then James began to sing.

Goose bumps prickled my arms and neck as every word flowed out of him delicately, his voice honeyed and warm. I wanted to go inside, touch his shoulder, and tell him that whatever sadness he was feeling, it would be okay.

But who was I to do that?

I barely knew him.

He was here for, what, a month?

And yet—

A dog barked in the distance, but I stayed frozen to the spot, my throat growing thick as he began the second chorus. And when his voice broke for the briefest of moments, warm tears trickled down my cheeks.

From somewhere in the store, Levi clapped.

I quickly wiped my eyes.

How long ago did he finish?

The spell now broken, I moved away to the brick wall next to the window and let my head fall back against the cool, rough bricks, moving my hand over my heart. My chest squeezed so tightly, I could barely breathe.

I had heard that song a million times before, but it had never made me feel like this.

James had sung like he ached for something he desperately needed.

While my heart ached for something I desperately didn't want to lose.

Chapter Eleven

"Christmas is not going to be 'clothing optional' this year. We've got company."

—THE FAMILY STONE

I awoke the next morning to the sounds of loud voices—some of whom were going in and out of Italian—and forks clanking on plates. After I threw on my favorite pair of flared jeans and a red sweater, I bounded down the stairs, stopping short at the entry to the kitchen where almost my entire family now sat or stood.

Mom scooped ground coffee into the pot, no doubt they had each drunk a cup already, and Nona stood at the stove, where she flipped pancakes.

Maybe if I back away really slowly, they won't notice . . .

"Ah! Ciao, bellezza!" Nona called.

Dang it.

"Sleeping Beauty has finally decided to join us," Aunt Helen said as she rested against the counter near my mom, and whispered, "Red is definitely her color, no?"

I glanced at the clock and rubbed my eyes. It was barely seven a.m. "Why are you all here so early?"

"Nice to see you, too," Marco said, standing and pulling out his chair for me to take.

I plopped down and grabbed a banana from the fruit basket on the table. "No, seriously. What's up?"

Nico leaned forward across the table from me and wiggled his eyebrows. "We're strategizing."

I groaned. "Oh God, please don't tell me you're going to go streaking through the town square at the Tree-Lighting again. 'Holly Jolly Christmas' is forever ruined because that image is burned into my corneas." I peeled the banana and went to take a bite, but the sight of the bare fruit brought back other . . . unwelcome images, so I put it down.

Aunt Helen snorted into her coffee as Nona set a heaping plate of pancakes in front of me. "Not that kind of strategizing, cara," she said, kissing the top of my head. "The kind where we convince that Scrooge to sell The Market back to us."

Sell it back to us?

Was that even possible?

I smeared some butter on the pancakes before drizzling them with syrup. "What have you come up with so far?"

Everyone's gazes darted around the room, but no one spoke up until Aunt Sofia stood, flicking her wavy hair over her shoulder. "Well, I had some ideas, but no one ever wants to do what I say." She muttered other inaudible words in Italian as she opened the door to the fridge before pulling out the creamer, closing the door with her foot. I smiled at her mismatched reindeer socks.

"That's not true, Mom," Bianca replied gently. "But doing a Christmas play *and* forcing both of them to be in it as shepherds would be a bit difficult—"

"We have a writer in the family!" Aunt Sofia pointed to me, and a piece of pancake caught in my throat.

I forced the piece of food down. "Uh, no. Sorry. I have finals coming up, and besides, I write *articles*, you know, the nonfiction type. I'm not a playwright."

Aunt Sofia deflated a bit. "Well, at least my idea was better than Mom's."

"What was wrong with mine?" Nona asked, turning around with the pancake flipper in hand.

"I can't pretend the B&B lost electricity for twentysomething days, Mom." Aunt Sofia threw her hands into the air before pouring cream into her coffee.

"Yeah, and I am not okay playing house with Mr. Bailey and his son either," my mom added, raising an eyebrow.

Oh dear God, no.

I already saw James shirtless once.

Having him living under the same roof as me for weeks? I'd never sleep.

"Uh, yeah, I'm with them," I added.

"Well, it was worth a shot." Nona smirked and went back to another batch of pancakes.

I ate a few bites of my stack before noticing that the room had gone quiet once again, and when I lifted my head, I realized why. Everyone stared at me, waiting for me to say something.

Why does it always have to be me?

But true to Steadfast G form, I swallowed and forced a smile. "Don't worry. I'll think of something."

Everyone smiled and immediately relaxed as Nona looked over her shoulder and winked. "Of course you will, bellezza."

Right.

Of course I will.

"Guys, I've got nothing." I plopped down next to Jo in one of the booths at the Wanderin' Eats Diner after school later that same day.

Across the table, Sam lowered his menu. "What about your idea to hijack Mr. Bailey's devices and make him go looking for them?" His eyes dropped back to the menu. "I liked that idea."

"Yeah, but breaking and entering to steal said devices is easier said than done. I am not the world's stealthiest person," I said, slumping down in my seat.

"True." Sam chuckled and then cried out after I kicked him in the shin under the table.

"Plus, you know, the whole illegal thing," I added. Pretty

sure I could kiss Italy and Sarah Lawrence goodbye if 'convicted felon' was included on my résumé.

"Here, have a cookie." Jo took the lid off a container next to her and held the spritz cookies out for me. "I baked these today in Culinary II, for Eve's consideration."

I took a bite out of one covered in sprinkles and shaped like a Christmas tree and sighed happily. Light and buttery with vanilla and something . . . different. "Orange?" I asked her.

Her eyes lit up. "Yes! I was inspired by Nona's batch of Befanini. Do you like them?"

I took another one and popped the entire thing in my mouth. "Duh."

After Sam ordered a sandwich and milkshake and Jo and I ordered a basket of fries to share, I grabbed Uno from the game shelf and brought it back to our table. This was the one way to tell the difference between a tourist versus a local in the diner at Mullings Creek. Tourists always ate in a hurry. We knew to take our time and enjoy the conversation while playing a game that would ultimately lead to arguing over whether or not we could stack in this version.

But after our third semi-civil round of Uno, our heads were as empty as Sam's plate and our fry basket.

"I'm starting to think we should let Nico and Marco streak through the town square again," I muttered as I laid down a Draw Two on Jo. "It's definitely more exciting than anything we've come up with."

Jo pulled two cards from the pile. "Sounds good to me. Ow!" She scooted back. "You didn't have to kick me that hard."

"Toes and heels of steel, that one," Sam said before quickly moving his legs so I couldn't do the same to him.

I groaned, laid my cards face down on the table and lowered my head into my hands. "There has to be a way to get them to buy into what we do here."

Someone tapped my head, and said, "Got room for one more?"

James stood smiling broadly at the end of our table, wearing a gray peacoat and collared shirt under a sweater, his cheeks and nose red from the cold. He looked like a completely different person than the one who sang in Chordcrafters last night, and my face flushed at the memory of it.

"Sure," I said, pointing to the empty spot next to Sam, opposite me.

Sam rolled his eyes but scooted further into the booth, sliding his copy of *The Two Towers* with him, as James took off his coat and hung it on the coatrack, which looked like a skinny Christmas tree with its garland and angel on top.

"Even coatracks are festive here, huh?" James asked as he slid into the booth.

"Everything gets a Christmas makeover," Jo said, collecting our cards and shuffling them. "Do you like Uno?"

"I don't trust anyone who *doesn't* like Uno," James said, tapping the table.

Glad we were on the same page.

James pointed to Sam's book. "Such a good movie."

"Book's better," Sam said as he picked up his cards and began to sort them.

"Agreed." James picked up his cards. "Although I'd be okay with fewer songs, especially from the Ents."

Sam snorted but didn't comment further.

We played another game as James ate a burger and fries, and we told him about the events coming up in town and which ones were our favorites.

"Gianna's is the Gingerbread House Contest," Sam said, smiling as he laid down a Draw Four against James.

"That's because she always wins," Jo added.

I laid down a Reverse. "I don't *always* win."

Sam and Jo made a face before the three of us cackled.

"I'm surprised you don't win, since you're the chef, right?" James asked her.

Jo took a sip of her water. "Gingerbread houses are more about engineering. Baking shouldn't be that stressful."

She also hated losing.

"We go caroling on Christmas Eve, too," I added, trying not to make eye contact with James for fear that he would know I'd spied on him singing.

"I don't sing, but that sounds cool." He laid down a Draw Two against Sam and smiled when Sam grumbled as he picked up two cards.

I raised an eyebrow. "You don't sing?"

James tilted his head to the side as he looked at me. "I mean, I sing, but not in public. It's not something my dad is a fan of."

Who would not be a fan of a voice like that?

"Sounds like your dad isn't a fan of a lot of things," Sam said, echoing my thought.

"He wasn't always that way." James popped a few fries into his mouth and shrugged. "Things just became different after he and my mom split. He likes Gianna, though."

"What does that mean?" Sam sat up straighter.

"Gianna gave him a great coffee recommendation, and my dad *lives* on coffee." He grinned at me. "He was impressed with her knowledge of old movies—"

"You do have a weird habit of knowing random film trivia," Jo added.

"And she also made him laugh harder than I've heard in a long time." James took a long drink of his Coke.

I mean, the stuff Aunt Sofia says is always good for a laugh.

"My parents invited you guys to our farm so they could give you a tour," Sam said, switching topics as he laid his cards face down on the table. "Did your dad mention it to you?"

"No." James frowned and fell back in his seat. "He probably hasn't listened to the voicemail yet. I can barely get him away from work at home, and it's even worse here and under this deadline from the bank." He played with the straw in his cup.

"I thought maybe being here around all this Christmassy stuff would . . . I dunno . . . bring us closer together. Kinda like we used to be. It's stupid, I know."

"That's not stupid." I laid my cards on the table.

James sighed. "Still. I really feel like if he took part in some of the stuff you guys do here that it could be exactly what he needs, but I don't think he'll listen to me."

"Your dad *does* seem pretty stubborn," I admitted. "I don't think this is something any one person can do alone."

None of us spoke for a while. The door to the diner opened and closed, bringing in a chilly breeze, which ruffled the fliers taped to the windows. One blew loose from its tape and floated over to our table, where it landed on top of our forgotten cards.

It was one of the advertisements about the annual Christmas Movie at The Market with the poster of *It's a Wonderful Life* at the center and one of my favorite quotes from the movie.

"'No man is a failure who has friends,'" James whispered, reading the flier before he made eye contact with me. A slow grin spread across his face. "I think I have an idea."

Phineas rang the bell for an order that was ready for a table as Jo took another sip of her water.

James clasped his hands in front of him and lowered his voice. "What if I pretend to date Gianna so she can bring her holiday flair closer to my dad?"

Excuse me?

Jo sucked too much of her drink and started coughing.

"What did you say?" Sam asked.

"I know it sounds crazy, and I barely know you." James turned back to me. "But I feel like you're already someone he trusts here, and if anyone has Christmas spirit in this town, it's you. Who better to help me get my dad on board with Christmas and everything Mullings Creek stands for?"

He does have a point. Why does he have a point?

My knee started bouncing wildly under the table.

"Won't it be a bit of a stretch, though?" Jo wiped her mouth with a napkin. "You've been here, what, like a few days, and you're expecting everyone, including your 'stubborn' dad, to just go along with the idea that Gianna is your girlfriend—"

"No, no. Not a girlfriend, per se." James stretched an arm behind him near Sam and then thought better of it, pulling it back to his side. "Look, I'm just a boy . . . standing—"

"Sitting . . ." Sam coughed into his fist.

"Sitting in front of a pretty girl, asking her out on a date. Well, a few dates. Is that really so hard to believe?" James smiled playfully.

Points on the movie reference, but . . .

"Gianna doesn't date," Sam said. "I mean, she hasn't dated . . . a lot."

Gee. Thanks for the reminder.

"Really?" James's eyes widened.

A quick, high-pitched laugh escaped me. "Well, when your

entire family lives in the same town and scrutinizes your every move, can you blame me?"

No one argued.

But fake dating James?

I barely knew the guy.

I mean, yeah, he was a semi-brooding secret musician with golden retriever energy. And sure, he was attractive—*okay, let's be honest here, hot*—and okay, even I could admit it would give me the best access to persuade his dad not to turn The Market into a commercial sellout . . .

My phone buzzed on the table. I swiped open a text from Mom, who sent me a few pictures of her latest work: beautiful ceramic vases with spring blooms and a couple of beautiful oil paintings of meadows with spring flowers and budding trees.

Mom: Like them?

Mom: Hoping to sell these in March if The Market is still open 🤞

Me: They'll sell out the moment you put them on display!

Me: Love you.

Mom: Love YOU ❤

I put my phone back down.

Screw it.

There was so much more at stake than just my nerves. "I'll do it."

"Really?" James and Sam said in unison.

"G, are you sure?" Jo asked, placing her hand on my arm.

"I'm sure." I reached across the table, offering my hand to James to make it official. "Let's save The Market."

James shook it with a smile. "And my dad's Christmas spirit."

Chapter Twelve

"I'm not going to fall in love with you. I promise."

—THE HOLIDAY

The only students who had to go into school today were those with state testing for science or language arts, so Sam, Jo, and I got to sleep in before meeting up for breakfast at Eve's. Frost in the shape of prickly, skinny Christmas trees stretched toward the center of each window from the pane, and dozens of new paper snowflakes dangled from the ceiling.

Within minutes, Eve brought out a tray of savory scones and three mugs of hot chocolate. "Here ya go, guys." She tucked the tray under her arm and motioned to our notebooks and Chromebooks sprawled on the two small tables we had pushed together. "Government final?"

"In two weeks," Jo said, sipping her cocoa. "There's so much to memorize."

"Be sure to know your amendments and focus on the judicial branch. Mr. Bennington has been giving the same final for years." Eve waved her hand in the air and turned to me. "Your dad would've given a much more inventive final, I'm sure."

I chuckled. “Something theatrical like dressing up as a historical figure and answering questions in character.”

“Exactly!” she said, laughing. As the bell at the door chimed, Eve added, “Holler if you need anything else while you’re here,” before she hurried back behind the counter.

“Is Nona holding up okay?” Jo asked, her eyes gentle.

I sifted through my flash cards, pulling out the ones I’d made on each amendment. “The chest freezer is already three-quarters full of meatballs, biscotti, and cannoli shells.”

Christmas had been hard in my family since Dad died, but we pushed through and had learned to lean on each other. Nona, though, preferred to pour her grief into cooking and baking. She claimed that if her hands were busy, that it distracted her heart long enough to not miss her Enzo and my dad, Tony.

“Gram keeps finding ways to get her out of the house,” Sam said as he pulled out his flash cards. “But she says Nona’s hand keeps going back to her locket. Like if she doesn’t touch it, they’ll disappear.”

“It’s a lot to deal with,” I said before taking a sip of my cocoa. “And with The Market’s future up in the air, there’s even more on her plate.”

Sam nodded grimly and broke off a piece of his scone. “I overheard Mom fussing at Gram about how she needed to slow down. That her blood pressure was too high—”

“Ha. The day your Gram slows down is the day my dads

forget to balance their checkbook." Jo stole a piece of Sam's scone and popped it into her mouth before grabbing her own from the plate beside the tiny snowmen in the middle of our table.

Jo's dads both worked at the local bank in town, and while they were notorious for their meticulous bookkeeping, they also were known for their "forgiveness" when it came to being behind on payments.

"Have they heard anything else regarding Mr. Paxton and The Market?" I asked her.

"Not really, other than the back taxes being really bad." She grabbed her cocoa and reclined in her chair. "They did say that Mr. Bailey came in a couple days ago while on a phone call, and that he was talking about an 'outdated gem of a property' in a town that held 'potential.'"

"Potential," Sam grumbled while flipping through his flash cards.

"Well then, I guess it's good that I've agreed to this whole fake-dating thing with James," I said while logging into my school account.

Another customer entered, bringing in a chilly breeze with her, as Eve switched her music over to an acoustic Christmas station. An older couple I didn't recognize settled in at a table on the opposite side of the café, pointing to the black-and-white framed pictures from our town's history decorating the walls.

Sam's eyes searched my face. "You don't have to do this, you know."

I avoided his stare and opened our Government Google Classroom instead. "I said I'd come up with something, and I did. Or he did."

"Yeah, but why you?" Sam gripped his mug and kept eye contact before glancing at Jo for support.

"Don't look at me," she said. "I literally called Mr. Bailey a Krampus to his face. Besides, James didn't ask *me*, did he?"

"That's exactly what I mean," Sam added. "We're just supposed to buy this whole 'Oh, let's fake date so you can save The Market' act? I mean, come on, it's *obvious* what he's doing."

I finally looked over my Chromebook. "And what *is* he doing, Sam?"

Sam flushed pink. "He's not interested in saving The Market, G. He just wants to . . . He's using you." He looked down and away before eating another piece of his scone.

"I appreciate the worry, Sam. Really I do." I took another sip of my cocoa. "But I'm a big girl. Do you really think I'm so naive that I can't tell the difference between someone who is sincere and who isn't?"

"That's not—"

"And okay, so maybe he is attracted to me. Is that really so hard to believe?" My heart pounded in my chest.

Sam held up his hands. "I didn't mean it like that—"

"Do you have a better idea for how to get closer to that family? Does James give you some kind of awful vibe?" I asked him, lowering my mug but keeping my hands around it to help ground me and give me the courage to say what I needed to next. "Or can you give me any other reason not to date him?"

Jo's eyes darted back and forth between the two of us as I waited for Sam to give me an answer. An honest answer.

Admit that he didn't want me dating James because he had feelings for me.

Explain why he almost kissed me in the den before running away.

Tell me I wasn't imagining the way the energy had changed between us.

But the only thing that had changed in those long, silent minutes was the song playing in the café.

Fine.

"I have to go." I tucked my Chromebook and binder back in my book bag. "I told James I'd meet him at my house in a bit. I need to be there before he arrives, or Marco and Nico will harass him from next door."

"Gianna, wait," Sam said, standing. He opened his mouth and closed it twice before grabbing the index cards on the table. "You forgot your flash cards."

Jo groaned and let her head fall in her hands.

"You can keep them," I said, zipping up my coat and tugging on my earmuffs. "I'm ready."

Over the next couple of hours, I did recon from my bedroom window, watching as Marco left for his shift at Hal's Hardware, and Nico drove away with the decked-out-for-Christmas delivery van for the florist. Nona had stayed at her home this morning, Mom was already at her studio, and Leo was at school, since fifth graders didn't have state testing for another week. With the house blissfully to myself, I blasted the soundtrack from *A Very Jonas Christmas Movie* as I got ready for my not-date date with James.

We had exchanged numbers yesterday before leaving the diner, and the plan for today was just a simple hangout in public—something casual to start people talking about the new guy hanging out with the local girl. Even someone as busy as James's dad would surely catch wind of that kind of gossip within the day.

I knew for a fact that Mullings Creek had multiple group chats dedicated to that kind of tea.

And that Nona was on most of them.

My phone buzzed with an alert, but I had to sift through the piles of sweaters and tops I had tried on after coming home from the café to find it.

James: Be there in a few!

James: Can't wait for our not-date date. ♥

I dropped my phone and hurried over to my mirror to quickly apply mascara before I remembered I already had. After a quick re-braid of my hair, I rubbed my palms over my black leggings and spun around in front of my mirror for a quick fit check. Beige hoodie under a long flannel. Black combat boots. Crossbody bag with Christmas pin.

The doorbell rang, and I jumped, butterflies now swirling in my stomach.

Why are you nervous?

"It's not like it's a real date," I whispered to myself as I half stumbled out of my room, catching myself on the wall. "It's *not* a real date. You can do this." I gripped the railing as I walked down the stairs, my heartbeat accelerating as James's shadow on the other side of our front door came into view.

You can do this.

I opened the door, and my breath caught in my throat.

James stood before me in aviators, beaming, with a dark green quarter-zip and dark jeans, with a fur-lined light wash jean jacket and a beanie. "Hi!" he said with a half wave before tucking his hand into his jacket pocket.

I can't do this.

No one in their right mind could fake date someone this hot and not get burned in the process.

"Hi." I tugged on one of my sleeves. "Any difficulty finding the place?"

"Nah." He laughed and rubbed his beanie. "But I swear your

neighbors have sensors on their homes, because lots of doors opened as I drove by."

"Neighborhood watch program," I said, closing the door behind me and locking it. "Sheriff Kingston is probably running your plates as we speak."

The color left James's face. "For real?"

I grinned.

He put a hand over his heart and exhaled. "Thank God. I've got some unpaid speeding tickets back home."

"You should probably pay those," I said, walking past him toward his red Jeep.

"I know, I know." He turned around and quickly hurried in front of me to open my door.

Wow.

And here I thought Sam was the only one with any chivalry.

After we both closed our doors, he faced me. "So where to?"

"You hungry?" I asked him.

He made a face. "Always."

"Let's go to the diner then. It'll be busy with the lunchtime rush, so a good place for people to see us, and it'll be loud enough that we can talk about our plan without everyone listening in." I buckled my seat belt.

"Speaking of the plan," he said as he put an arm behind my headrest and backed out of my driveway. "I've been thinking we need like an official name for it."

"I like that idea," I said, turning on the radio and adjusting it to the local holiday music station. "What about . . . Operation Holly Jolly?"

He pinched his lips together and hummed along to "Sleigh Ride" before replying. "Operation Mistletoe Magic?" His eyes twinkled with mischief.

I hit his arm. "This is supposed to be about getting your dad into the spirit. Not kissing."

Dear Lord, did I just say that? But more importantly, did fake dating lead to fake kissing?

And if so, how did you fake kiss someone?

What if I liked it?

What if he liked it?

"Got it. Sorry." He chuckled and turned onto Mistletoe Lane, slowing down to find a spot near the diner. "I promise I won't bring up kissing unless it's absolutely necessary. Deal?"

"Deal." I pointed to a spot a couple spaces down. "How about Making Spirits Bright?"

He shook his head and cut the engine. "Ho Ho Humbug?"

"That's it!" I laughed, and he joined in before he realized I was watching him.

"What?" he asked, wiping his face. "Did I cut myself shaving again?"

"No, no." I unbuckled and opened my door. "You and your dad have the same laugh. Did you know that?"

He nodded. "That's why it was so nice to hear it again after what you made up about your aunt—"

"Oh, that wasn't fake." We crossed the street.

He paused on the sidewalk. "You definitely have an interesting family, Gianna."

"You have no idea," I mumbled.

James held open the door, and I grabbed a couple fliers as we entered Phineas's Wanderin' Eats Diner, laying them out in front of us as we took our seats in the same booth as last night. "So we have a lot of events coming up," I said. "Gingerbread houses, Reindeer Games . . . Breakfast with Santa . . . Oh! Saturday night is the Tree-Lighting. Everyone will be there, and there's usually some singing."

Not that I would know anything about your singing ability.

" 'The best way to spread Christmas cheer is singing loud for all to hear,' " James quoted. "What if me and my dad meet you there?"

"That works," I said.

"Is it a real tree?" he asked me as a waitress brought us some water.

I made a face. "Our town *literally* has its own Christmas tree farm, and you ask if we go plastic?" I pressed a hand against my chest and winced.

"My bad." James held up his hands before he took a sip of water. "We've only ever had a fake tree at home."

"There's nothing like a live tree." I closed my eyes and sighed. "The smell, the texture . . . It just *feels* like Christmas. It's beautiful."

"I think so, too," James said.

I opened my eyes and immediately flushed as I caught him staring at me.

"I mean . . ." He cleared his throat and quickly put his menu in front of his face. "I'm sure they . . . *the trees* . . . are beautiful."

A smirk tugged at the corners of my mouth.

Several minutes later, the diner was suddenly filled with chatty folks from town. A few waved at me and then stared curiously at James before going back to their menus or conversations.

"Oh, my texts are about to blow up," I said, shaking my head as I tried to decide what sandwich to get.

"From who?" James asked, turning the menu over.

"My family. See those women over there? They're in a book club with Nona, only they don't actually read books. They just use it as an excuse to drink mulled wine and gossip."

A smile slowly formed on his face. "Sounds like my kind of club."

I laughed. "Do you want to play a game? Phineas keeps a stocked shelf over there by the door."

"I was wondering if you guys just brought your own Uno cards last night. Sure!" He laid his menu down.

I brought back Scrabble, but James frowned. "Any other options? Not really my game."

"Oh, sorry. Yes. Be right back." I hurried back to the shelf and scolded myself.

No one likes Scrabble, Gianna.

Except Sam.

His flustered and disappointed face from the café this morning flashed in my head, making my heart squeeze a bit before I pushed the memory away and returned to James with Battleship.

"Oh, big mistake." James clapped his hands and rubbed them together. "I happen to be a champion at this game."

"Is that so?" I asked, taking the red and blue game boards out of the old box. "Care to up the stakes then?"

"Absolutely." James drummed his fingers together. "Since this is our first non-date date, how about this: Winner gets to ask the loser three questions, *any* three questions, and the loser has to answer."

My palms started sweating at the potential embarrassment, but before I could spiral too hard about it, I said, "Deal."

I learned that James and I had one big thing in common: We were loud board game players.

So much so that half the diner came over to find out which of us would spot the other person's tiny tugboat first—the last untouched piece on each of our boards.

James ate the final bite of his sandwich and then leaned back in his seat, pursing his lips together as he studied his board. "I-8."

"We already know you ate!" Phineas called out from behind the counter.

The entire diner burst into laughter, but I stayed quiet and stared at my small tugboat resting on the exact spot he just called. "Hit," I mumbled.

"Hit!" James yelled, throwing his hands into the air.

Everyone started shouting "Hit! Hit!" so loudly that I wondered why more people hadn't come inside from the street to see what the heck was going on in here.

My next guess missed, naturally, making the smug smile on James's face only grow wider. And it was then that I noticed the tiniest of dimples on the right side of his face. If this was a real date, and I wasn't about to lose a game I normally won, I'd admit that I found dimples adorable. But this was war.

And we did not think about dimples during war.

Or a fake date.

"I . . . 7?" James asked.

Dang it.

The entire diner stilled, the only sounds coming from the soap opera on the TV mounted in the corner and the sizzling of the griddle.

I sighed. "Hit . . . and sink."

Napkins flew into the air. Someone hit the order bell several times near the kitchen, and people started giving James high fives and patting his back before laughing and returning to their seats.

I grumbled and sank further into mine.

Hi, remember me?

The girl who has helped all of you more times than she can count?

James, oblivious to my pouting—or maybe not—whistled happily as he started to clean up his board.

"Yeah, yeah," I said to him, separating my white and red pegs. "Enjoy it while it lasts."

"Oh, I will." He stood and grabbed our checks from the table before pulling out his wallet.

I reached into my crossbody. "Here, let me—"

"Absolutely not." He made a face and lowered his voice. "This may be a 'fake date,' but I clearly have a reputation now." He gestured to the crowd in the diner, still watching him. "I've got this one."

"Fine," I said, putting my money away. "But I get to pay for cocoa at Eve's, then."

"Deal. And then I get to ask my questions." He smirked.

Great. More embarrassment for me.

But as I watched him walk away to pay for our lunches, he smiled, shaking hands with several people like he'd known them for years and not an hour. It was like they had forgotten who he was and the powerful position his father was in.

Or maybe they just didn't care, didn't worry about him.

Maybe they saw something good in James Bailey, something promising.

Maybe going on a few dates with him wouldn't be so bad after all.

Chapter Thirteen

"One thing about trains: It doesn't matter where they're going. What matters is deciding to get on."

—THE POLAR EXPRESS

The bell rang behind us as we made our way out of Eve's Drop, me with my special cocoa and James with his plain one. The sun decided to finally come out, giving our fingers and noses a bit of a reprieve from the cold as we walked toward The Market.

"Are you sure you don't want to try mine?" I asked him, holding up my to-go cup.

"Positive." He sipped his and sighed contentedly. "I'm not a huge fan of peppermint."

Who isn't a fan of peppermint?

"Your loss, then." I drank mine and stopped as we reached Chordcrafters. "Did you want to pop in?"

James's eyes lit up with hope as he peered in through Levi's holiday-decorated window, but then he shook his head. "Maybe another time."

The guy plays and sings like he's done it his whole life.

He lights up like a Christmas tree when he's near the music shop.

So what's holding him back?

As we crossed Cherry Street, my mom stepped out of the main entrance of The Market and buttoned up her coat. She saw us and smiled, her face curious.

"Hey, Mom!" I called as we got closer. "You remember James?"

"Of course I do. Hi." Mom reached out her hand and then drew it back, frowning at it. "I really should wash the paint off myself more before offering my hand. Sorry."

James chuckled. "No problem, Mrs. Mancini. Gianna was just showing me around town."

"Is it okay to visit your studio?" I asked. "We won't stay long."

"Sure." Mom pulled a scarf out of her pocket and wound it around her neck. "Just be careful moving around the stuff on the easels. It's still wet."

After showing James around the main floor of The Market and introducing him to some of the vendors and Sandy, he followed me up the stairs to Mom's studio. The smell of fresh paint and clay lingered in her space as Nat King Cole crooned softly on the radio in the corner. Potted plants covered an entire wall with an LED tree illuminating them, and several more hung from the exposed beams above. The opposite wall had floating shelves covered with paints, stains, glues, and a small tin filled with dark chocolate "for emergencies." A long desk with an open sketch pad and trays of more paints, brushes, and different sizes of pens and markers sat next to the largest window that faced the street.

"This place is incredible," James said as he ran his fingers along the fabric draped next to one of Mom's oil paintings from last season. "Your mom created all of these pieces?"

"Mm-hmm." I sat down in the swivel chair my dad once gave her many Christmases ago and spun back and forth. "More, but she's sold quite a bit over the last several years, and the rest is already downstairs at her booth."

James stopped near the wall of plants. "Why hasn't she tried getting an agent, or I dunno, selling her stuff in the city somewhere? Is she not a city person?"

"She used to be. Grew up in the city, went to college there for a while too, but got stuck here during a bad winter storm." I stopped spinning. "My dad worked late grading papers that night and saw her slip and fall on his way home. He helped her up and walked her over to the café—before it was Eve's—and the two of them stayed there till after closing. Just talking.

"A few days later, Mom's ankle was better, and her car was fixed up and ready to go, but she didn't want to leave." I paused and smiled at the memory of my parents telling me this story to get me to sleep. "Long story short, she said goodbye to my dad but promised to write. And they did. For a year. She finished up art school and decided to move here.

She said that Mullings Creek got into her heart and didn't let go, and that she couldn't imagine living anywhere else."

"And she's been here ever since," James added, crossing the room to me. "Wow. Sounds like a movie."

"Yep." I got up and spun the chair back toward her desk. "Everyone's told her she could make tons of money if she sold her stuff elsewhere, but Mom doesn't want to. She says it just . . . brings her joy."

"I still think I'd always wonder 'what if.'" James ran his fingers over the desk's edge. "But I can respect that."

After showing James the studio, we headed back toward the B&B, where we took a seat on a front porch swing near a tall patio heater. James pushed the swing a bit with his feet as mine swung freely.

"My dad is kinda the opposite of your mom," he said, eyes watching the wispy clouds move over the sun on the tops of the trees. "He grew up in a small town. Said it was suffocating, so he moved to the city and stayed there. He did photography in college before he switched majors."

"Photography? Really?" I tried picturing Mr. Bailey behind a long lens instead of his phone but couldn't manage.

"I know, right?" James pushed his hands into the pockets of his jean jacket. "But his dad convinced him to switch to law. Said photography wasn't solid enough to rely on."

Aha.

Realization settled over my shoulders.

I bet Mr. Bailey tells James the same thing about music.

James stopped pushing the swing. "Anyway, I don't think he likes being in the city anymore."

I angled my body to face him. "How can you tell?"

"He's just more short-tempered now. Rubs his face a lot like he's frustrated. The stuff he used to find exciting he now finds annoying. Like taxis—"

"And noise?" I guessed.

James nodded. "He told me once that he hears sirens in his sleep and can't tell if he's awake or dreaming."

Oh. Would that happen to me and Jo if we stayed in the city for too long in college?

I scooted further back in the swing and brought up my legs toward my chest, wrapping my arms around my knees. "But there are good things about living in a city, right?"

"Of course." He stretched and leaned back. "It's the best place to people-watch and make up stories about who they are or where they're going. You have infinite options for food and entertainment. I've even seen entire streets blocked off for movies and television filming."

"Sounds awesome." I sighed.

"I bet you'll love it so much, you'll never want to come back home." He nudged my shoulder.

Never come back home?

True, Jo and I were both super excited to start school in

New York City next fall, but was I the kind of person to live there full-time?

Clearly, I was ready to leave Mullings Creek. I mean, I *was* skipping the second half of senior year to be an ocean away.

Once I signed the commitment form, of course.

If I signed it.

The clock tower chimed just as my phone buzzed. I groaned at the dozen or so missed messages from different people in my family and held up my phone. "Told you it wouldn't take long before my family started grilling me for info."

"Impressive." James leaned forward, resting his elbows on his knees. "Would it help if I was there to answer the questions with you?"

"Oh, absolutely not." I stood and adjusted my hoodie and flannel. "If we want Operation Ho Ho Humbug to work, it'll need to last longer than a day."

James cocked his head. "I don't scare that easy."

"Noted, but I'll spare you this time." I pulled out a Gingerbread House Contest flier from the diner and handed it to him. "Don't forget to leave this lying around where you dad can see it, and really push the whole competitiveness of it, since you said he's big on that."

James gave me a mock salute as he read over the flier again.

I started down the garland-wrapped steps and opened the text chains from my family when James called my name.

"Whatever happened to your dad?" he asked. "I'm assuming they didn't divorce, like mine did. You made it sound like they were super close—"

"They were." My limbs turned cold and heavy, and my chest tightened. Telling people about it had never gotten easier. "He was killed by a drunk driver when I was eight. Leo was barely walking."

James took in a sharp breath and hurried down a couple of steps before stopping. "I'm so sorry. I shouldn't have . . ." He sighed and shook his head. "I'm sorry."

"It's okay. You didn't know." I turned to go but looked over my shoulder. "See you Saturday night for the Tree-Lighting?"

"It's a non-date date." He smiled, the dimple appearing once more, and a small part of me started to warm up. "And don't think I've forgotten: I still get to ask you three questions."

Strangely enough, I was actually looking forward to it.

Another dozen or so text messages waited for me when I checked my phone the next day. Apparently, the family wasn't a fan of my short, straightforward replies to their questions about why I was seen around town with James Bailey. And based on the noise coming from downstairs, most of them must've invited themselves over for breakfast, too.

Yeah, that's a hard pass from me.

The last thing I needed this morning—or any morning,

really—was a family roundtable discussion about my love life or lack thereof. I got dressed as quietly as I could, thankful I had showered last night, so I wouldn't make any more noise than necessary. After successfully sneaking across the hallway to the bathroom to brush my teeth, I crept down the stairs and reached stealthily between the balusters to grab my keys from the mail table before going back up to my room to hatch an escape plan.

It had been years since I snuck out my window and scaled the lattice on the side of the house. The last time I did was to meet Jo at a drive-in movie that Mom had deemed too scary for me. In the end, she had been right; the movie gave me nightmares for weeks—not that I'd ever admit it. But that was during the summer.

I opened my window, the condensation drips on the glass running together like snakes playing tag, and grimaced at the sparkly frost on the roof.

Are you really going to risk death for the sake of avoiding your family?

Silverware clattered below as someone, probably my Aunt Helen, yelled my name, followed by Nona echoing her.

Yep.

I threw my book bag over my shoulder and climbed through the window, closing it gently behind me. Scooting slowly across the roof, only semi-slipping twice, I reached for the lattice and gave it a couple tugs to make sure it was fastened tightly. The descent was successful until the entire thing started to groan and wobble.

Crap.

I leaped off the lattice—thankfully only five feet from the ground—and landed on my feet. My hands went up in a silent cheer before I hurried toward the sidewalk as the frosty grass crunched under my shoes.

A little while later, Jo and Sam came into AP Lit, and Jo dropped something warm and heavenly smelling on my desk.

"A bacon, egg, and cheese bagel?" I asked, unwrapping it quickly.

"Well, seeing as you skipped breakfast and nearly tumbled to your death—"

"You fell?" Sam whipped around in his seat. "Are you okay?"

"I'm fine," I replied, doing my best to avoid his worried expression. "Even landed on my feet."

He mumbled something that sounded like "good" before turning back around as the bell rang.

Jo leaned across the aisle. "So how was your . . . date?"

"Um, it was a non-date." I ran my hands over my hair, tucking it behind my ears before I pushed the last couple of bites of my bagel to the side to take out my binder. "But it was great, actually."

Did Sam seriously just stiffen?

I fought the urge to smack the back of his stubborn ginger head with one of my Flair pens.

We all pulled out our copies of *A Midsummer Night's Dream* and flipped open to act 3 while Mrs. Bartlett did a quick recap of the love potion mix-up on the ViewBoard.

"Isn't it weird how what we read in class mirrors what we're dealing with in real life?" Jo said, pulling out her study guide.

Sam shifted in his seat and mumbled something I couldn't hear.

"What do you mean?" I asked, my voice low.

"Love triangles." Jo made a face and nodded toward Sam, tapping her pen on her play. "Falling for the wrong person—"

"Falling for a donkey," Sam said over his shoulder.

The three of us cackled and immediately quieted when Mrs. Bartlett gave us one of her infamous "don't push it" looks. Jo and Sam followed along silently a minute later as a few of our classmates began reading their parts aloud, but my brain couldn't stop circling back to the way Sam responded to my leaping from the lattice.

The panic in his voice.

How his shoulders squared when Jo asked me about my date with James.

And then there was that mumbling about love triangles—

Oh my God, Gianna, why does it matter? I sighed and rubbed my temples.

I had given Sam the opportunity to tell me his real feelings, to give me a reason not to date James, and he said nothing.

He did nothing.

So as much as I hated to admit it to myself, those two things told me everything I needed to know.

Chapter Fourteen

"We make our own magic."

—DASH & LILY

On Saturday, after successfully sneaking out again to hang with Jo while she worked a morning shift at Eve's, I finally forced myself to go home, cringing when I saw the familiar cars parked in my driveway.

You knew what you were signing up for, G.

I did one of Leo's four-count breathing things before opening the front door, and no sooner had I closed it than my entire family swarmed me from different areas of the house. Questions and comments flew at me all at once.

"Cara, what is going on?"

"—you barely know him!"

"Is this like a serious thing—"

"Or are you two in the 'talking' phase?"

"Everyone just slow down and take a breath." I held up my hands. "Yes, James and I went on a date." I held up my hand to cut off Bianca, who was about to interrupt. "Yes, it is new, and yes, I barely know him . . ." I thought back to our game of

Battleship. Of our conversation in Mom's studio and on the porch of the B&B. And how he jumped up and hurried halfway down the stairs after asking me about Dad, and I smiled. "I know the timing is off, but I'm excited to get to know him and to see where this leads."

I thought it would be hard to do that. Lie to them.

But surprisingly, it wasn't.

Because maybe I wasn't actually speaking a lie.

James was, in fact, pretty interesting. Charming, even.

Did it go against the fake-dating pact that a small part of me was actually kinda excited to hang out with him some more?

Leo must've walked down the stairs at some point, because as I finished, his pinkie finger found mine, and he smiled up at me.

I ruffled his hair and turned back to my family. "We can talk more about it later. I've got finals to study for."

Most of them separated into different rooms, whispering among each other as they left the hall, but Marco and Nico lingered behind and cut off my escape path to the stairs.

"Just make sure he knows that we know people," Marco said, cracking his knuckles.

"What he said." Nico nodded toward his brother and crossed his arms over his snug, pink crewneck sweatshirt that said LILAC THE ABILITY TO CONTROL MYSELF.

I bit back a smile. "I'll do that."

The temperatures were already dropping below freezing by the time I searched for the Baileys that evening in the town square. As was tradition, every business on Mistletoe Lane turned off the lights on their buildings so that the tree could be the true center of attention when lit for the first time.

Jo, Sam, and Isaiah walked up together and waved at me before coming over. Jo pulled out her gloves and slipped them on, rubbing her hands together in front of her face. "So have they arrived yet?"

"Not yet." I craned my neck and jumped up and down a couple times, but it was no use. I couldn't see over anyone in this crowd.

Sam sighed and crouched down in front of me. "Get on," he said.

"Excuse me?" I looked to Jo, but she shrugged in confusion.

He patted his shoulders. "You'll never see them coming from down there. Hop on."

I stepped back. "I dunno, Sam, what if—"

I break you.

Or I break me if I fall to my death from your super-tall shoulders.

Or . . .

"I won't let you fall, G." He looked down at me, his freckles glowing under the nearby lamplight. "We've done this a million times."

Yeah, like, in elementary school.

But the lighting would start any minute, and I did promise James I'd be with him and his dad to kick off Operation Ho Ho Humbug. I sighed. "Okay. But if I'm too heavy just—"

"I've got you," Sam said.

I walked up and swung my legs around either side of his neck, trying not to think about the way my entire body pulsed with heat from being this close to him. He tucked both forearms around my shins, and stood up faster than I expected.

I squealed and threw my hands over his face.

"Can't see, Mancini," he said, his voice muffled.

"Oh, sorry." I moved my hands to the top of his head, adjusting the beanie that I'd messed up.

"You good?" he asked.

The dormant butterflies stirred back to life once again, bouncing around my stomach so wildly that I wondered if Sam could feel them too. "I'm good," I lied.

After a couple of minutes of slowly spinning around, I spotted James and Mr. Bailey at the edge of the crowd on Mistletoe Lane and called out to them, waving. James tapped his dad's shoulder, and they both wove through the crowd toward me.

Sam lowered me to the ground just as the Baileys appeared in front of us—Mr. Bailey was on his phone, naturally—and stood back up, adjusting his hooded winter coat.

"Thanks," I said, my heart still pounding.

Because of the spinning and heights.

Obviously.

He gave me a small smile and said, "Anytime," before disappearing into the crowd. Jo had gone a moment ago, too, probably not wanting to remind Mr. Bailey of her "Krampus" comment.

"Good evening, sir," I said to Mr. Bailey after he hung up.

He tapped on a few things.

"Dad." James nudged him. "You said you were going to leave it behind."

"Well, that was before I got a hellacious email from Milton . . ." He mumbled something inaudible before putting his phone in his coat pocket. "Good to see you, Gianna." He spun to face the huge tree. "Quite a turnout."

"It's always a big event here," I replied.

"How was school yesterday?" James asked as he came around to stand on my other side.

"Pretty chill. Most classes are having makeup days or finishing up projects before state testing and finals."

"Bleh. Finals." James shoved his hands into his pockets. "I like that we take ours early and are off for all of December, but I do hate starting the beginning of August."

"Yeah, mid-August is early enough for me." I adjusted my earmuffs. "So, what did you guys get into today?"

"Dad went to go work at the diner, of course." James rolled his eyes. "And I went to a couple places—the bookstore, Eve's—"

"Chordcrafters?" I asked.

James looked shocked but amused. "You spying on me?"

"No," I said, quickly dropping my eyes to my boots.

Except that one time, of course.

"Did James tell you about our upcoming Gingerbread House Contest tomorrow?" I asked Mr. Bailey, who was once again scrolling his phone.

"He did." He looked up and put his phone back in his coat pocket. "It's been years since I've made a gingerbread house, though."

"Oh, that's okay. We give you all the supplies." I pointed behind us. "Everything gets displayed in The Market for the judging. And there's live music and food afterward, too."

Mr. Bailey pursed his lips together and stayed quiet.

I nudged James. "Maybe hide his devices so he doesn't have any excuses," I whispered.

"Already scoped out a few places in the suite," he whispered back, giving me a fist bump.

Mayor Moore took the stage and after the applause died down, he was joined by several kids, including Leo, from the elementary school, all with scripts in their hands.

"What's going on?" Mr. Bailey asked. "I thought this was a tree-lighting."

"It is," I said. "But with a twist."

On cue, the crowd started humming the Whoville song from *How the Grinch Stole Christmas*, and the kids on the stage recited the Grinch's monologue from the mountain-top scene where he realizes that "Christmas doesn't come from a store." And as Leo slowed down the final line of "Maybe Christmas . . . perhaps . . . means a little . . . bit . . . more." Mayor Moore flipped the switch. Hundreds upon hundreds of multicolored Christmas lights now illuminated the big tree.

Everyone clapped and cheered, although Mr. Bailey's hands remained in the pockets of his fancy coat. "Well, I've never seen a tree-lighting like that before."

I smiled proudly. "We do things a little differently here in Mullings Creek."

"I loved it," James said, taking my hand.

His gloved fingers threaded through mine, and I was surprised at how normal it felt. Natural, even. The butterflies didn't dance around the way they had moments ago when I was on Sam's shoulders, but they did flutter a bit.

"Is this okay?" James whispered near my ear.

"Yes," I said, surprising myself at how quickly I answered.

Mr. Bailey's phone rang, and he stepped away to answer it.

James checked the time. "Shoot, I have to head back. I've got a FaceTime date with Jenny in ten minutes."

Date? I angled my face up to James and tried my best to sound indifferent. "Jenny, eh? She sounds . . . cute."

"I mean, sure, she is." He smirked. "For my stepsister." He angled his head. "Was that a flash of jealousy I detected?"

"No." I looked away.

Okay, maybe.

He laughed and nodded toward Leo, who was still on the stage with his classmates. "She's a year older than Leo, I think."

"What's she like?"

"She's great. Super smart and funny, too." He grinned. "The only redeeming quality about my stepfather."

"James, I need to head back to grab some files so I can finish this call," Mr. Bailey said, his hand covering the bottom of his phone to mute his voice. His eyes darted down to James's fingers, still laced with mine. "You should get going, too, so you don't miss Jen." He turned and started weaving his way through the crowd.

"Sorry we can't hang out some more," James said, facing me as the clock tower chimed.

Same. "I'll see you tomorrow at the Gingerbread House Contest, though."

"It's a non-date date." He leaned in, his lips a breath away from my cheek before he stopped and stood up straight. "Sorry. I was on autopilot."

"It's okay."

Was I on that too, since I didn't pull away?

The fluttering inside my belly thumped a bit harder. "I mean, everyone is here, so it didn't hurt the act, right?"

I regretted it the moment I said it.

The moment his sweet smile vanished off his face.

"Right, of course," he said, his voice clipped. "All part of the act." And without another word, he turned around and hurried away to catch up with his dad.

Ugh.

Way to go, Gianna.

"Leo killed it!" Jo said as she and Sam joined me. "And that might've been the first time the town didn't sound horribly off-key, too."

"Did Mr. Humbug stay off his phone long enough to hear it?" Sam asked.

"He did." *Sort of.* I rubbed my hands together. "And he loved it."

I think.

It was hard to get a read on him when his face was always in his phone or perpetually scowling.

Jo gave me a quick hug before saying, "I gotta go help Eve finish closing up, since we left early to come here. But I'll see you two tomorrow."

Sam flicked one of the candy canes framing the big tree and blew out a long breath, making steam puff up in front of his face. "You hungry?"

I smiled. "Does La Befana deliver gifts to children?"

A few minutes later, we found two open seats at the bar of Phineas's diner and took off our coats, draping them over the backs of the chairs. I reached across the counter and spun the dial on the radio till it reached our local station. WQRB played twenty-four-seven Christmas music, and it earned us some cheers from Hal and his son, who sat a couple chairs over. Sam grabbed Scrabble from the game shelf as I ordered our usual late-night meal of bacon cheeseburgers, fries, and milkshakes—mint chocolate chip for me, because of course.

After our meals slid across the counter, we exchanged my lettuce for his tomato, since Phineas—bless his heart—always forgot to do it, and then we started playing the game quietly while we ate. Sam used his current read, *1984*, as inspiration for words. I fell back in my chair and spun it back and forth while figuring out which letters to put together next, and took a minute to look around the garland-draped room.

Every person in here had known me my whole life. They could probably fill a book with their stories and anecdotes about my family—multiple chapters on Marco and Nico alone. I loved how safe I felt here. How predictable things were, down to the wonky sounds of our clock tower to the mishaps with my burger. And yet part of me did think that maybe I really was ready for a change. Maybe it was time to see new people and make new stories.

"You must have crappy tiles," Sam said, bringing me out of my head.

"Oh, sorry." I picked up my tiles and spelled *J-I-N-G-L-E*.

"Fourteen. Not bad," Sam said as he started to write the score on the napkin, but I laid my hand on top of his.

"Twenty-eight. Double word points." I grinned. "Tie game."

Sam scoffed and then his eyes dropped to my hand still covering his.

"Sorry," I said, drawing it back.

"No worries." He fixed the score and laid the pen down, letting his hand fall to his side but not before I caught him flexing it.

My own fingers had that same kind of numbness from when you placed freezing hands under warm water. I busied them with picking up the last of my fries, but the ticklish pinpricks lingered.

"You good?" he asked, taking the final bite of his burger before placing a couple of tiles onto the board. "You seem far away tonight."

I finished chewing and pushed the basket away. "I was just thinking about next semester. Next year."

"Of leaving?" he picked up more pieces and switched them around.

"Yes," I said, "but also the coming back part." *If they'll even want me back if I can't convince Mr. Bailey not to sell our Market to some random outsider.*

Sam spun to face me, placing his arm on the back of my chair. "Mullings Creek will always be here, G. It'll always be your home."

Will it, though?

I looked around, at everyone chatting or playing games while they ate, and my heart squinched up a bit. "But what if it's not the same home I leave behind?"

Sam drummed his fingers on the top of my coat for a

moment before responding. "Places change. People do, too. But I think home is more of a feeling than a location on a map."

"Not bad, Holt." I grinned. "Maybe you should go into writing like me."

"Nah." He spun back around and waved his hand at Ms. Donna for the check. "I'll be quite happy just running the family farm someday."

When she dropped the check in front of us a moment later, Sam scooped it up. "I've got this one."

"You sure?"

"Yep."

Before I could process what he was doing, Sam picked up my earmuffs off the counter and carefully slid them onto my head, pushing a couple flyaways off my forehead afterward. I froze, my boots glued to the floor.

The last time we were this close was in my den, when I so desperately wanted him to kiss me. And just like that night, I felt myself getting lost in the almost twinkling golden ring around his irises.

How do we keep getting here, Sam?

He cleared his throat and hopped off his chair, avoiding my eyes as he took out his wallet. "I'll just go take care of this at the register."

"Okay," I said, trying to not read too much into the fact that normally Sam and I split the bill and what his paying for me could mean. "I'll clean up the board, then."

But when I started picking up the pieces, I noticed that Sam had, in fact, laid down his tiles for a final word, one threaded through two others.

He got ten points.

And I got an instant uptick in my heartbeat as I ran my fingers over his winning word.

S-O-U-L-M-A-T-E-S.

Chapter Fifteen

"I can't put my arms down!"

—A CHRISTMAS STORY

Before the sun rose Sunday morning, Nona, arms full of materials from The Market for the annual Gingerbread House Contest, knocked on our door. Leo had already been awake for over an hour, too excited to sleep and desperate to get started on our contest entry. This was his favorite part of Mullings Creek's Holly Days—probably because of the sneaking of treats while we constructed our design rather than the competition part.

"Buongiorno, my dears," Nona said, giving us each a kiss on the forehead before heading to the kitchen to lay the supplies on the table. "Can you two carry in the gingerbread? It's in the crate in the back of my car."

"On it," Leo said before practically springing through the front door and leaping off the front porch, then he stumbled onto the sidewalk in his boots.

"So will James be joining us today?" Nona asked from the kitchen.

I slipped back into my boots. "No, he's going to be doing an entry with his dad, actually."

"Interesting." Nona rummaged through one of our drawers. "Donna said she saw you and *Sam* last night at the diner."

My finger froze on the doorknob.

Did she see the moment with the earmuffs before we left?

Then again, could we really even call it a moment?

I made my voice as casual-sounding as possible. "We eat there all the time."

Nona's head popped out of the kitchen. "I'm just surprised you ate there with him, when you're dating that other person—"

"James. And it was one date," I corrected. "You literally just asked about him, Nona. You know who he is."

"I'm just making sure *you* do, too." She shrugged before disappearing back into the kitchen.

My God, that woman is going to give me an ulcer before I'm twenty.

After Leo and I carried the large gingerbread house into our kitchen, we stepped back with Nona and started brainstorming our design. Every competitor received the same basic house structure, since not everyone had the time or money to make their own gingerbread. We were also allowed to use any of the candies and supplies laid out in The Market with the houses, but we had to use our own frosting, which was where Nona famously came in.

"I feel like we should do something different this year," I said, tying my apron around my waist. "But I'm not sure what."

Leo cocked his head from side to side and then clapped his hands. "I got it!" He hurried closer to the table and crouched down next to the house. "What if we make ours The Market and add some of the other fun stuff from town around it?"

"That's perfect." I hugged him and then folded his apron down so it wouldn't loop behind his neck—he hated that feeling—before tying it around his waist.

"Nona, can you make—"

"Red frosting for the poinsettias and wreaths and green for the roof? I'm on it," she replied, already dumping powdered sugar into a mixing bowl—no measuring necessary when Nona was in charge.

Leo and I began sorting the candy into different piles, taste-testing for quality purposes as we went. We pulled gumdrops to line the roof, Pull 'N' Peel Twizzlers to line the windows, and candy-coated chocolate chips for the walkway.

Leo then grabbed a box of Rice Krispies cereal and a bag of marshmallows. "Let's mix these to make our Christmas trees and barrels."

"You are a genius!" I grabbed a stick of butter from the fridge to melt before we'd add the marshmallows.

A couple of hours later, with our mouths and fingers sticky from the marshmallow treats, Leo and I had finished molding our barrels and Holt Christmas trees for outside our gingerbread

Market. Nona had successfully tweaked her recipe so that the icing would harden faster, which she then cut out into the shapes of the shutters and metal sheets for the roof. I piped white frosting onto the top of the gable, and Leo pressed the gumdrops into it, creating a pattern of green, white, and red.

Nona always said Italians were meant to celebrate Christmas in a big way, since our flag had the same festive colors.

While we separated the Twizzlers into smaller ropes to outline the windows and shutters, the doorbell rang. Leo hurried to answer it, and a moment later he was followed into the kitchen by Sam.

"Smells amazing in here," he said, taking off his gloves and then his beanie, which had made his hair stick up at all angles.

My heart skipped a beat at the messiness of it and the brightness of his eyes before I forced it to chill out.

He is your friend, Gianna.

Something he has made abundantly clear.

"Gianna," Nona said, waving a hand in front of my face. "Did you hear him?"

I blinked. "Sorry. What? Who?"

Nona laughed and wiped her hands on her apron. "Sam came over to borrow some butter for Gram. Could you spare two sticks?"

"Oh, sure." I hurried over to the fridge and grabbed two sticks while Sam crouched over by the table, listening intently to Leo explain everything we were still planning to do for our gingerbread Market.

"This was a genius idea, little man," he said, ruffling Leo's hair.

"That's what I said." I smiled at them both.

Sam stood and tugged on his hat as I held out the butter. "Thank you," he said.

"No problem," I replied. "Did you guys enter this year?"

"No, Gram's been feeling a bit tired lately, so she wasn't up to it."

"Tell Suzie I said to make a large Amaretto and then go to bed," Nona said, waving her spatula at Sam. "She has all winter to bake."

"Yes, ma'am." Sam saluted Nona with the butter sticks and then turned back to me. "Oh, you have something just there."

Sam brushed the end of his sweatshirt sleeve against my cheek. "Powdered sugar," he said, his voice low.

Shivers moved down my spine and all the way to my Christmas-slipper-socked toes.

"Always a mess, Mouse," he said, grinning.

I dipped my finger in red frosting next to me and bopped his nose. "Whatever, Rudloph."

He wiped the frosting off with his thumb before sucking on it.

My goodness.

I braced my hand on the back of the closest chair and tried to think of the non-sexiest things I could.

Marco's armpit stink after hockey practice.

Nico's drool when he remembered to wear his retainers.

Nona cleared her voice loudly, making us both startle. "Don't forget to tell Suzie what I said."

Sam nodded and zipped up his coat before hurrying out of the kitchen.

Once the front door opened and closed, Nona chuckled and went back to mixing more frosting before she said, "Crack open a window, will you, Leo? It's quite warm in here all of a sudden."

Tell me about it.

While we waited for everything to set, Leo and I grabbed our new outdoor Christmas lights to wrap around our front bushes and surprise Mom. But just as we stepped onto the front porch to start detangling them, my phone rang with a call from James.

I swiped it open and put it on speaker so Leo and I could keep working. "Hey!" I said. "How's the gingerbread construction going?"

"Uh, not great," James said. The sounds of clanging pots and pans echoed around him.

Leo stopped untangling lights and stood up. "Oh no, what happened?"

"I can't move!" Mr. Bailey shouted from somewhere nearby.

"What does he mean, he can't move?" I asked as Leo and I exchanged worried looks.

"I think we made the frosting wrong, because every time Dad lets go of something, it falls." James's breathing quickened like he was pacing. "He's been stuck with his arms up, holding some pieces together on the roof for ages—"

"I can't feel my arms!" Mr. Bailey shouted. "My arms are asleep! It's these gumdrops. I told you we should've used the mints, James!"

Leo chuckled, putting a gloved hand over his mouth to cover it.

"We'll be right over," I said before I hung up and joined Leo's giggles.

My brother and I quickly piled some supplies into our bike baskets and pedaled over to the B&B.

When we got there, Aunt Sofia was nervously pacing on her front porch with her hands around a mug of something steaming hot. "Oh, thank God you're here," she said as we hurried up the walk.

I really do need that printed on a shirt.

"They're making an absolute mess of my kitchen." She pinched the bridge of her nose. "It's like the time Francis came home from college all over again."

That was a story I knew to be true. It involved all of my male cousins, Aunt Sofia's famed punch bowl, a large bottle of cognac, and an eggnog recipe gone wrong.

Or as Nico still put it: "Oh so right."

"We'll take care of it," I said as Leo and I rushed by her and into the B&B.

James and Mr. Bailey sighed with relief as we pushed open the door to the kitchen.

"Holy cow!" Leo set his stuff down on the breakfast nook table. "This looks like a war zone!"

And he wasn't wrong.

The gingerbread house had spires sticking out of it with lumps of frosting dripping down its sides. Red Hots speckled the floor, and powdered sugar covered almost every surface, including James's and Mr. Bailey's hair. And that was when I noticed their Christmas aprons. Mr. Bailey had on my Uncle Gabriel's, which had LET'S GET LIT spelled out in Christmas lights, and James wore my Aunt Sofia's SANTA'S FAVORITE HO.

I pinched my lips together and tried to hold back a laugh but failed, eventually doubling over snorting and crying.

"When you are *quite* done, could someone please give me a hand, since I can no longer feel mine?" Mr. Bailey asked, his face red. "I can't believe I skipped a Zoom call for this . . ."

"Honestly, sir, you should just drop your hands and let those gumdrops fall," Leo said, propping his elbows on the island in the middle of the kitchen, where most of the mess was. "You're going to have to start over anyway."

"Oh, thank God." Mr. Bailey let his arms go and fell back against the cabinets behind him. "There was no way I was going to allow my name on *that*."

"Come on, Dad," James said, crossing the kitchen. "It's not that bad."

The four of us exchanged glances, there was a pause, and then we all burst into fresh laughter.

I wiped my eyes a moment later. "Okay, so first, we need to remix your icing so it's less runny."

"How do we do that?" Mr. Bailey, asked straightening his apron.

"More powdered sugar," Leo said matter-of-factly.

"Oh, for the love of God, please, no!" Aunt Sofia yelled from the foyer.

Leo giggled and then picked up the bag that had fallen over and stepped carefully around the candy-covered floor to the stand mixer.

I grabbed two clean spatulas from my bag, having assumed theirs were either broken or caked with something impossible to clean, and handed one to each of them. "You two carefully scrape off that frosting and then sort your candy by weight. You don't want to place too much heavy stuff on top."

"But what about the spires?" James asked.

I pointed to the plastic tub behind me. "We can make those with our leftover Rice Krispies."

"Brilliant!" Mr. Bailey yelled. "Quickly, James, let's do what she says."

Brilliant?

Maybe it was the plume of powdered sugar in the air, but that Scrooge just sounded almost . . . excited?

An hour and a half later, we had created our best version of St. Patrick's Cathedral in New York City. The new batch of frosting worked perfectly to hold up the crispy rice spires, and James even added some indentations. Gumdrops were placed around the entire structure, and Twizzlers ropes hung down to make each spire look longer and taller.

But Mr. Bailey surprised us all when he melted the Red Hots to give the appearance of stained glass. He dripped them inside mini pretzels before sticking them to the sides of the cathedral.

This Scrooge was definitely on his way to finding some Christmas spirit.

"Not bad," he said, stepping back to survey our work. "Not bad at all."

"It just needs one final Christmas touch," I said, gently lifting up the small wreath I'd made from halved green gumdrops.

"Here, let me help," James said. He took one of our bowls of frosting and a small knife, smearing some onto the front of the graham cracker door. Together, we pushed the wreath above the door, our fingers touching as we did.

Tiny sparks prickled their way around my wrist and up my arm.

Well, this is . . . new.

"Thank you," James said, his face close to mine.

I tried to slow down my heartbeat but failed. "No problem."

What the heck was wrong with me, swooning twice in one day?

My conversation with Nona ran through my head.

You know who he is.

I'm just making sure you do, too.

And I did.

This is James, and we are fake dating.

But since when did fake dating make someone so breathless?

"Can I eat the rest of this?" Leo asked, holding up the bowl of frosting and melting whatever that was between us.

I made a face and said "No" at the same time James said "Sure!" and the kitchen erupted with laughter once again.

Chapter Sixteen

"Traditions change. Right? The new ones are scary, but they might be great."

—NOELLE

Later that afternoon, Mullings Creek's annual Gingerbread House Contest was in full swing at The Market. Per tradition, everyone who participated wore their favorite ugly Christmas sweater. Mine said MEOWY CHRISTMAS with a huge fuzzy cat draped in tinsel, and Jo wore one with a lit-up goat dressed as Scrooge that made noise thanks to a button near the hem. We pushed the stands to one side, making room for a new row of foldouts for the contest entries. Then Jo and I draped each table with deep green cloths.

"So, Eve was looking at sales reports the other day, and she said my Christmas pastries and cookies have doubled the café's numbers from last year," Jo said, smoothing out one of the cloths.

"Why am I not surprised!" I said. "She's probably regretting not letting you sell your stuff in mid-November like you'd wanted."

" 'Christmas falls *after* Thanksgiving.' " Jo mimicked Eve's voice, which had the slightest New England accent, before pressing the button to make her sweater scream, *BAAA HUMBUG!*

I handed her another cloth that we opened and shook out together. "Well, at least she's appreciative of you."

"My dads said the same thing." Jo helped me drape the final cloth on the table before we moved over to everyone's entries, and my phone pinged with an email alert.

Crap.

I didn't have to open up the notification from Adventure Italy Academy to know what it was about.

"You good?" Jo asked as she and I took the different sides of one entry and carefully moved it over to a contest table.

"Yeah, just got an email from AIA." I took the nameplate of the entry and flipped it around so the judges wouldn't see. "A reminder to sign the commitment agreement before December twentieth."

Not that I needed it.

No matter how busy I stayed, that deadline was always on a loop in my brain.

Jo and I grabbed another entry that looked like Santa's workshop. "Why haven't you signed it yet?" she asked.

I shrugged.

"Don't put off your dreams because of what's happening here, G." She made a face. "This is the chance of a lifetime. You deserve this."

"I know. I just don't know that I'll really be able to celebrate it if The Market goes under." *Which is why I can't let it.*

Once all the entries, including our Market-themed structure and the Baileys' cathedral, were in place to be judged by the Mullings Creek Town Council, Sam pulled up in his father's cherry-red vintage 1952 Chevy truck. The driver and passenger doors had their Holt Christmas Tree Farm logo, and a fresh wreath hung on the front grille. As his family, including Gram, piled out, my throat grew thick while I watched Sam offer his arm to Gram. Family and tradition were everything to him. To them.

The Holts loved helping out this town, watching it flourish.

I knew Jo was still semi-optimistic, but what if the new store in place of The Market took away some of their business or made it harder for them to sell their stock?

I couldn't let that happen.

No sooner had they entered The Market than the music from our local band Restless Dad Syndrome began their set. Normally, this group of retired dads played covers of classic rock favorites, but today and over the next few weeks, they'd be heard around town doing only seasonal hits.

Jo hurried off to the stage where she would, no doubt, dance till they took a break. She didn't need a partner, but that never stopped her from grabbing anyone standing nearby. As I backed up a bit to avoid being her next victim, I bumped into someone, earning a loud grunt and a pair of large hands grabbing on to my elbows to keep me from falling.

"I'm sorry!" I whirled around and came face-to-face with Sam and Gram.

"No apologies needed, honey," Gram said. Her eyes dropped to Sam's hands, still holding on to my arms.

He dropped them the same time I took a big step back.

Gram winked, and I looked for the nearest exit or sinkhole to disappear into. "Sam's gotten so strong that nothing takes him down anymore, right, Sam?" she asked.

He kept eye contact with me for a beat longer than I expected before looking at Gram and saying "right."

"I think I'll go find Silvia." Gram patted her grandson's cheek. "Why don't you just ask the girl to dance already before someone else does, hon."

Oh, sweet Lord.

And with a knowing grin, she scurried away before either of us could remind her that Sam didn't dance.

Or that I was already dating someone.

Sort of.

Sam ran a hand through his hair. "She spends far too much time with your Nona."

You can say that again.

He smoothed down the front of his *Home Alone* sweater and then motioned toward the dance floor. "Um, did you maybe want to—"

"Gianna!" James hurried over and casually placed his hand on my shoulder. "Love the festive cat, but I think Sam has you beat."

He wasn't wrong.

Sam held his hands out and spun around to show off Mrs. McCallister's panicked face and KEVIN! embroidered underneath.

James sighed and pointed to his plain sweatshirt. "I don't have an ugly Christmas sweater, and Amazon wouldn't have gotten it here fast enough. I'm surprised you guys don't have next-day delivery."

Sam rubbed the stubble on his chin. "We don't really need it. Most everyone here gets by fine with what they have."

"Well, you don't know what you're missing," James said before pointing to Sam's sweater. "All yours needs is a—"

Sam pressed a button and the classic *KEVIN!* screech cut through the air.

"Nice!" James laughed and clapped.

"It's one of my and Gianna's favorite movies," Sam said, the freckles on his face turning the slightest shade of pink.

Well, it used to be.

But now I don't know what to think about it.

Or how our socked feet touched under the fleece blanket.

Or how our faces were just inches from each other.

Or the way his eyes sparkled from the Christmas tree lights . . .

James nudged me, bringing me out of the memory that I was almost convinced had been a dream. "Wanna dance?"

I gulped. "Now? Here?"

James looked around the room. "Is there somewhere else where dancing is happening I don't know about?"

"Gianna doesn't dance," Sam said.

I made a face. "You're one to talk."

"Doesn't like the attention—"

"Doesn't like her family having more ammo to throw at her is more like it," I said, hitting his arm.

"Ah, that makes sense." James's smile vanished faster than fresh snow on warm pavement.

Oh, what the heck.

"You know what? Yes, I will dance with you," I said. "But first, you need a wardrobe update." I turned around to the contest table and grabbed a strand of garland that lined the front of one table, draping it over James like a scarf. "Perfetto."

He beamed and took my hand, leading me to the floor where Jo waved wildly at us before pressing her button again, activating that all-familiar shriek.

"How exactly do we dance to 'Run Run Rudolph'?" I asked him as a dozen or so people from town bumped and shuffled around us.

James pursed his lips and studied them for a moment before grabbing my hand and twirling me quickly. "You just make it up as you go!"

So I did, letting myself be twirled back and forth with James till I was dizzy. He started moving like one of the characters from *A Charlie Brown Christmas* and I followed, flipping my head from side to side while hopping like a bunny. The next thing I knew, Nico and Marco had joined in, and by the time Jo circled us, pressing her shrieking goat like a freakin' drumbeat, we were all laughing so hard I could barely breathe. The song ended, and after a loud applause, the band slowed it down with "White Christmas."

James, panting, held out his hand and I took it as he put his other hand on my back near the bottom of my sweater. We swayed quietly to the music for a few moments before I spoke, remembering our "mission."

"Where's your dad?" I asked.

He nodded to the side. "Doing what he does best. Watching from a distance."

"Well, Operation Ho Ho Humbug doesn't allow watching." But I no sooner finished the words than Nona crossed the room and held out her hand to Mr. Bailey, who smiled a bit forcefully as he shrugged out of his long peacoat.

He wasn't in his typical suit and tie, but he did wear slacks and a dark green button-up with an open collar. Nona guided him to the dance floor, and they moved slowly for a moment or two before she stopped abruptly, pressing a hand to her side as if in pain. I let go of James to check on her, but she had already waved to the other side of the room where I could see a familiar head of dark curls working her way through the crowd.

Nona motioned from my mother to Mr. Bailey and then backed away.

"Oh, that woman takes meddling to a whole new level," I said, putting my hand back on James's garland-draped shoulder.

"Who?" he asked, looking around.

I spun us around so he could see and bit back a laugh as Mom made a face at Nona.

So relatable.

James smiled as his dad started slow dancing with my mom. A minute later, both were talking and laughing about something.

Jo hurried over to us with a cup of punch in her hand and nodded toward our parents. "Hey, maybe you two don't need to fake date after all, eh?"

"Yeah."

Why did that thought make my heart sink?

"Maybe," James added, his breath warm against my forehead.

"Can I have your attention, please!" Mayor Moore announced suddenly from the stage, cutting off the music.

Or had the music already stopped?

James and I dropped our hands and faced the stage.

"First, the council and I wanted to say what an excellent showing of gingerbread creations we had this year . . . Maybe our most inventive yet!" Mayor Moore smiled as he pulled out three envelopes. "So, without further ado, let's hear the results!"

Dr. Penhallow, former pediatrician for Mullings Creek and current drummer of Restless Dad Syndrome, gave a small drumroll on his snare.

"The award for Funniest Creation goes to . . ." Mayor Moore paused as he opened an envelope. "Levi Phillips of Chordcrafters!"

Everyone clapped as Levi stepped onto the stage to receive his medal.

"Be grateful you didn't get that one," I said to James, keeping my voice low.

"Why?" he asked.

"Funniest Creation is our town's way of saying 'It was so horrible, we had to do something.'"

"Well, had you and Leo not come over when you did, we would've given Levi a run for his money." James nudged my arm.

"It was no big deal," I said, brushing off the compliment.

"It was, actually." He looked down at me and cocked his head. "You always seem to drop everything to help anyone when they need it. That's admirable."

Admirable?

I never realized how nice it was to hear someone say something like that to me—someone I wasn't actively helping.

"Winning the Most Creative Gingerbread House is . . ." Mayor Moore paused dramatically after opening another envelope, his eyes widening in surprise. "Oh! Would you look at that! It's Mr. Travis Bailey and his son James!"

I jumped up and down and pushed James toward the stage as my mom did the same to his father. The crowd cheered and whistled as they climbed the short flight of stairs to Mayor Moore, who stepped away from the mic and draped a medal over each of them. James held up his hands in celebration, earning more applause, and then he grabbed his father's and held it in the air. Mr. Bailey gave his son an incredulous look that slowly morphed into a genuine smile. He followed James off the stage and the two of them came over to me.

"Congratulations!" I said. "That's a tough category to win."

"We wouldn't have won without your help." Mr. Bailey stuck out his hand, but I made a last-second decision and went in for a hug.

"We're all family here," I said against his shirt.

He patted my back a few times, awkwardly, before chuckling. "I'm starting to see that."

Mayor Moore took the mic one final time as I let go and caught eyes with James, who looked at me with an expression I hadn't yet seen.

Wonder?

Mayor Moore took out his last envelope and opened it. "And now, for our final winner. This year's Most Festive Gingerbread House goes to . . . Gianna, Leo, and Silvia Mancini!"

The Market erupted in cheers as James now pushed me toward the stage where Leo waited with the most precious excited face I had seen on him in weeks. The two of us linked pinkies and waited for Nona, who was escorted up by her bestie, Gram, the two of them beaming.

After we received our medals, Leo and I started back down the stairs, but Nona lingered behind and moved toward the mic. The sharp screech of feedback sounded, and she stepped back quickly.

"Oh, good grief, who thought to give her the mic again?" I asked to no one as I stood frozen in front of the stage.

Please don't say anything embarrassing.

"I just wanted to say thank you to everyone who participated this year." Nona looked around the room before her gaze stopped several feet behind me where James and his father still stood. "Christmas is a time for family," she said, and then she turned and looked at me. "We are a town that thrives because of tradition. And I know we may be seeing some changes sooner than we expected, but remember: Just because something is new doesn't mean it can't also be wonderful. Thank you."

The crowd clapped once more as Nona stepped down from the stage. She squeezed my arm and kissed my forehead before saying, "Briallare mentre cresciamo," one of her favorite phrases.

Glow as we grow.

As the crowd dwindled down, Leo snuck away with some of the leftover candy from the contest entries, and I snuck away for a quiet moment near the firepit out back. The air was crisp, and not a cloud moved across the late-afternoon sky.

"Almost smells like snow," Sam said as he sat down next to me, holding his bare hands near the fire to warm them.

"We haven't had a December snow in so long," I said, holding my hands closer to the flames, too.

"I feel like it was, what, five years ago, Mouse?"

"Six," I replied, bringing my hands back and pushing them into the fleece lining of my jacket pockets.

"That's right." He settled back in his chair. "You and I snuck out to make snow angels while Nona fussed that we'd catch pneumonia. Your hair was covered." He chuckled.

I smacked his arm. "Only because you dumped a metric ton of snow over my head."

"It was a watering-canful, don't get dramatic." He smiled at the flames.

The band announced their final song for the day, "Last Christmas," and the others gathered around the fire hurried inside to listen, leaving Sam and me alone with the crackle and spit of the flames.

I picked up a stick and poked at the logs. "Hey, can I ask you something?"

"Shoot."

I took a breath and held it for a moment before releasing it. "When we played Scrabble the other night—"

"You mean when I won?" He winked.

"Yeah, yeah." I took another deep breath and then swallowed over a lump in my throat. "Um, that last word, though."

"What about it?" He faced the flames again, picking up his own stick and poking the logs.

"You played that word to . . ." I paused, giving him an in.

"To win?" he asked, still staring at the fire while he rubbed the back of his neck. "Yeah. Of course. Why else would I play it?"

"Right." *Stupid question, Gianna.* "Play to win."

My stomach knotted, and I suddenly didn't feel very warm anymore.

I stood and tossed my stick into the flames before passing by him to go back inside, but his hand closed around my wrist.

"Gianna, wait," he said, standing.

I looked down at our hands and then back in his eyes, searching for an answer.

Just say it, Sam.

Say what I've wanted you to say for a stupidly long time.

He opened his mouth. "I—"

And then James called my name from the back door.

We dropped our hands, and I immediately shoved mine back into my pockets, which did nothing to quell the numbing tingles on each finger.

"Dad wanted to thank you again before we left," James said, his eyes narrowing on Sam.

"Be right in," I said as James went back inside.

I turned around to Sam, who looked completely deflated, making me feel ten times smaller.

A mouse indeed.

I cleared my throat. "So, will I see you and your family at Nona's later tonight?"

"Of course. After all, Sunday Supper Club only comes around one Sunday a month," he said. His eyes dropped to his hands, where he rubbed the one that had touched mine with his other thumb before he added, "See you later, G."

"Bye, Sam." I turned my back on him, the warmth of the fire, and walked toward the guy I should've been focusing on.

But how did you focus on one person and ignore the way the energy around someone else tugged at your core?

Like those old dolls Nona had, where you'd pull a string to make it speak, Sam had that same effect on me.

In any room, at any moment, I could find him, and he could find me.

Because at some point over the years, we had formed an invisible string between ourselves.

Or at least, that's what I had always thought.

But lately, I wondered if maybe that string, like the evening in my den with *Home Alone*, was just another thing I had imagined.

Chapter Seventeen

"I just love meeting people's families. I find it so revealing."

—FRED CLAUS

Sunday Supper Club was something Nona and Papa had been doing for longer than I had been alive. One Sunday out of every month, they would host the entire family, and sometimes local friends like the Holts, for a big, traditional Italian meal.

Dinner was always ready by seven, but the real ones knew to show up ahead of time for the antipasti—platters filled with cured meats, cheeses, artichoke hearts, and my personal favorite, olives. Though Nona always put some aside for me, in case Nico and Marco got to the platter first.

By the time Mom, Leo, and I arrived, the driveway was crammed with everyone's cars except the Holts' truck, which was honestly fine with me. I needed the extra time to prepare for being in the same room as Sam *and* my nosy cousins.

Whatever brief "moment" Sam and I had at the firepit after the gingerbread contest had melted faster than spring snow.

You'd think after being on this carousel with him for

several cycles, I'd have gotten used to the back-and-forth, but nope.

That thread between us held fast, even the parts that were all knotted up.

I knew I should probably just cut it and stop waiting for him, but I couldn't.

I'd rather endure the knots and unexpected loops than not have him in my life at all.

The enticing smells of manicotti, tomato sauce, and garlic hit me the moment we walked through the door and shrugged off our coats. As we neared the kitchen, the echoes of my cousins arguing intermixed with the sizzling of Nona's famous meatballs in a cast-iron skillet.

Everyone was gathered around the small island in the center of the kitchen, deep in conversation, hands gesturing wildly. Aunt Helen and Aunt Sofia stood near the meatballs, taking turns stirring and flipping, and Nico fixed Leo a plate of his favorite meats and cheeses. I bypassed the platter and went straight to the fridge for my specially reserved olives.

God bless you, Nona.

"Are we expecting more company?" Mom asked, gesturing to the extra leaf inserted in Nona's table.

"But of course." Nona pulled a loaf of Italian bread out of the oven and carefully transferred it to the bread basket on the table. "The Baileys should be here any minute."

I inhaled a piece of olive and nearly gagged. "Did you say 'the Baileys'? As in Mr. Bailey and—"

"James, your *boyfriend*?" Marco added, a mischievous glint in his eye. "Yes, yes, she did."

"He's not my boyfriend." I gulped down some tap water quickly. "We're just—"

"Hanging out, sure. We got it." Nico popped a chunk of mozzarella into his mouth. "But since you're spending time with him, and since his dad has control over The Market, Nona thought it would be good to invite them, right, Nona?"

"Precisamente." Nona ruffled Nico's dark hair before kissing his cheek.

Right.

"Mom, what is this?" My mother held up a couple of place cards with names written in Nona's signature sloping cursive.

"Name cards," Nona said matter-of-factly.

Name cards? Since when did Nona use name cards?

I hurried over and found mine placed in between James and Marco.

Phew.

I could elbow Marco anytime he crossed a line.

Which meant I'd be sore by the first course, but sacrifices had to be made.

Mom put the two she was holding back on the table. "Care to explain why *mine* is next to Travis Bailey's?"

The doorbell rang, right on cue.

"Ah, go get that, will you, cara?" Nona pointed to me. "And make sure they take off their shoes."

Mom grumbled and grabbed her empty wine glass off the table before heading toward the back door while I walked toward the front.

James smiled as he kicked off his Nikes, his eyes darting around to take in Nona's cluttered Christmas home.

I snorted and pointed toward his feet. "I like your socks."

"Aren't they great?" He lifted one of them, showing off the big face of Chewbacca. "I got Dad a pair, too. Early Christmas gift."

Mr. Bailey stood awkwardly near the doormat in dark jeans and a button-up, holding a bottle of wine. My eyes trailed downward to his exposed socks, which sure enough, donned Han Solo's enormous face.

I bit back a laugh. "I like yours, too, sir. Why don't you guys come into the kitchen? Dinner's almost ready."

"Smells amazing." James hurried in front of me, and shouted, "Hey, everyone!" the moment he stepped into view of my family.

Poor guy.

So adorably naive as he enters the lion's den.

After quick introductions, Mr. Bailey cleared his throat and crossed the kitchen toward Nona, who was bending over three glass dishes of bubbling manicotti in the open oven. "Thank you for inviting us, Mrs. Mancini—"

"Silvia, dear," she said before wrapping her arms around him. "We're so glad you could join us."

Mr. Bailey stood as still as a tree, arms at his side, before he brought one up and patted her back. "Um, Gianna told James you'd be serving a pasta dish, so I brought over a bottle of merlot." He held it out for Nona, whose nose scrunched up ever so slightly.

"Thank you." She passed off the bottle to Aunt Helen, who immediately shelved it in the corner cabinet with the other dust-covered bottles of yore. "Alice, why don't you fill Travis's glass with some Chianti."

Mom's left eye twitched, but she did so. And when she brushed Mr. Bailey's arm as she walked by, I swore I saw the slightest bit of pink bloom on his cheeks.

Interesting.

Uncle Rick moved all the meatballs to Nona's big serving bowl and spooned some sauce over them before grating fresh Parmesan on top as Uncle Gabe and my Aunt Sofia took turns handing each other plates from the table for the manicotti. A few minutes later, once every plate was filled and the meatballs and salad were placed on the table, we all moved to our seats, only mine wasn't next to James anymore.

Marco and Nico's were.

"Who moved my seat?" I asked.

My cousins shrugged and flicked their napkins out before placing them daintily on their laps.

I glared at both of them. *One day, I swear, they will pay.*

"You're here by me," Bianca said, patting the chair next to her.

Based on her grin, I knew exactly who the empty chair on the other side of me belonged to.

And because the universe just loved comedic timing, the doorbell rang again.

"I'll get it," I mumbled.

I opened the door to a red-nosed Sam, standing alone on Nona's stoop under the porch light, holding up a bouquet of flowers.

"Where's everyone else?" I asked, stepping aside so his tall frame could fit through the front door.

"Gram's got a head cold and didn't want to get anyone sick," he said as he moved past me.

I held my breath, fighting the urge to smell him.

That pine and soap mixture was a real doozy.

"Dad had some last-minute orders come in for a church a couple towns away, and Mom stayed home to make sure Gram didn't overdo it." He took off his coat and hung it on an open hook. "Have you guys started yet?"

I made a face.

He chuckled and ran a hand through his messy hair before picking up his flowers off the small table where he had laid them. "Okay, I know Nico and Marco probably destroyed the antipasti, but am I too late for the main course?"

"You're right on time, but hold on." I reached up and folded down part of his flannel collar near his stubbled jawline. "There. Better."

"Thanks," he said, his voice surprisingly smoky.

His freckles reminded me of a constellation, but I could never remember which one.

Cassiopeia?

Perseus?

Someone cleared their throat, and I instantly fell back on my heels.

"Nona sent me to make sure you didn't get lost," Bianca said from the kitchen doorway, arms crossed over her sun-yellow sweater. "Who are those for?" Her eyes flickered toward the flowers in Sam's hand.

"Nona. Gram told me to give them to her." He passed by me, but I took a minute to follow.

This is fine.

Everything is fine.

You can sit at a table with the best friend you almost kissed and across from the guy you should be kissing, surrounded by your entire extended family.

The grilling started the moment James spooned a single meatball out of the serving dish.

"Don't you like meatballs?" Marco asked him.

"Of course." He used a fork to cut it in half on his plate, steam pouring out. "I just didn't want to take too much before everyone else."

Nico snorted.

"We have another batch on the stove." Marco took a spoon and dropped three more meatballs onto James's plate. "Bon appétit."

"This ricotta mixture is so fluffy," Aunt Sofia said to no one.

"So, James." Nico sat back in his chair and took a sip of Chianti. "Crunchy or creamy?"

James paused mid-bite. "Like, peanut butter?"

Nico nodded.

"Creamy, obviously." James took a heaping bite of manicotti and groaned. "This is the best manicotti I've ever eaten, Mrs. Mancini."

Mr. Bailey's phone chimed, and when he took it out of his pocket to check it, Nona clicked her tongue and pointed her fork at him. "No phones at my table."

He put up a hand in surrender and tucked it away.

Nona then turned her attention back to James. "The secret is in the pasta. You must roll out your own dough, and you need to undercook it."

"France is known for their flour. Good for pastries," Uncle Rick said from one end of the table. "Would love to get my hands on some."

Nona muttered something under her breath in Italian, and though I couldn't be positive, I was pretty sure she told my uncle he was blasphemous for saying such things.

"Bradley Cooper is French," Bianca added.

"No, he's not. He just speaks it." Marco grabbed the big salad bowl and helped himself to some.

"I've had dreams where people speak French to me and I understand it," Aunt Sofia said before taking a sip of her wine.

Oh Lord, here we go.

"Then you must know someone French, because you can only dream of faces you've seen," Aunt Helen said to her.

Aunt Sofia frowned. "That's not true."

"Yes, it is."

Aunt Sofia waved her fork toward my uncle. "Then how did I dream about Gabriel before I met him?"

Bianca stopped eating. "You dreamed about Dad before you—"

"I did take a little French in high school," Uncle Gabe said as he rose with his empty wine glass and walked toward the back door.

"Surely, you don't eat any peanut butter now, right?" Nico asked James.

"Wait. What?" James asked. "Why wouldn't I?"

Crap.

The entire room went still.

Nona's oven timer dinged.

The back door banged shut, and Uncle Gabe stood frozen by the door, holding his refilled glass. "What'd I miss?"

"Oh, not much," Marco said.

"Just Gianna's *boyfriend* possibly killing her," Nico added.

Sam tensed next to me.

"Whipped to perfection." Aunt Sofia pushed some of the cheese around her plate, inspecting it.

I held up my hand. "He didn't know—"

Bianca leaned forward. "How does your boyfriend not know you're deathly allergic to peanuts?"

"And tree nuts!" Leo added.

"Boyfriend?" Mr. Bailey turned his head toward our end of the table. "Is this true, James? I mean, you barely know the girl—"

"She's not my girlfriend." James shifted in his seat. "I mean, we're not ruling that out someday, but . . ."

"But we're just getting to know each other," I finished. "I haven't told him things like my food allergies yet."

Or my shoe size.

Or how I still check under my bed before I go to sleep.

Must've missed that memo.

"Seems like an important thing to mention to someone you're kissing." Marco's eyes narrowed in on me.

Sam coughed into his water glass.

"Ew," Leo mumbled.

"We're not kissing," I said, staring down my cousin.

"Yet," James added with a smirk.

Okay, definitely not helping here, bud.

"Bradley Cooper rowed crew in college," Mom blurted. "Did you know that? He went to Georgetown."

"I could've been great at crew," Uncle Gabe added wistfully as he came back to the table.

"He's fluent in French, too," Aunt Helen added as she reached for another piece of Italian bread.

"No, I'm not." Uncle Gabe looked at her in confusion.

"I meant Bradley Cooper," she replied. "Jodie Foster is, too, I believe."

"Parmesan adds a great bite." Aunt Sofia took another mouthful of manicotti and sighed.

As Marco and Nico moved on to ask James who he thought was the strongest Avenger—a topic often argued about in this house—I made eye contact with my mom and mouthed a silent "thank you." She winked.

Mom could always be counted on for a quick subject change.

Later, Mr. Bailey's phone rang again, and he stood up and left the kitchen to take it.

"I'm sorry," James said to Nona. "That thing is literally attached to him twenty-four seven."

Nona, her eyes kind, pressed her fingers together in front of her face as she looked down the table at him. "A child shouldn't have to apologize for their parents. Ti deve delle scuse."

James turned to me, eyebrows raised in question.

"She said, '*He* owes *you* an apology,'" I explained.

And I couldn't agree more.

We all chipped in to clear the table as Nona put on a pot of coffee and some water for tea. Uncle Rick then pulled out a container of his cannoli to dust with powdered sugar before placing a platter on the table.

James and Sam were soon deep in conversation about whether or not movies like *Solo* could be considered *Star Wars* movies.

"None of the original actors from the *Star Wars* canon are even in it," Sam said, crossing his arms over his chest.

"What would you have them do, CGI them in? That would be terrible." James picked up a cannoli and took a big bite, his eyes widening before he took another.

"They did it with Leia in some of the later films."

"Fair." James set down the cannoli as his father entered the kitchen again, tucking his phone back into his pocket. "But just because it doesn't have a Skywalker plotline doesn't mean it can't be considered a *Star Wars* movie," James added.

"Doesn't it say 'A *Star Wars* Story,' though?" I interrupted. "Like, under the title?"

I only watched it once, because Sam and Leo made me, and I'd ended up falling asleep halfway through, but I had a weird photographic memory for these kinds of things.

Sam reached to put his arm around my shoulders but quickly caught himself and tried to make it look like he was picking something off my purple sweater.

James's gaze went back and forth between the two of us a couple of times before Nona placed a cup of tea in front of him.

"Milk or lemon, dear?" she asked.

"Milk, thank you," he replied, his voice short.

"So, James," Mom began, clearly sensing that we needed a subject change again. "Levi tells me you're quite the musician."

"Levi?" Mr. Bailey set his coffee cup down. "Who's Levi?"

Oh crap.

Maybe not the best change of subject, Mom.

"The owner of the music shop in town, Chordcrafters," Mom said. "He toured with a couple big names back in the day before he quit that scene and settled here."

"Gives lessons to kids who want to learn guitar and piano, too," Nona added. "Nice man."

"James?" Mr. Bailey turned toward his son. "What's this about?"

James stared down at his tea. "Nothing."

But . . . it's not nothing. "Your son is an excellent guitar player, sir. I heard him play the other night." The words came out of my mouth before I could stop them.

James's eyes shot up. "I thought I saw someone outside. That was you?"

I nodded, my ears now burning. "Sorry," I whispered.

"It's okay." He smiled and then sat up straighter to face his dad, oblivious to the extra twelve pairs of ears that had tuned in to listen. "Yeah, Dad. I played guitar in Chordcrafters. I've actually gone back there a couple times. Levi's cool."

"Sicily makes the best cannoli," Aunt Sofia mumbled. "Their ricotta is perfect."

Mr. Bailey's jaw ticked. "I thought we spoke about this.

How you should be using that time to study. You have college app—"

"I don't want to go to college." James moved his hands to his lap. "I've told you that. I want to play music—"

"We'll talk about this later," Mr. Bailey said, his voice firm.

"Yes, sir." James swallowed hard before going back to staring at his tea while I sat on my hands to keep them from shaking him.

"Hendrix or Clapton?" Marco asked James, his voice low.

"Neither." He turned toward my cousin. "B. B. King."

"Good choice," Sam said.

Marco nodded. "Agreed."

The two of them dug into their cannoli, and multiple conversations began to buzz around the table again. Nona and Mom listened intently to Mr. Bailey speak about the "horrific" state of Mr. Paxton's back taxes on The Market while Uncle Gabe and Uncle Rick argued about who was the best Bond, but I continued to watch the boy across from me. The one who had held his own while in the ring with my cousins but who seemed so hesitant, so scared, to admit what he wanted to do with his life to his own father.

I was surprised at how much I really wanted to know more about him.

"Would you like to go on another date?" I asked, and the room fell quiet again.

A slow smile spread across James's face as he said, "That

depends." He tilted his head to the side. "Do I get to finally ask you my three questions?"

Bianca leaned forward. "What three quest—"

Aunt Helen shushed her.

"You may," I said, keeping eye contact. "But you just used up one, so choose your next two carefully."

Hold up.

Am I flirting?

In front of my family?

And . . . enjoying it?

James pursed his lips and drummed his fingers on his cup for a long moment before smiling once again. "Yes," he said. "I'd love to."

I swear the entire room exhaled.

I know I did.

But . . . what did that mean?

Were we officially moving past the fake dating to, like, actual real dating?

Is that what I wanted?

I turned to Bianca, who beamed and gave me a quick nod of approval, before I let my eyes meet James's once more. He always looked at me with such sweet kindness and curiosity and respect. This city boy not only agreed to a plan to help save a stranger's town but also trusted that same stranger to help him bring back his father's Christmas spirit.

Who does that?

Maybe James had seen the same thing in me that I saw in him, even more so now.

Hope.

I broke eye contact as my cheeks began to warm, sneaking a quick glance around the table and immediately regretting it.

Sam sat with his shoulders slumped and a defeated expression that filled me with a hollow, empty feeling, but honestly, it kinda pissed me off. A lot.

What the heck, Sam?

I gave you a chance. Multiple ones, in fact.

And you said nothing. Did nothing.

"Hands off the nuts, though. For real," Nico said, bumping James's arm.

"Ricotta really is the most underrated cheese." Aunt Sofia took a sip of her coffee as the entire table stared at her.

The Mancinis, everyone.

Chapter Eighteen

"Oh, you know how the elves exaggerate. They get excited at the drop of a hat."

—THE CHRISTMAS CHRONICLES

On the following Wednesday, schools were closed for Mullings Creek's Reindeer Games, as was tradition. I pulled on my favorite pair of leggings and warm socks followed by a red flannel and grabbed my white puffy vest before looking in the mirror.

I didn't look any different. Same blue eyes. Same dark, unruly hair. Same olive complexion and dark under-eyes—shoutout to Nona and Dad—and yet, I felt . . . different.

Maybe it was the fact that I had asked out the guy I was fake dating in front of my entire family and Sam.

Or maybe it had happened slowly over time, after my one hundredth rewatch of *The Holiday* and seeing Kate Winslet finally taking charge like a leading lady.

All I did know was that I liked this new Gianna, radiating with confidence.

For the first time ever, I didn't dread walking into my kitchen that I knew was already filled with most of my family—noise always gave us Mancinis away.

I said a singsongy "Good morning" as I joined my Aunt Helen by the coffeepot and reached for one of my favorite holiday mugs from the cabinet.

"So, when were you going to tell us?" Marco asked, propping his arm on the back of his chair. Everyone else followed suit, stopping their conversations to stare at me.

Oooo-kay, so maybe I could've been a little less chipper.

"You have to go, G," Nico added before taking a drink of his coffee.

Go? "Go where? On the date?" I asked.

"No, cara." Nona took the skillet filled with eggs and bacon off the burner. "Italy."

Oh.

Bianca threw up her hands. "I already bought you a present—"

"Me too." Aunt Helen nudged me.

"Just be mindful of the trees there, dear." Aunt Sofia waved a biscotti at me. "Your Great-Great-Great-Uncle Giuseppe was taken by one during—"

"Sofia," Uncle Gabe said, lowering his newspaper. "He was not taken by trees. It was a fishing accident—"

"Boating," Uncle Rick chimed in. "He wasn't fishing, he was—"

"Enough about Uncle Giuseppe!" Mom shouted, pushing off

the counter before turning to me. "Gianna, I'm sorry. Half of them were here when I came down this morning, and I promise we'll change the locks."

The family gasped as if Mom had stabbed them with her grapefruit spoon.

I bit back a laugh.

This family, these people, could push me to my breaking point, and yet I knew that if I ever needed them, they would drop everything for me.

Heck, Marco, Nico, and Francis had already proven that when I was teased by a horrible girl named Julie in the sixth grade who said I had a big nose and cheap clothes. They hid rotten eggs in various spots of her yard, tree house, and locker—apparently, Francis had a spreadsheet of all the locker combos used at Mullings Creek Middle for "emergencies."

And then there was the time when Aunt Sofia and Aunt Helen had stayed up past midnight to mend my Dorothy costume and shoes when I accidentally ripped mine while racing Sam on our bikes the day before opening night.

Or how Uncle Rick and Uncle Gabe took shifts at our house for months after Dad died when Leo had a bad case of croup.

But my Nona . . .

My eyes filled with tears. Next to my mother, she was the strongest woman I knew. When I first told her about the opportunity to study abroad, she immediately started contacting her cousins who still lived there so that I could stay connected with my family.

Papa would be proud to know I was going back to the place that brought him such joy.

"Don't worry, Aunt Sofia." I pulled out my phone and opened up my confirmation email from the Adventure Italy program. I smiled as I clicked "Yes" and then held up the confetti-exploding "CONGRATULATIONS!" screen to my family. "I'll watch out for the trees when I go to Italy."

The room erupted into cheers. Nona and Mom hurried over to me and hugged me tightly before Nona held up her hands to quiet the group. "I will throw a party to celebrate, and we'll finish it with a movie under the tree, yes?"

We all agreed just as a knock sounded from the front door.

I opened it to find Sam with cold-kissed skin and wearing his usual flannel, jeans, and boots.

"Hi!" I said, surprised at how chirpy it came out.

"Hi." He smiled. "I was wondering if you'd want to walk together to town? My mom said they could still use a few hands to help finish setting up some of the Reindeer Games."

"Love to. Just let me grab my keys."

Bianca, who had suddenly materialized like the freakin' Ghost of Christmas Present in the kitchen doorway, winked at both of us before I rolled my eyes and closed the front door.

The air was crisp and cold, and our breaths lingered in the air like steam as we walked toward Mistletoe Lane.

"Sounded like a lot of noise in there," Sam said before breathing into his hands and shoving them into his pockets.

"Yeah." I kicked a small rock toward the road. "I just accepted the invitation to Adventure Italy."

"Congratulations!" Sam shouted.

"Thanks!" I fixed my earmuffs. "Nona wants to throw a party and then watch a movie under the tree. It's been years since we camped out on her floor."

He bumped my shoulder. "Am I invited?"

"Of course!" I said, then quickly added, "Your whole family, too."

"Cool." He paused. "Will James and his dad be coming, too?"

Oh. Didn't think of that. "Nah. This feels more like a family and close friends kinda thing."

"Close friends." Sam gave a short nod. "Gotcha."

His tone sounded different then, almost distant.

I mean, was I wrong to say that?

We continued walking and a few minutes later turned down Mistletoe Lane. I ran my hands along the candy cane fence that surrounded the big tree in the town square. "It really is one of the best trees you guys have donated."

"I think so, too." He stood and peered up at it with a satisfied grin on his face. "I hope they continue to do this even after I take over."

I gawked at him. "Of course they will. You're like the smartest arborist I know."

He waved a hand at my comment and turned to start walking again. "Being book smart doesn't mean I'll be as good as my dad."

"Hey," I said, grabbing his sleeve to slow him down. "Maybe it's not about being as good as your dad but about bringing something different to the table, or in your case, to the trees."

He smiled. "Yeah, maybe."

I skipped toward the nearest light pole and swung around it, then hurried over to the next one to do the same.

"You always get dizzy when you do that," Sam warned.

"No I don't!" I shouted, spinning away and directly into Sam, who grabbed my hand and twirled me.

"Well, now I will," I said, laughing as he spun me back toward him.

I pressed my hand against his chest as I tried to catch my breath, but the feel of Sam's racing heartbeat beneath my palm only made mine move that much faster.

"I . . ." Sam swallowed hard. "I've been meaning to talk to you. Since that night by the firepit after the gingerbread contest when you asked me about my Scrabble word—"

"Oh?" I didn't dare look up at him. He was standing too close. We were standing too close.

He took a breath. "I didn't play it just to win."

I swallowed. "You didn't?"

"No."

I raised my eyes to his, and my body hummed with so much energy that everything felt supercharged.

This was what I had been waiting for.

The moment I had imagined—*Be real, G, maybe even dreamed of*—for longer than I'd ever admit out loud.

And yet a quiet voice in the back of my head whispered . . .

James.

I had just asked him out. In front of my family and Sam.

Wait.

Was this why he decided to bring this—whatever this unspoken thing was between us—back up?

I dropped my hand and stepped back.

Screw spinning on light poles. I was so over the dizziness of this emotional whiplash.

"We should go," I said, the cold air wrapping itself around me once more. Cold air was good for that—clarity.

He moved forward. "Gianna . . ."

No.

I couldn't do this. Not now. Not anymore.

I hurried past him and ran down the street toward The Market and its comforting sounds of holiday music that spilled onto the sidewalk.

Thank God for Christmas.

You could always count on familiar, predictable Christmas to keep you grounded.

Chapter Nineteen

"What right have you to be dismal? You're rich enough."

—THE MUPPET CHRISTMAS CAROL

I was roped into helping Ms. Louisa Mae and Ms. Donna set up the prize table and a couple of the silent raffle tables for two hours. Sam kept his distance but stole glances at me more than once from across the room where he helped his family with their poinsettia and fresh wreaths display. All the games were held outside in Mullings Creek Park, directly behind The Market. The land and pavilion were the most sought-after spots for outdoor parties and town gatherings, and during the spring and early summer, youth soccer practices and games took over the field.

But my favorite part was the massive hill that embanked the far side of the property opposite the playground. It was the perfect spot to sled, and my Uncle Gabe was known for going out early on snow days to build jumps on the hill before the kids got there.

I pulled on my light-up reindeer antler headband and paced back and forth, waiting for James and Mr. Bailey to show up. Jo's dads were running the first shift at the ticket table behind me.

"Would you look at her," Mr. Eric said.

Mr. Josh nodded. "A bundle of nerves, that one."

I stopped pacing. "Sorry. I don't know why I'm so fidgety," I said to them.

"Boys will do that to you," Mr. Josh said while taking someone's money and giving them a wristband.

Preach.

"Well, I'm just waiting for one." I helped snap bracelets on the kids for the next family in line after they paid.

"Mm-hmm . . ." Mr. Eric put the cash into the money box. "But the big question is, which one?"

Good grief.

Was there a Gianna community newsletter everyone subscribed to?

James finally walked up in a hoodie and jeans—the most casual I had seen him yet. I waved, but my hand quickly fell to my side.

Walking next to his dad were two people I didn't recognize. They both wore dress pants and button-ups just like Mr. Bailey, only their skin looked like it had never seen the sun.

Like the real-life versions of Marley and Marley with Scrooge himself.

Great.

The three of them looked as out of place in our cozy town as bathing suits in department stores mid-February.

I pushed aside the icy feeling of dread in my gut and forced my best and biggest smile. "Welcome to the Reindeer Games!" I said, arms wide open. "Love the headband, James. Where's yours, Mr. Bailey?"

"He refused to wear it," James said. "I told him he didn't know what he was missing." James smiled and shook his head, making his antlers jingle.

Mr. Bailey made a face at his companions. "Clearly."

Marley No. 1 looked at the listed ticket prices and scoffed. "Do you actually pull a profit during this?"

"Probably one of those towns that expect donations, too," Marley No. 2 mumbled loud enough for all of us to hear.

Mr. Eric's eye twitched ever so slightly. "We find that it's more about the experience. Raising ticket prices would exclude families that come here to make memories they may not have the means to give their children themselves."

"But think of what *else* you could provide at next year's Reindeer Games in your little town if you did," Mr. Bailey countered, crossing his arms.

Mr. Eric stood, his palms flat on the table. "Our low prices keep families coming back year after year. Believe it or not, that draws others from outside our *little town*. Now, how many tickets would you like to purchase today?"

Mr. Bailey looked to the Marleys, who both waved their hands as if saying, "I suppose we can find time in our busy schedules to attend," before he took out a couple of large bills and said, "No change."

But Mr. Eric thrust the change back into Mr. Bailey's hand anyway. "And we don't need donations, especially from people like—"

"Would you all like your wristbands on your right or left wrist?" Mr. Josh stood up and gently touched his husband's arm before placing the bands on the Baileys and their guests.

I knew it was a good thing—what Mr. Josh did—and yet, part of me wished Mr. Eric had finished what he was about to say.

I may not have had the same lie detector superpower that my Nona and Bianca did, but I *was* a Mancini.

We could smell trouble from two towns over when the wind blew the right way.

And right now, that cold December breeze told me these two outsiders were trouble.

"Come on," I said, taking James's hand to lead him into the Games. *Maybe I can get him to tell me what the heck is going on!*

But Mr. Eric spoke up first. "Oh! Gianna, could you be a dear and take Jo her water bottle? She's horrible about remembering to hydrate."

"We can take it, right, Dad?" James suggested, a peace offering. "Where is she?"

Mr. Eric handed him the pink stainless steel tumbler. "Inside The Market at the booth for Eve's Drop."

"Eve's place?" Mr. Bailey perked up a bit. "Bret, Milton, you should come with us. Their coffee is some of the best I've ever had."

Bret and Milton—*totally could've guessed those names*—began walking with Mr. Bailey toward The Market, asking him if Eve's did a "proper" slow drip.

Jo was going to just love those two for sure.

"We'll meet you at the Games soon," James said, smiling before he let go of my hand and walked away with his father.

"By the Santa Sack Race!" I called after him. "I promised Leo I'd race him."

"Ms. Donna mentioned something about two outsiders eating at the diner this morning." Mr. Josh sat back down. "Said they were drawing up blueprints for some high-end boutiques."

High-end boutiques?

Here?

Mr. Eric sighed and shut the money box. "How can we expect to win over a man who clearly doesn't get small towns?"

But that's just the thing.

Mr. Bailey *did* grow up in a small town.

He hadn't been all-in on our holiday traditions yet, but he did compliment Eve's coffee more than once, and he seemed to loosen up a bit at Nona's, which was not easy to do at a table with all my family.

So, if I could just get him to buy into even a small bit of our Christmas magic, maybe it could be enough in the end.

I ventured into the Games, breathing in the delicious scents of cider, hot cocoa, and funnel cakes from Phineas's Christmas Trolley, immediately feeling my spirits lift. Each of the booths looked like gingerbread houses outlined with colorful baubles or garland. A golden star centered in each apex cast sparkles atop the cotton-fluffy fake snow that blanketed their canvas roofs. I sent Mom a quick text to remind her to stop working and come down to enjoy herself before we were due to work the face-painting booth in an hour.

Usually, I was pretty good about spatial awareness, but my eyes were on my phone, and before I knew it, I'd walked head-first into a tree.

Or rather, Sam.

"Sorry!" we said in unison.

I laughed and tucked my phone into my vest pocket. "I should know better by now to not text and walk."

"Same, honestly," he said, chuckling before adjusting his plaid-printed reindeer antlers.

"Can we race now?" Leo began jumping up and down and tugging on Sam's hand.

"I thought you were racing me?" I asked him.

"I am!" he replied, taking my hand, too. "I'm racing both of you."

"Let's go, then," Sam said before he crouched down and let Leo jump on his back. He laughed and called out the reindeer names as if Sam was his chariot.

Every game at the Reindeer Games came with prizes and medals. Like events at a track meet, there were multiple heats so that no game would be too crowded. This also gave everyone a shot to play in each event regardless of the time of day that they came.

The Santa Sack Race wasn't my favorite, because I usually fell down at least once before getting to the finish line, but Leo had always been a bouncer, preferring to jump and skip places rather than walk or run. The sack was normally two sizes too big for him, but he never let that slow him down.

By the time I got to the starting line, Marco and Nico were in their sacks ready to race, and Leo and Sam were getting into their Santa-themed bags. Sam tossed me mine. "Let's see what you've got, Mancini."

"I'm gonna smoke you both so bad!" Leo announced as he lifted his sack to his chest, gathering it tightly in front of him.

"We'll see about that." Sam pointed two fingers to his eyes before turning them toward Leo, who did the same.

Ann held a megaphone in front of her mouth and spoke. "Are my racers ready?"

The ten of us shouted, "Yes!"

"That's the Christmas spirit!" Ann smiled. "Remember, your entire body *must* cross the finish line. If you fall and throw an arm out, it doesn't count. Got that, Marco?"

"That was *one time*!" he yelled before smacking Nico, who laughed at him.

Ann yelled, "Go!"

And then the chaos started.

Marco bumped Nico who bumped another small child who cried out and fell on their dad, who then shouted at my cousins and charged them while still in his sack. He ended up knocking them both out-of-bounds before continuing on.

Sam and I were neck and neck, but Leo was already yards ahead of us and everyone else.

"Is that . . . the best . . . you can do?" Sam asked, breathless.

"I don't see you . . . doing any better!" I replied, trying to pick up the pace, but then my right foot caught on the fabric the wrong way.

I fell sideways and took Sam down with me with a loud *thump* onto the cold ground.

The disgruntled dad and several others hopped by us while we both just lay there on our backs staring at the cloudy gray sky.

I turned my head toward him at the same time he did to me, and a second later, we broke into a fit of laughter.

"You did that on purpose," he said, his eyes narrowing at me.

"Did not." I smacked him. "It's not my fault I suck at this game."

The whistle blew, and Leo hurried over, his face appearing above mine. "I won!" He held up a fake gold medal, but looked prouder than an Olympian. "Three years in a row!"

Sam and I both clapped from the cold ground.

"Are you guys going to stay there all day or what?" Leo asked before hurrying away.

Sam sat up and slid out of his bag before offering his hand for me to take.

I reached for it and then stopped. Every time I touched his hand, my brain turned to static and my insides turned gooier than Jo's molten chocolate lava cake.

"I've got it," I said, sliding out of my own bag on the ground and standing.

"Okay, then." He tucked his hand into his jeans pocket and slung the Santa sack over his shoulder. "I guess I'll catch you later."

James hurried over with powdered sugar on his face just as Sam walked away. "You didn't tell me they had funnel cakes here!" he said. "I haven't had these in ages."

Mr. Bailey followed, surprisingly with a headband on his head. "Did you win?"

I rubbed the back of my neck. "Yeah, no. I'm not really coordinated enough for this game."

"Too bad," he said, taking a sip of his steaming hot coffee.

"So where are *Brett* and *Milton*?" I looked around him.

James snorted.

The corner of Mr. Bailey's mouth almost lifted into a small smile. "They had a couple of important calls to make, so they headed back to the B&B for a bit."

Important calls?

Like the kinds that carelessly tore down people's way of life?

"So, where's this Snowman Bowling event?" James asked, clapping his hands. "Dad apparently used to bowl in a league back when he was still athletic."

Mr. Bailey laughed, the kind of full-belly one that James had said he rarely heard anymore. James looked so elated that he was the one this time to bring it out of him that my heart pinched with sadness.

Was it—laughter—really such a rare thing in the Bailey house?

"All right, son," Mr. Bailey said. "I'll take that challenge. Gianna, show us the way, please."

After pulling James away from Phineas's funnel cakes, the three of us made it to the Snowman Bowling. White spray paint outlined the "lanes" in the grass, and the snowmen-painted bowling pins, complete with little blue hats and matching scarves, sat waiting at the far end of each lane. The balls used to knock down the pins were red kickballs with painted-on flames.

"Oh, I get it," James said as he picked up one and rolled it in his hands. "They're meant to be fire so they can *melt* the snowman." He chuckled. "Clever."

Mr. Bailey squinted down the lane. "Are those real pins?"

"Yep." I picked up a ball and handed it to him. "The bowling alley just outside of town donated a few sets for this event."

"Very generous of them," Mr. Bailey said, lifting the ball up and down to inspect its weight.

I nodded. "Small towns take care of each other."

"Gianna!" My mom's voice rang out as she hurried over. She must've brought a change of clothes, because she wore a different outfit than her usual paint-splattered overalls. Her dark, wavy hair was pulled into a loose bun, and her cream-colored cable-knit sweater hung loosely over her skinny jeans.

"Alice." Mr. Bailey's gaze moved quickly over my mother before pulling back toward the lane.

What's this?

"Travis," my mother replied as she grabbed a ball from the crate next to me.

"So, we're on a first-name basis?" James whispered next to my ear. The warmth of his breath and the smell of his cologne gave me unexpected shivers.

I made a mental note to ask my mom about this later. "Girls versus boys?" I suggested.

James motioned to our parents with a confused face. "But—"

"Trust me," I mumbled under my breath.

"Think you can handle that, Travis?" my mom challenged.

"Absolutely." Mr. Bailey set the ball down and rolled up his sleeves to his forearms, and my mother's eyes wandered over him before she cleared her throat.

Oh, she has some explaining to do.

"It's best score out of three turns," she added.

Mom and I went first. I knocked down seven, and Mom got eight.

Then Mr. Bailey launched the ball down so fast that it looked more like a red blur, getting a strike. After a quick celebration, James went and knocked down nine.

Several minutes, two "team meetings" on the Bailey side, and one creative curse from my mother later, the Baileys whopped us 56–40.

"Beginner's luck," my mom said as Mr. Bailey, wearing his medal, brought her a cider and James brought me a hot cocoa.

"He used to be in a bowling league," James said, quickly dodging a smack to the back of the head from his father.

Mom threw her hand up. "Well, we should've had a handicap, then!"

"Would you have really taken it?" Mr. Bailey asked her.

"Probably not," she admitted.

James wandered over toward me and lowered his voice. "So, how do you think we're doing?" He propped an elbow over my head against the tree behind me and nodded toward our parents. "I personally think Operation Ho Ho Humbug is a rollicking success so far."

"A 'rollicking success'? Really?" I lowered my cocoa. "What about those two businessmen who were with your dad this morning?" The nearness of him made my head a bit fuzzy, but I tried to stay focused. "Who are they? Why are they here?"

"Whoa, Gianna. Calm down." James lowered his arm and held up a hand innocently. "I've never met those two snobs before today, but I think they work for the same firm as my dad. I googled them, and, um, they're known for . . ." He paused.

"For what?"

His eyes dropped. "Property development."

Great.

Just great.

I should've been more focused on The Market. On our original plan.

Not asking the guy I was supposed to be fake dating on a real date.

And now it was probably too late. The Market would get turned into some tacky, bougie spot.

Several families would lose their small businesses and probably have to move.

Mom would have to take out a second mortgage to afford a space to rent for her studio.

And meanwhile, I'd be overseas, dreading coming back home because I wouldn't recognize it when I did.

"Hey, hey, hey." James took my hand. "We're not done yet. There's still time. We can do this."

"How can you say that when failure is literally staring us in the face?"

He smiled. "You see failure. I see opportunities."

I sighed.

Not really a concrete plan, but it wasn't like I had anything better to go on.

Leo hurried over a second later with two more medals in his hands. Sam moseyed up behind him, eating a funnel cake, as James let go of my hand.

"I love these games!" Leo squealed, chocolate around his lips.

Mom gently lifted his chin. "Were you in Ms. Louisa Mae's chocolate again?"

"No." He stepped back and smirked before adding, "I was in Eve's!" He laughed and hurried off.

Sam chuckled. "I offered to carry the medals for him, but he wanted to keep them close."

"Why doesn't he just wear them?" James asked.

Sam and I spoke at the same time. "Doesn't like the feel of them on his neck."

We stopped and smiled awkwardly at each other before my mom stepped closer.

"Sam, I was going to take them to Ringing Rudolph. Would you like to join us?" she asked him.

"Thanks, but I told Mom I'd give her a quick break at our table so she could get some funnel cake." He held his now-empty paper tray.

"Those were ridiculously good," James said, his focus now on Phineas's stand. "He must be a magician or something."

"Phineas adds a pinch of nutmeg to his powdered sugar." Sam pulled out a napkin from his back pocket and wiped his mouth.

"Ooooooh, *that's* why it tasted like Christmas," James muttered to himself.

Sam and I exchanged a knowing smile before he cleared his throat. "I should be going. I'll catch up with you guys in a bit."

Ringing Rudolph was our town's version of a ring toss, except you had to get the highest number of rings on Rudolph's antlers. I explained to the Baileys that the reindeer's face and body were made from logs donated from the Holt Christmas Tree Farm and the legs were dowels donated from Hal's Hardware.

"Who carved the large antlers?" Mr. Bailey asked. "Those are pretty impressive."

"Thank you," my mom replied, her cheeks going red.

"You?" Mr. Bailey did a double take.

"It's not a big deal." Mom waved a hand in front of her face and took a sip of her cider.

"She actually *is* a pretty big deal around here." I looped my arm around her shoulder.

"You should see her studio," James added.

Mr. Bailey walked closer to one of the reindeer and ran his fingers over the antlers. "I know some interior designers in the city who would pay top dollar for this, Alice—"

"My work is here." Her voice had gone cold, hard.

James raised his eyebrows at me before snapping his fingers. "So, guys versus girls again?"

But then—right on cue—Mr. Bailey's phone rang. He held up his finger and took the call, stepping away before shouting, "What? No, no. Just wait for me. Be right there." He hung up and quickly walked back to us. "I'm sorry, but I have to cut this short. Bret and Milton need me at the B&B for one of their Zooms."

"But, Dad. You promised . . ." James frowned, and I wanted to grab one of those reindeer and use it to knock some sense into his father.

"It's important, son. They came all this way. I'll see you later tonight." He patted James's shoulder before he smiled rather forcefully at the rest of us. "You all enjoy yourselves."

Mr. Bailey took off his headband as he walked away, disappearing into a sea of antlers. "Jingle Bell Rock" played over the speakers, and several couples and groups of kids sang along while bustling back and forth to different games and booths.

There was so much more that I could've shown him.

Mom and I had to forgo Ringing Rudolph to get to the face-painting booth, and James followed, gently talking to my mom about some of the woodwork and pottery he had seen in the city and how much it sold for. But Mom just smiled and shrugged after letting him speak and again said that she was happy right where she was.

James watched us both paint different holiday-themed pictures, chosen from a laminated card, on people's cheeks.

"You're a natural," he said to me as I gave the finishing touches to a Christmas wreath.

"She is," Mom said, nudging me as she finished a gingerbread man.

Sam walked up, and the peaceful scent of pine wrapped around me like a warm, comforting blanket.

"How's your family's table going?" Mom asked him.

"Great. We sold out of wreaths already, and we have several deliveries scheduled for tomorrow, too." He beamed proudly.

The little girl whose face I had just painted said thank you as she got up to leave, and then James plopped down in the chair.

"*You* want your face painted?" I asked him, dipping my brush into the water before rolling it back and forth on the towel under the cup.

"Of course." He picked up the card of options and tapped his chin for a moment before putting the card down and saying, "Surprise me."

Although I was tempted to do something semi-embarrassing like the butt of a reindeer, I suddenly had the perfect idea for him. Leaning this close to James while Sam watched nearby was not how I envisioned today going, but I pushed away my jumbled feelings and got to work.

Several minutes later, I had a guitar with a sprig of holly

painted on his smooth cheek. "What do you think?" I asked, handing him a mirror.

He held it up and placed his fingers just below the guitar. "I love it." He lowered the mirror and cocked his head, his nose crinkling. "And you painted mistletoe with it?"

I cleared my throat. "Holly, actually."

"Aren't they the same thing?" he asked, rising to his feet.

"Actually, no." Sam straightened up, and I bit back a smile, knowing full well what he was about to say.

"Holly is a shrub or small tree," he continued, pulling his shoulders back the way he always did when he proudly talked about plants. "Mistletoe is parasitic, latching itself onto trees to steal their water and nutrients."

James blinked. "So . . . definitely *not* the same."

"Nope."

I bit back a smile.

Ladies and gentlemen, Mullings Creek's resident arborist, Sam Holt.

Chapter Twenty

"Leaning is whole bodies moving in like this. Leaning involves wanting, and accepting . . ."

—WHILE YOU WERE SLEEPING

After the run-in with Bret and Milton, I decided to call an emergency meeting with James, Jo, and Sam. We met in Mom's studio, since she was outside at the games with most of the other vendors while our local Boy Scout troop set up the tables and chairs for Blitzen Bingo inside The Market.

"I've only got a few minutes before I need to go back down there to help Eve," Jo said. "What's going on?"

I quickly relayed everything that had happened this morning, and how Mr. Bailey's guests meant bad news for our town.

"Crap." Jo grabbed the tin of Mom's chocolate and handed us each a piece of the good stuff before she sank down into the desk chair.

Mom always said there was nothing a little 75 percent cacao couldn't fix, but I wasn't too sure about it this time.

"I'm sure we can think of something," Sam said from where he sat on the windowsill. He gently rotated one of Mom's plants so another side would face the midday sunlight. "Won't he be at the movie tonight? Maybe you guys could stage something then?"

James cleared his throat and rubbed a hand over his jaw. "I mean . . . he might go, but, um, Gianna and I were going to . . . go—"

"On our date," I finished, my throat suddenly dry. "Alone."

Which was fine, right?

Just because we were going alone didn't mean we couldn't strategize more for Operation Ho Ho Humbug.

"Right." Something flickered over Sam's face, but before I could ask myself what it was, it disappeared and a fake smile stood in its place. "Sorry, I forgot."

Jo looked back and forth between the three of us before blurting, "What if I put something in Bret and Milton's coffee, and they got sick—"

Sam and I shouted "No!" at the same time James excitedly shouted "Yes!"

There was a beat of silence, and then the four of us burst into laughter.

"Jo." I wiped my eyes and took a breath. "Promise me you won't do something stupid with their coffee . . . or food . . . or just in general . . ."

Jo shrugged and grabbed another piece of chocolate out of the tin. "I mean, if no one else comes up with a solid plan, I think a couple days of delay on the toilet is what we need to go with." She stood and crossed the room, stopping at the door to go back downstairs. "Text me later about what you decide, G!"

"I'm with her, to be honest." James said after she left.

Sam snorted.

From somewhere below in The Market, the sweet voice of Sam's mother could be heard singing "Silver Bells." The hum of the other conversations quieted, and even the sliding of chairs and tables against the floor stopped, not that I was surprised in the least.

When Sam's mom sang, everyone stopped to listen.

"She sounds like an angel," I said.

Sam smiled. "Yeah, she does."

"Who is that?" James asked, opening the door.

"My mom," Sam said. "She's in charge of the church choir." He chuckled and rubbed the back of his neck. "I swear she sings more than she speaks, but I've always loved that about her."

James leaned his head against the doorframe, keeping his back to us. "My dad used to sing with my mom when I was little."

"Really?" I couldn't imagine someone like Mr. Bailey singing, let alone with another person.

James closed the door and turned back around. "They used to fight over who got to sing harmony." He laughed. "Dad always wanted it, but he was never good at staying in key."

"That must've been fun to listen to," Sam said with a smile.

"It was." James looked at him, his eyes now a bit misty. "But then he got too busy to be home in time for dinner. And she got too busy on the weekends . . ." He sniffed and stared at his feet, and my heart squinched. "So, I started playing music. Learned guitar. Sang. But by then they didn't want to listen, and Dad became convinced music was a lost cause."

Sam cleared his throat. "I don't agree with my parents on everything. And Lord knows I have some different opinions about how I think the tree farm should be run, but at the end of the day, we're still family." He shook his head. "I'm sorry your dad doesn't get that."

"I mean . . . I honestly don't know what he wants from me half the time. I get good grades, play sports, am involved in clubs." James ran a hand through his hair. "But because I don't want a desk job when I'm older or to go to law school like he and my granddad did, I'm 'wasting my talent.'"

I started toward him, but Sam surprised me by doing it first, crossing the room in just a few steps. "Does your dad have a favorite Christmas song?" he asked him.

James shook his head. "Not really. Not anymore."

"But he must've had one once, right?" I asked, walking over to join them.

James stared off toward the wall of windows for a long moment, his lips pinched together, before he came back to us. "'In the Bleak Midwinter,'" he said. "He and my granddad used to listen to it on repeat every December before he passed away."

Sam slowly turned to look to me, his face illuminated with a new idea.

What?

Oh.

Hope began to bubble inside of me.

"Great idea!" I clapped him on his shoulder. *Wish I had thought of it first.*

James raised an eyebrow at us. "I feel like I'm missing something."

"Don't worry. Sam's got it," I said, taking James's hand and squeezing it. "Right, Sam?"

Sam's focus briefly dropped to our clasped hands before coming back to James. "Right."

Nona had apparently signed Sam and me up to work the ball cage for bingo like we did last year, so after James left to go FaceTime his mom and stepsister, Sam and I headed back downstairs to take our places on the stage.

The room was now filled with long tables draped in burgundy. Dozens of people sat in folding chairs with their bingo cards and daubers with red ink. Although everyone smiled at each other and made small talk, tension lingered among them.

I didn't know what it was about bingo, but it always brought out the drama in Mullings Creek.

"You ready for the chaos, G?" Sam asked, pulling out the chair next to him.

I sank into it and took a swig of water from a bottle he had grabbed for me. "Let's just hope Marco keeps his shirt on this year."

"I think Jo would hope otherwise."

I smacked his arm as he pulled a new book out of his back pocket, laying it on the table next to him.

"*A Christmas Carol*?" I touched the cover. "Didn't you read that last Christmas?"

"And the one before that." He tapped it. "It's a good book to read this time of year. A reminder of the important things."

"I get that."

Ms. Louisa Mae hurried over to the stage. "Oh, Sam, I'm glad I caught you before we got started." She beamed up at him. "I wanted to let you know that the *Lord of the Rings* trilogy you donated for the silent auction received the highest bid of the day!"

Hold up. What?

"Donna thinks that money alone should really help offset some of the back taxes Arthur left behind," she added.

Sam donated–

Mayor Moore clapped and tapped the mic at the end of the stage. "Ladies and gentlemen, if you'll take your seats, we will begin Blitzen Bingo in just a few minutes!"

Ms. Louisa Mae waved at Sam and thanked him one more time before hurrying back to her bingo cards.

"Why the heck did you donate your *Lord of the Rings* books?" I asked him. "Aren't they, like, super valuable?"

He waved a hand at my question and then jumped up. "Crap, we still need the cage and master board."

"Sam . . ."

He hurried off the stage toward the storage closet, but I followed closely behind him.

He didn't get to dodge something this big.

Not with me, at least.

The storage room smelled like mothballs, cedar, and dust. A small light bulb above us flickered, spilling shadows onto the board games, decorations, and rolled-up yoga mats stacked on the shelves.

I gently closed the door behind us as Sam began to search the shelves.

"How could you give up those books?" I asked him. "That's your favorite series—"

"I'll buy another set from Ann." He held out a couple of board games for me to take as he continued to dig.

"But it's not the same—"

"Aha!" He held up the cage and shook it. "Let's count these just in case."

I narrowed my eyes at him but opened the master board as he dumped the bingo balls onto the counter.

Forget tree farming.

With the way he avoided answering questions, Sam could be a top recruit for the CIA.

We started placing each one in their right spot on the master board to double-check that we weren't missing any.

"So . . ." He set two more down. "Excited for your big date?"

Redirecting like a pro.

I reached around him for a couple more to place. "Yeah." *Nervous is more like it.*

Sam must've heard it in my voice, because he nudged me. "It'll go great, G."

"You think?"

He handed me the last three. "I mean, he knows about your allergies now, so if he . . . um . . . if you two want to . . ."

"Kiss?" My neck started to prickle with heat. *Why don't contractors think to put better ventilation in places like this?* "I doubt *that* will happen."

"I wouldn't count it out." We started putting the balls back in the cage. "He definitely wants to."

"How can you tell?" I asked, immediately regretting the question, because in what world would a conversation like this in a closet with my best friend who I still sorta wanted to kiss *not* be awkward?

But Sam wasn't fazed by it. In fact, he just blinked at me like I had grown reindeer antlers.

"He leaned." He tossed the last couple of balls in the cage and then closed it.

"He *leaned*?" I asked. "What does that even mean?"

Sam sighed and folded up the master board. "Earlier today, before the face-painting, I saw him lean toward you."

"And that . . ." I moved my hands around. "Means something?"

"Of course it does." And before I knew what was happening, he took a step closer to me. "Look, G, if a guy leans in like this . . ." He paused and reached his arm behind my head, leaning his elbow against the closest shelf. "That means he wants to be close to you. Like he's . . . waiting. You know what I'm saying?"

"No." I smiled. "But I'm having fun watching you try."

He rolled his eyes and bopped my nose.

"Why'd you give up your books, Sam?" I asked.

He let his cheek fall against the hand still above me. "I told you. It's not a big deal."

"You're so full of crap." I crossed my arms over my chest. "You said those books had original dust jackets. That there were even some errors on the page, which made them priceless."

"You remember that?"

"Of course I remember that."

They meant something to you.

And you mean something to me.

Even when I'm trying so desperately hard for you not to.

"Why'd you do it, Sam?" I pressed.

He groaned. "You're not going to drop this, are you?"

"I'm a Mancini. Since when do we drop anything?"

He closed his eyes for a moment—like it would make whatever he was about to say next easier—before opening them again. "It's important to you, right? Saving The Market?"

I nodded.

"That's why." He stood up straight and grazed his fingers over the bottom of one of my braids. "I did it for you."

Thank God for the shelves behind me, or I would've 100 percent dropped to the floor.

I did it for you.

How could he just say something like that and not expect me to . . .

Screw it.

I uncrossed my arms and ran my fingers down the front of his flannel shirt, settling them near the hem before pressing my forehead against his broad chest.

He sucked in a sharp breath, and the air between us sparked with tension. As I inhaled his familiar scent of sweet pine, the butterflies that were hibernating after our almost-kiss at my house startled awake, going full circus-mode with death-defying loops, leaps, and spins in my stomach. Every single one of my senses was aflame, prickling with so much heat that I felt I would literally combust if I didn't get closer to Sam that instant.

I lifted my gaze.

He swallowed hard, and I counted the times both our chests rose and fell together.

One.

Two.

Three.

He lowered his chin.

I tilted my head.

And then the door banged open.

"Are you two about done—" Bianca stopped short. She stared at the two of us for a long and extremely uncomfortable moment before grinning. "You know what? Take your time." She winked and scurried away.

Oh, she's never going to let me live this one down.

Sam cleared his throat and stepped back. "Yeah, so, um, that's what I meant by the 'lean' thing." He grabbed the bingo cage off the shelf. "But maybe just ask James if he's eaten any peanuts recently before . . . you guys . . . you know."

"Sure. Yeah." I tucked my hair behind my ears and grabbed the master board. "I'll do that."

Right after I crawl under the nearest Christmas tree and stuff myself into one of the fake presents for the remainder of the season.

You're literally going on a real date tonight, Gianna.

And you just tried to kiss your best friend.

Again.

I followed him back to the stage, acting as natural as possible, despite the fact that half the town and most of my family just watched the two of us exit the closet together.

Totally normal.

Nothing to see here, folks.

"But, I mean, as long as he brushed his teeth afterward, he's good. It's not like I'd ask him to completely give them up for me." I laid out the board between us before taking my seat again. "My own family hasn't even done that."

Sam rolled the cage a couple of times. "I did."

"You did . . . what?"

"Gave up peanuts for you," he said simply before pulling out the first ball and calling it aloud, but all I heard was white noise.

Sam gave up peanuts for me.

Sam gave up peanuts for me?

When?

How had I not noticed this?

My mind spun backward in time so fast, I had to put both my hands on the table to steady myself.

Think, Gianna. Think.

When is the last time you remember a conversation about Sam and peanut butter?

Early December?

No.

October?

Or is it September?

Yes. That's it.

He had come to the cafeteria a little late that day because of a makeup test, and when he opened his packed lunch, Jo said his sandwich smelled different.

Sam had held it up triumphantly, and replied, "It is! I switched to sunflower butter."

Oh gosh.

I turned and watched him continue to roll the cage and pull another ball out as if he hadn't just dropped a major truth bomb on me.

Sam *had* given up peanuts, for me.

I never asked him to. He just did.

How had I overlooked something so meaningful? So significant?

And if I had forgotten something as big as that, what the heck else had I missed?

Chapter Twenty-One

"Why don't you kiss her instead of talking her to death?"

—IT'S A WONDERFUL LIFE

A couple of hours later, I stood in front of my long mirror, fidgeting with the ends of my dark green sweater, wondering if the soot stain on my right cuff was small enough to go unnoticed on my date.

My date.

It still felt weird to think it or even say it, and yet here I was, getting ready for a real date with a real boy who I was pretty sure liked me.

And who, to my biggest surprise, I kinda liked as well.

Even though I still obviously had feelings for my best friend.

Who I'd tried to kiss earlier today.

In a closet.

God, you've really made a mess of things, Gianna.

I unplaited my two braids and let my hair hang loosely around my shoulders, something I rarely did because it drove me crazy to have it in my face, but this was what girls did when they went on dates, right?

Wear their hair differently than usual?

Bet those girls don't have hair as freakin' frizzy and heavy as mine, though.

I groaned and grabbed some smoothening cream for the ends before sending a selfie to Jo, who quickly responded with a few fire emojis.

Jo: You look AMAZING!

Jo: Green makes your eyes pop

Me: But am I trying too hard wearing a color I know HE likes?

The conversation bubble popped up and then quickly disappeared before reappearing with her response.

Jo: I've seen you wear that sweater lots of times

Jo: If it makes YOU feel good, then wear it!

A knock sounded on my bedroom door before it opened, and my mom stood in the doorway. She beamed and then her eyes turned glassy.

"Mom," I warned, holding up my hands. "Don't make a bigger deal out of this than it needs to be."

"I won't. I promise." She sniffed. "It's just . . . times like these I really miss your father."

Shoot, now I'm going to cry.

Mom crossed my room and gently placed her ring-covered

hands on my shoulders. "You have his eyes, his smile. Even his hair." She ran her fingers through mine and chuckled. "Beautiful waves . . . although his was a bit more unruly than yours."

"I dunno." I looked back at the mirror. "Have you seen what happens if I go to bed with it wet? I'd make an excellent home for any magpie."

We laughed before she wrapped her arms around my shoulders, squeezing me tightly as I pressed my nose against the hood of her sweatshirt and breathed her in.

Clay.

Oil paint.

And eucalyptus—her attempt at covering it all up.

When she let go, she wiped my cheeks. I hadn't even realized tears had fallen.

"You look beautiful, but you *are* missing one thing." She stepped back and put a finger on her chin.

"I am?" I checked my wrist for my watch and my right ring finger for my claddagh ring. *Yep. Both there.*

"Yep." She reached into her back pocket and pulled out one of my favorite pairs of earrings, small white drops in the shape of irises. Her favorite flower.

I gasped. "Are you sure I can borrow these?"

"For my daughter? *Psh.* Anything." She laid them in my palm and pressed my fingers closed around them. "Your father gave me these before I opened Designs by Alice, and they've brought me luck ever since."

I kissed her damp cheek and hurried over to the mirror to put them on.

Mom appeared behind me and rested her chin on my shoulder. "Perfetta, cara."

I ran my fingers over them, the way I'd seen my mother do before a big event in town, and smiled. She was right.

They were perfect.

"I miss him, too, you know," I whispered to our reflections that blurred behind new tears, my throat tight. "Sometimes I miss him so hard that I can barely breathe."

Mom kept her chin on my shoulder and tilted her head against mine. "Me too."

"It's been so many years." I sniffed. "I worry I'm starting to forget things."

"Like?"

"I dunno. Little things?" I turned around to face her. "Like the way he'd throw open our front door every day after school . . . or how he took his coffee at the breakfast table, or the sound of his laugh—"

"Gianna," Mom said, cupping her hand on my cheek. "Some memories will fade over time, but others will always stay with us." She sighed and released her hand. "He used to drop his bags on top of everyone's shoes after he got home. It drove me nuts because he could've easily hung them up on the wall, but he would say that he couldn't wait. He was too excited to see everyone."

I laughed. *He did say that.*

"He drank his coffee with a tiny splash of whole milk," she added.

"That's right!" I said, suddenly remembering how he used to tease my mother about her sugary creamer.

"And as far as his laugh goes, well . . ." She brushed a stray hair off my forehead. "I get to hear it every day, thanks to you and Leo."

"Well, it's not hard when you have annoying cousins who live right next door . . ." I nodded toward my Aunt Helen's house.

"Good point." She winked.

The doorbell rang, making us both jolt.

"That'll be your hot date." She beamed. "Better get down there!"

I grabbed my crossbody, double-checking that I had my neffy, before hurrying down the stairs. I did some of Leo's deep breathing as I slid into my boots, but my nerves were still jumpy when I opened the door. James stood before me beaming and wearing dark jeans, boots, and a collared shirt under a light blue sweater, which turned his eyes a stunning robin's-egg blue.

"Green is definitely your color," he said, a light pink spreading over his cheeks. "Shall we?"

I nodded and took his hand, which only made my heart thrum faster.

I peeked over my shoulder and caught Mom smiling at the window with two thumbs up.

This is good.

I'm going on a date with a nice guy who is super attractive and interesting and . . .

But as I took my seat in his Jeep, I couldn't shake the guilt-like syrup slinking into my stomach.

Because even though a part of me was really excited to find James waiting for me outside my front door, another part of me had still secretly hoped it would've been Sam.

As usual, it was a packed house at the annual Movie in The Market. The bingo setup was gone, and the vendor stands had been pushed to the walls, leaving the floor open for everyone to sit with their favorite quilts and blankets for the movie. The room smelled of old wood, warm popcorn, and hot cocoa, and the air buzzed with excitement.

Most of us in here had seen *It's a Wonderful Life* more times than we could count, but it was still a Mullings Creek tradition to show it every year. Mr. Paxton used to say that it was the best movie to watch during Christmas because it reminded people of the impact just one person can have on a community. But it was one of Nona's favorites because of Jimmy Stewart, who was in her top three Hollywood men she would've married had it not been for Papa. Gene Kelly and Christopher Plummer held the top two spots.

I pinched my lips and looked left and right, but every spot of the floor was taken.

"Over here," James said, nodding to his left.

I followed him, weaving and stepping around several families and couples who waved at me politely. Some others, who I recognized from bingo earlier, stared at me questioningly.

Most likely coming to the real-time conclusion that James was *not* the boy I was found in the closet with earlier.

James finally stopped in the front row where a large, familiar quilt and a couple of throw pillows sat waiting.

"I borrowed these from your Aunt Sofia." James put his hands in his pockets and rocked back on his heels. "I hope that's okay."

I smiled. "Of course it's okay!"

Reader, it is not okay.

The last thing I wanted was to be literally front and center when I already was the other 364 days of the year.

I sat down on the plush quilt and pulled off my boots as James did the same.

"I didn't realize everyone took off their shoes for this thing until I got here . . ." He made a face and pointed to his feet clad in bright blue socks with someone's face all over them.

"Well, he's certainly not Chewbacca." I snorted. "Who do we have here?"

"That's Pete, my best friend back home." He chuckled. "He's got a pair with my face on them, too. We had them made for Crazy Sock Day during last year's Spirit Week."

"And what is Pete doing during his winter break?" I asked,

sitting cross-legged. "I doubt he's stuck in a small town like this."

"No, he's probably skiing with his brothers up in Vermont at their vacation condo." James sighed wistfully. "Perfect time of year for skiing."

"I've never been."

"Really?" He leaned back on his hands.

I nodded. "Flying down an icy hill standing up is a bit too risky for me."

"Maybe you just need the right kind of teacher." James grinned.

My face warmed. "Maybe." I pointed to the basket resting on the corner of our quilt. "Is that from Aunt Sofia, too?"

"The basket, yes." He reached around me to grab it and set it between us. "What's inside, no. All me."

I peered over the lid expectantly.

James cleared his throat and opened the lid. "I have an assortment of snacks for us this evening, Ms. Mancini. Crackers, cheese, dark chocolate, pretzels, and strawberries." His eyes lifted to meet mine. "I wasn't sure what kind of movie food you liked, but everything in here is nut-free, and I was really careful when preparing it, too."

He remembered. "Thank you, James. That's really sweet. Can I treat us to the cocoa, then?"

"I'm sorry, I can't allow that." He stood. "Be right back!"

I laid out the food onto a large plate packed inside and shot Jo a quick message.

Me: He packed us nut-free snacks!

Her response was immediate and all emojis.

Jo: 😘🖤🖤

I tucked my phone away as James returned with two steaming cups of cocoa.

"Peppermint and cinnamon added, courtesy of Eve," he said, handing me mine.

"Thank you." I blew across it before taking a cautious sip and sighing contentedly. As usual, Eve knew the exact proportion of peppermint to cinnamon I liked.

The lights dimmed, and everyone clapped and cheered with the familiar opening credits and the instrumental score that came with it. We snacked for a bit and finished our cocoa before lying on our stomachs and propping ourselves up with our elbows. James laughed along like the rest of us when George and Mary accidentally danced themselves into the gym pool.

And I couldn't help but think how natural this all felt—hanging out with him while surrounded by the people who had known me my whole life.

Maybe . . . maybe this *was* something.

"I love this part," I whispered to him a few minutes later as George spoke to Mary about throwing a lasso around the moon for her.

He nodded. "Yeah, this is iconic—and that part at the end about angels getting wings."

"Totally."

He popped a pretzel in his mouth and angled his head toward me. "Okay, so time for me to ask my three questions."

"Two," I corrected, bumping his shoulder.

"Fine." He made a face. "First question: Why do you want to be a journalist when you grow up?"

"How did you know that?" I turned my head to the side.

"Your aunt has one of your articles taped to her refrigerator. I asked her about it, and she mentioned it."

She still has that one?

"I guess I've always liked writing and telling stories," I said, grabbing a piece of dark chocolate. "But I really like focusing on people and places that might get overlooked or forgotten."

James nodded. "I like that. You can help a lot of people that way."

That's the idea.

"Favorite dessert?" he asked.

I laughed. "That's your final question?"

He put a hand on his chest. "I take dessert very seriously, Gianna."

"Fair." I bit my lip and smiled at the current scene on the

projector, George talking excitedly about his favorite sounds at the train station. "Cheesecake. I love the cookies and cannoli my Nona bakes, but my dad once brought me back a slice of cheesecake from a teacher's conference, and I still dream about it on a nightly basis."

"There are a couple of great places to eat cheesecake in New York City." James sighed wistfully. "Junior's is a staple, but Birdland has an amazing one, too."

"Birdland?" I asked.

"It's this old jazz club. Great food. Even better music. Tourists could walk right by it and never know the history inside, but, man . . ." He stared off toward the right of the stage. "You can feel it when you walk in there. All the greats who played there—Davis, Fitzgerald, Coltrane—that kind of music stays with you. Leaves its mark, you know?"

I nodded.

Listening to him talk about music was like listening to Sam talk about plants and books. It was easy to get excited even when you didn't quite understand everything they said.

"Promise me you'll visit that spot when you and Jo are there next year, okay?" he asked.

I gave him a small salute. "You got it."

"Or . . . or maybe I could take you there sometime?" His voice softened.

"I'd like that." I smiled.

He grabbed another few pretzels before adding, "I know I

only get two, but can I *please* have one more? It's a good one, I swear."

I raised an eyebrow. "If you must."

He beamed. "Top ten Christmas movies?"

My mouth dropped open. "I can only pick ten?"

"Ten is a lot."

"Not when it comes to Christmas movies." I let my cheek rest against my fist. "I mean, I can try to narrow it down to musicals or movies made before 1970, or maybe animated versus live action, but do I group *Rudolph* and *Santa Claus Is Comin' to Town* with animated or are they different because of stop-motion—"

"Whoa, Gianna." He placed a hand on my arm and chuckled. "I didn't mean to make you spiral. I was just curious."

"Sorry." I bit my lip. "It's hard for me to pick when I watch them all year long."

"I forgot you did that." James pulled back. "Don't you get tired of them?"

I shook my head. "Christmas movies bring me joy. I love the magic and the comfort that comes with them."

He smiled. "My favorite is *Die Hard* . . . in case you were wondering."

Oh, good grief. "*Die Hard* is *not* a Christmas movie."

"Don't enter the ring with me on this one." He held up a hand. "You will lose."

I chuckled. "I suppose you're also like Sam and think that *Lord of the Rings*—"

"Is definitely one, too! The Fellowship begin their journey on December twenty-fifth. It has elves and—"

"Gandalf is like Santa . . ." I deadpanned. I had heard that one from Sam for years. "We'll agree to disagree."

"Okay." He held out his hand. "But I want your top ten list before the new year."

"Deal." I shook it before we both settled back in to watch the rest of the movie in a comfortable silence.

After the credits finished and the lights were turned back on, I helped James pack up the food and fold the quilt before carrying it all back to his Jeep. I really didn't have anything to compare it to, but it really felt like this date went the way dates were supposed to go. Good food, lots of laughter, and just . . . easy.

On the short drive home, we made small talk about the differences between our schools and the programs they offered. James really wanted to switch to a public school for his senior year so he could finally be in a solid music program, but his dad apparently wouldn't hear of it.

"It's hard when he is on me about everything, but I can't imagine what you must go through," he said. "I'd go nuts having my entire family breathing down my neck all the time."

"Oh, I dunno." I drummed my fingers on the doorframe. "It's not terrible—"

"Come on, Gianna." He made a face. "I've seen the way they

bombard you. Not to mention the entire town when you walk down Mistletoe Lane. Doesn't it get old? I mean, why you? Why not your cousins?"

"It didn't used to be this way, but . . . after Dad died, I think everyone just felt like they needed to look after Mom, Leo, and me," I said, my voice growing quiet. "I don't think they do it to be intrusive."

They do it out of love.

And realizing that made my heart fill with something I didn't expect.

Gratitude.

By the time we reached my driveway, the ease of the evening vanished and was replaced with jittery nerves that made my leg bounce wildly in the passenger seat. As James turned off the Jeep and jogged around to my side to open the door, I had to remind myself how to walk and prayed he couldn't hear the way my heart pounded in anticipation.

This was it.

He was walking me to my door.

We'd go up the front porch steps and . . . then what?

How would I know if he wanted to kiss me?

Did I need to like . . . linger or something?

Did I want to linger?

Honestly, yeah. I do.

"Thank you for coming with me tonight," he said, his voice a little high before he cleared it. "I had a great time."

I swallowed over the lump in my throat and managed a semi-coherent "Me too."

"The last time I saw a movie like that was in the park back home, but we had a bit more people around us."

"How many?"

"A couple thousand." He grinned.

"Thousand?" My voice rose. "I can't imagine."

"Well, by next year, you won't have to." He tucked his hands into his pockets. "You'll be among millions in New York City."

Millions.

My stomach rolled.

All my life I'd dreamed of breaking away, exploring the world and then writing it all down so others who were stuck like me could live that life, too.

But who was I to tell that story, really?

When there were millions more who could probably do it better?

"Gianna?" James's voice broke through my daze. "You good?"

I spun my claddagh ring a few times and took a slow breath in through my nose, grounding myself. "Yeah, I'm good. Just . . . thinking about the future, I guess."

"Exciting, isn't it?" He rocked back on his heels.

Ha. "A bit, yeah." *And terrifying.*

The cold wind moved around us, rattling the Christmas

lights hanging on our porch railing, and I smiled at the familiar, cold scent. "Smells like snow."

He looked at me skeptically. "Snow has a smell?"

"Absolutely."

"Okay, I'm game." He leaned against the nearest post. "What does snow smell like?"

I closed my eyes and pictured all the times I stood in our yard, face up to a cloudy sky, waiting for what I knew could be minutes or hours away, remembering how my stomach always fluttered with excitement, and then later, the pure joy I'd feel at that first snowflake touching my skin.

"The air goes very still," I whispered to James, almost reverently. "It's clean and crisp, sharp . . . in a way that only happens right before the snow falls. Only then, you get the briefest hint of earth, deep and woodsy."

I opened my eyes and found James watching me intently, his mouth opened just a little.

He blinked quickly and then a slow smile spread across his face. "I've been around snow my whole life but never noticed *that* before."

"Most people don't." I shrugged. "They're just too busy speeding by to stop and pause." I looked around at the quiet stillness of my street, the lazy glow of the lamplight and their outlines stretched across the cold ground. "Small towns are good for slowing down and appreciating those moments."

He tilted his head. "I'm beginning to see that—"

"You gonna just stand there all night?" a familiar voice heckled from the next house over. "Or are you gonna kiss her?"

"Marco Ulderico Mancini, get your head back inside this house and leave your poor cousin alone!" Aunt Helen yelled.

"I'm helpin' the guy out, Ma!" he yelled back before someone yanked him back inside.

"I'm going to kill him," I mumbled, my entire body now burning with embarrassment. "Sorry."

"No, it's okay. I, uh, kinda needed the boost." He stepped toward me and leaned in, angling his head just a bit, waiting for me to move closer, to allow what I knew was a kiss to happen. "Is . . . is this okay?"

Before I could conjure up three scenarios about everything that could go wrong like bumping noses or having food in my teeth, I closed the space between us, stretching onto my tiptoes and placing my hands on his chest before I, too, leaned in and let my lips brush his.

He tasted of chocolate and strawberries and a smidgen of salt, and I blushed even more at the feel of his rapid heartbeat underneath my fingertips.

A whistle sounded through the air followed by the distinct sound of a hard smack and then Nico cursing.

We pulled away laughing, and I dropped back to my normal height, tucking my hair behind my ears. "My cousins are . . ."

"Family." James shrugged. "I don't see mine much, but when

I do I have to remind myself that they're not perfect, but they're mine."

I chuckled.

"Goodnight, Gianna." He leaped off my front porch steps and walked backward, grinning goofily all the way to his Jeep, stumbling once before giving an awkward half wave.

"Goodnight," I whispered, feeling lighter than I had all day.

Chapter Twenty-Two

"It's going to be easy. Like peeling a turtle."

—HOLIDAY INN

At school the next day, Jo and I worked in the library helping Ms. Diaz with her midyear inventory. Each of us took a Chromebook and scanner and went to work scanning every book on the shelves. Jo and I took the nonfiction section, since it was all grouped relatively close together, allowing us to talk quietly while we worked.

"I can't believe Marco and Nico did that," she said, gently pulling one book out just enough to see the barcode and scanning it before pushing it back on the shelf.

I huffed. "Yes, you can. Because I definitely expected it."

"Still . . ." She stopped scanning for a moment. "If you had to rate this kiss . . ."

"I really don't have much to compare it to, Jo."

Especially when all of them were pretty cringey.

I used my foot to roll a kickstand stool next to me so I could sit to scan the bottom two rows. "There was that time two years ago under the bleachers at that home football game—"

"With Oliver Young!" She pointed her scanner at me with eyes wide. "I forgot about that one. I was thinking more about Steven Scott in—"

"Ninth grade." I nodded while I scanned. "Our first homecoming dance. Totally didn't expect that one, which was why we bumped noses." I snorted.

So awkward.

Marco had followed me around for a week asking if I needed ice for my face.

"You're right; I guess that isn't too much to go on," she admitted before going back to her row of books. "But still . . . it wasn't terrible, was it?"

"Not at all." The back of my neck prickled with heat. "It was . . . nice."

"Nice like 'comfortable and a bit exciting' or nice like 'out-of-body experience'?"

I thought about it as I finished my bottom row before I stood to stretch. "Comfortable and a bit exciting."

Which wasn't a bad thing, right?

Comfortable was good.

And it must've been exciting enough, since it kept me up late in my thoughts last night.

So then why do I feel like a kid who opened every present under her tree but still went searching for one more?

A few minutes later, the bell rang for early dismissal—except for those who had a final in the afternoon, which neither of us did. So, Jo and I headed toward our lockers as Mrs. Bartlett came up, holding a candy cane clipboard. "Gianna! Glad I caught you."

Well, I know where this is going.

"The Ladies Bible Study group was hoping you could help wrap gifts for their angel tree again this year. Can I put you down for a shift this afternoon?"

"Oh . . ." I bit my lower lip. "Jo and I actually had plans—"

"She can help!" Mrs. Bartlett said, giving a quick smile to Jo. "You've helped them out the last few years. You know how they like things done—"

"Or maybe it's a good time to find a different volunteer." Jo shifted her book bag to her other shoulder. "Since Gianna will be in college next year, right?"

Mrs. Bartlett winced and made a noise in the back of her throat. She crossed something off her clipboard—*a bit aggressively, if you ask me*—before saying, "I'll just let them know that Gianna is unavailable for the foreseeable future."

Well, that seemed a bit harsh.

I mean, who's to say I won't be able to help when I come home from college break?

But before I could speak up, Mrs. Bartlett moved on down the hallway toward a crowd of seniors watching someone stand on a chair with a stereo over his head as he sang "All I Want for Christmas Is You" with words switched out for the Mistletoe Masquerade.

"It's okay to say no to things," Jo said as we walked toward the main entrance.

I opened the front door for us. "I say no to things."

She made a face. "You're about as good at saying no to people asking for help as Sam is."

Sam is way worse, but whatever.

"Speaking of Sam . . ." She zipped up her coat to her neck. "Has he talked any more about going to the dance?"

"Nope." *He apparently just enjoys confessing secrets about peanut butter and what it means when a guy "leans."*

"Do you think James will ask you?"

"He probably doesn't even know about it." I flipped up my hood and burrowed deeper into my jacket, hoping it would protect me from the biting wind.

"You'd have to live under a rock to not know about it while staying in this town," Jo said. "What about Mr. Bailey? Think you guys can get him to go?"

I kicked a loose stone on the sidewalk into the street.

Why hadn't James and I talked about that—about ways to get his dad to buy into Christmas at Mullings Creek—on our date?

Oh wait.

We were too busy ranking Christmas movies and discussing stupid cheesecake.

"You off in your thoughts?" Jo asked.

I nodded as icy guilt snaked its way around my stomach. "I

should've thought to talk to him more about Operation Ho Ho Humbug last night. I mean, I didn't even look to see if his dad came to see the movie! What the heck was I thinking?"

She looped her arm through mine. "You were thinking about yourself and your feelings and enjoying your date. And there's nothing wrong with that, G."

"So it definitely was a real date, right?" I asked. I mean, it felt like one.

Jo tilted her head. "Do you want it to be?"

I swallowed. "Yeah, I do." Even though my stomach still felt tighter than my hair when Bianca braided it.

She smiled. "Then that's that!"

That's that? But what about—

"Hey." She nudged me. "You've still got time to win over his dad."

Psh. "Not really." It was already December seventeenth. Eight days till Christmas.

And less than two weeks till the Baileys leave Mullings Creek.

All I had done since they arrived was help fix a chaotic mess of a gingerbread house and a couple rounds of Snowman Bowling.

Some help I've been.

A bark sounded behind us, making us stop and turn around to find Sandy waiting with something shiny in her mouth, her tail wagging. The red antler cap Aunt Sofia crocheted sat crooked on her head.

"Whatcha got now, girl?" I asked, letting go of Jo's arm before I crouched down in front of Sandy and fixed her hat. She gently lowered her head to the ground and dropped an old, tarnished compass at my feet.

Something about it looked familiar, but I couldn't put my finger on it.

"Did you want me to have this?" I asked her.

She replied with a short bark and then sat expectantly.

"You're such a smart girl." I smiled at her before bringing my book bag around front and opening one of my smaller pockets. I pulled out a Ziploc bag of small dog treats and tossed one to her.

She caught it mid-throw and then promptly got up and trotted back down the street.

"Where'd she get the hat?" Jo asked as I stood back up.

"Aunt Sofia." I tucked the compass into my jacket pocket.

"That checks out." Jo chuckled. "Wait till you see my plans for my new tastings for Eve. You're gonna flip."

But then my phone dinged.

I checked it and cringed at the calendar alert. "Crap. I forgot I promised to swing by the stables to brush Shadowfax for Sheriff Kingston."

Jo made a face. "Since when are you Shadowfax's groomer?"

"Since . . ." I opened my mouth and then closed it, thinking.

"The sheriff started helping out with Toys for Tots at the fire department."

"Gianna . . ."

"I know. *I know.*" I held up both hands and backed away. "But I promise I'll be at your place in like an hour. Hour and a half, tops, okay?"

Jo crossed her arms and tapped her fingers. "If you're later than that, you don't get to eat any of my samples."

I saluted her. "I won't be late."

I was late.

Only by a half hour, but Jo being Jo took pity on me and saved some of the prep for a new cookie recipe she created. Her dads were out Christmas shopping, so we had the house to ourselves. Each year, they chose a different theme for their interior decor, and this year's choice was a *Little Women* Christmas in honor of Jo's namesake.

Every room was adorned with burgundy and gold accents and scented with cedar, dried oranges, and cinnamon. New needlepoint stockings hung from their fireplace, which was draped with a soft garland covered in bronze sleigh bells and small bows. Their coffee table had a centerpiece arrangement of citrus fruits with tall, drippy candles framing it.

Their live tree, though, was my favorite part. It was simple yet elegant, with strands of popcorn and cranberries and ornaments made of dried oranges and paper-star shapes. There were no twinkle lights to be seen. The only light came from dozens of small battery-operated candles clipped to its branches.

"Everything is so beautiful in here," I said as I tossed my coat over the back of their couch and unwrapped my scarf.

"Thank you," Jo said from the kitchen, which was open into the living room.

I hopped up on a barstool and rested my elbows on the counter. "So, what can I do to help?"

She tossed me two boxes of candy canes and a gallon Ziploc bag. "Unwrap these and then toss them into the bag. Once you do that, I'll give you a hammer to beat the crap out of them."

"You got it." I pushed up my sleeves and got to work while humming along to the music of *Holiday Inn* playing on the TV in the background.

Thirty minutes in, I had most of the candy canes unwrapped, but I was interrupted by a pinching, pulsing sensation in my forehead above my eyebrow. I kept stopping to try to rub the pain away, but it didn't work.

"You okay?" Jo stepped away from the stand mixer, which was humming away as it spun on a low setting.

"Yeah." I pinched the bridge of my nose. "Just can't shake this headache."

"When did you last eat?"

Um . . .

"Gianna, when you don't eat, your body will remind you about it in not-so-nice ways." Jo laid her hands on mine over the bag.

"I know." I hopped off the stool and did my best not to look as dizzy as I felt before grabbing a glass from the cabinet for some water. "It was a busy day."

"It didn't have to be."

"What does that mean?" I leaned against the counter and drank almost half the glass. Guess I was thirsty after all.

She switched off her stand mixer and spoke with her back to me. "There's a reason you put your own mask on first before you help others on an airplane."

"Okay . . ."

"You can't keep giving everything to everyone else and leave nothing for yourself." She turned around and tucked her hands into the pockets of her apron. "Have you even started packing or thinking about your trip to Italy in a few weeks?"

"No," I mumbled.

"Then maybe you should say that word 'no' more so you can." She sighed and then pointed to the fridge. "We have some gnocchi from your Nona in there. Why don't you heat it up and eat that before beating up the candy canes?"

"Thanks, Jo." I smiled and crossed the kitchen and gave her a hug. "I don't know what I'd do without you."

She patted my back.

"Oooh, I love the green of that mixture!" I said, pointing to the bowl. "Did you use food coloring?"

Jo made a face. "What kind of pastry chef do you take me for? I used matcha. It pairs perfectly with peppermint."

"Brilliant."

She did a quick bow and then pushed me back toward the fridge so I would eat, reminding me that she had fresh Parmesan in the fridge for the pasta.

Making Nona's gnocchi was an all-hands-on-deck affair. The whole family got involved. We would lay out tea towels over her extended dining room table. Each of us would then roll out long logs of the potato pasta before using a knife to cut off small pieces, pinching it with our fingers, and finishing it with a quick press of a fork.

I sighed happily as I ate this batch, which was sautéed in a garlic, onion, basil, and tomato sauce, and watched Jo expertly pipe macaron dough into perfect circles.

After scraping the bowl clean, I relaxed and spun back and forth in the chair.

"Better?" Jo asked as she slid the cookie sheets into the oven and then grabbed a hammer, placing it next to me.

"Much better," I said. And it was true. My headache had all but vanished, but then I glanced at their large whiteboard calendar hanging on the back door of the kitchen, at the big "Countdown to Christmas" numbers on the bottom, and my eye began to twitch.

"Oh no. Was the gnocchi bad?" She set the heart sprinkles

on the counter and hurried over. "You look like you're about to throw up all over the candy canes."

"No, it's not the gnocchi." I picked up the hammer and began hitting the candy canes.

Oh, this is satisfying.

I hit them harder.

"I'm running out of ideas for convincing Mr. Bailey not to sell The Market to outside buyers." The candy canes continued to break under my infinite power.

WHACK.

"But also, like, even if he doesn't, who in town would have the money to buy it?" I wondered aloud.

WHACK.

"And if someone *could*, what if they change a bunch of stuff anyway?" I focused on one stubborn piece that wouldn't break and hit it over and over until Jo caught my hand mid-swing.

"I think the candy canes are thoroughly crushed, hon," she said.

Maybe this was why Sam loved chopping wood with his dad?

Great stress reliever.

"Focus on one problem at a time, okay?" She laid the candy cane bag near the sink before picking up her mixing bowl to clean out. "We need to think about what gets Mr. Bailey out of his shell."

I rested my cheek on my fist. "Uh, alcohol?"

"Well, that's true for most people." She chuckled and turned off the water. "You said he got really into the Reindeer Games before he took off, right?"

I nodded.

"So, he's competitive?" She grabbed a towel from the oven handle.

I nodded again.

Jo dried the mixing bowl and pinched her lips together, her focus moving around the kitchen until it landed on the bag of crushed candy canes, a slow smile then spreading across her face. "I think I have an idea."

Chapter Twenty-Three

"Peppermint! What I've been searching for all my life!"

—RUDOLPH THE RED-NOSED REINDEER

Jo, true to form, held off telling any of us about her "brilliant master plan" until we were all together at Wanderin' Eats Diner for lunch after our Pre-Calc final the next morning. She sat next to Sam, who was busy looking anywhere but at me—which was fine.

It's not like I've replayed our second almost-kiss a hundred times in my head since it happened.

I was far too busy thinking about my super-awesome, exciting kiss with someone who actually wanted to reciprocate.

But by the time that someone came in, our multiple orders of fries and chocolate shakes were already half empty.

"Sorry!" James announced as the diner door flew open, bringing in a bitterly cold wind that blew two menus off the counter. "I had to help Dad find his laptop, and it took longer than expected."

He threw his jacket on one of the empty hooks by the door and slid into the booth next to me, absentmindedly kissing my cheek when he did.

See? How is that so hard?

Sam's attention immediately snapped toward the two of us, but I pretended not to notice as I tucked a piece of hair behind my ear and cleared my throat. "Your dad lost his laptop?"

James smirked. "Well, he didn't *lose* it, per se. I hid it."

Jo laughed. "And how did that go?"

"Honestly, it was a great plan for the first hour." James grabbed a fry and dunked it into some ketchup before popping it into his mouth. "I convinced him that he left it at Eve's, so he went there first and got a coffee. And then he called me all flustered and said it wasn't there, so I told him to check The Market—"

"Brilliant," I said before taking a sip of my milkshake.

"Thanks." He rested his arm on the back of the booth seat behind me. "But apparently when he got there, he ran into your mom, who was arguing with your Nona. Something about how she left mistletoe all over her studio?"

God, not again.

I thought Mom had changed the locks after last year.

I fell back against the seat. "I bet I'll hear all about that later."

"Without a doubt." James reached for another fry at the same time Sam did, but Sam pulled his hand back and said, "Go ahead."

"Thanks!" James grabbed it and took a bite. "Long story short: Nona asked my dad to help your mom with some cookie deliveries—"

"Santa works hard. Nona works harder." I rolled my eyes.

"And by the time he made it back to the B&B, he was pretty pissed, so I did this whole 'Oh, look, here it is!' bit, but he didn't buy it." James took a long sip of his milkshake. "He told me to go down and ask your Aunt Sofia for a vacuum and duster and then made me clean the entire suite." He sighed. "Those Christmas villages and elf statues were brutal."

"Hermey's hat is a nightmare," I mumbled.

Bianca, Nico, and I had "elf statue" duty a few years ago when we forgot to close the freezer all the way after sneaking some ice cream.

"But I'm here now!" He clapped and looked at Jo. "So, what is this great plan?"

"Okay, here we go." Jo rubbed her hands together and then pulled a piece of paper out of her jacket pocket. She hastily unfolded it, then pushed the fries to the side and flattened it out in the middle of the table.

Sam and I both tried turning the paper at the same time, and zips of electricity pulsed through my hand when our fingers brushed.

"Sorry," I blurted, pulling my hand back and sitting on it. "You go ahead."

"You sure?" He swallowed hard.

"Yep. All you." I pressed my leg harder on my hand, but it still felt tingly.

Sam picked up the paper and then smiled. "A candy cane scavenger hunt?"

Jo nodded excitedly. “Each riddle will lead you to a different place in town where you’ll have to find the next clue.”

“Mellon,” Sam whispered, a quote he commonly said from *Lord of the Rings* anytime we spoke about puzzles.

James inclined forward on his elbows and spoke to him. “Okay, I have to ask, which one is your favorite?”

“*Return of the King*, easily.” Sam shifted back in his seat and crossed his arms. “Except for the fact that they left out—”

“The scouring of the Shire!”

“I know!”

James threw his hands up. “I don’t know what bothers me most, that or how Faramir’s story gets totally overlooked compared to the book, but the movies are still amazing.”

“Unparalleled.” Sam tilted his head to the side before he picked up the basket of fries and held it out for James. A peace offering.

Apparently, all it took was Tolkien.

James took a fry before reading over the puzzles. “And the prize for the winner?” he asked.

“A free handcrafted ornament from Glass Works,” Jo said.

I pointed to the paper. “You already wrote the riddles? I could’ve helped with that.”

“I know.” Jo crossed her arms. “But once I got started, they just kinda poured out of me.”

“Well, how about I swing by the stores on Mistletoe Lane to let them know people will be coming—”

"Already did that, too." Jo smiled. "I also printed the riddles on cute candy cane tags and attached them to candy canes."

"So they just need to be hidden?" I asked.

Jo shook her head. "My dads and I did that early this morning after our sunrise yoga."

I frowned. "I would've helped you."

The boys began speaking enthusiastically about *The Hobbit* as Jo reached across the table and took my hand. "I know you could have." She spoke softly. "But now you have time to, oh I dunno, pack for your trip to Italy?"

Packing for Italy while blasting Pentatonix did sound wonderful, but I couldn't quite shake the heaviness that had settled in my stomach.

Did Jo not think I could do the job correctly?

Was I not smart enough to write a riddle?

I mean, I thought I was the writer of our group . . .

"G," Jo said, snapping her fingers in front of me. "Stop overthinking."

"I'm not—"

"Yes, you are." She tilted her head, her expression softening. "I took charge because it was a last-minute idea that I wanted to happen tonight and because you don't have to do *everything* in this town." She took another fry and dunked it in her milkshake. "Now go home and have fun making lists and organizing. Anyone who wants to participate has to meet at the town square at eight p.m. tonight."

"Okay." I sighed. I did love making lists.

James slid out of the booth and helped me into my coat before putting on his own. "Can I walk you home?"

"Sure," I said, smiling.

We were quiet for most of the walk until we turned down my street.

"Did I do something wrong the other night?" he blurted. "I mean, the kiss. Was . . . Should I not have done that?"

"What? No." I stopped and faced him. "I thought the kiss was . . . nice."

He pursed his lips. "Nice like, 'Wow, can't wait for another one,' or nice like, 'Meh, I've had better'?"

I laughed and hooked my arm through his, leading him toward my driveway. "Definitely nice like 'Wow, can't wait for another one.' "

He exhaled dramatically and put a hand over his chest. "Whew. Thought I had really lost my stuff there for a moment."

I bumped his arm.

We stopped at the bottom of my front porch steps, and I was overcome with déjà vu, waiting for Marco or Nico to poke their head out of their windows next door and heckle us. But they didn't. In fact, the entire street was quiet except for some kid playing basketball a few houses down.

"So, I'll see you tonight, then?" James brushed something off my shoulder.

"Eight o'clock by the big Christmas tree," I replied.

"Operation Ho Ho Humbug will commence once again." He leaned in and gave me a quick kiss before heading back to the B&B.

I smiled as I watched him walk away.

And later, that same smile returned after I had made two lists and a pile of "maybe" clothes as I ran my fingers along the large map that hung over my desk, stopping at each red dot.

I had so many places I wanted to go, and now I finally get to cross off one of them.

This was my time to do what Dad and I had planned out years ago.

To get out, explore, try new things.

Like kissing a boy I had only known for a couple weeks.

My door flew open, and Leo came bounding in like a puppy, landing on my bed with a loud *thump*.

"Mom said I could join Marco and Nico's team for Jo's candy cane hunt!" His powdered-sugar-covered lips broke into a wide smile.

Someone has been in the pizzelle tin again, I see.

"Come on! We're going to be late!" He hopped off my bed and squeezed me around my waist before running out of my room. Several thumps and a door slamming shut later, I watched my little brother hurry across our yard toward Marco and Nico's, where they were waiting by their front porch steps. Marco scooped him up and threw him on his shoulders before the three of them galloped off under the streetlights, and something heavy pressed itself against my chest.

Yes, I did have so many things I wanted to do and to see.

But how do you leave a place that already has so much of your heart?

"Ladies and gentlemen!" Jo stood on a bench near the big town square tree, shouting through Mayor Moore's megaphone. "Thank you for coming out for Mullings Creek's first-ever Candy Cane Scavenger Hunt!"

A crowd of about two dozen people clapped and cheered.

Amazing turnout for something created so last-minute, but then again, when Jo had her mind set on something, she always delivered.

"My friends and I will be handing out your first riddle momentarily. Once that happens, you and your team will need to solve that riddle, which will lead to the next location where another riddle and a candy cane will be waiting for you. And don't worry, we've mixed up the order for each team so you can't just follow one person around all evening, *Marco*."

"Why does everyone take shots at me?" Marco asked innocently, but his smirk told a different story.

After Jo revealed the prizes for the teams that finished the hunt first, she handed me and Sam a few small envelopes each to distribute.

Mr. Bailey tucked his phone away as I handed him an envelope. "You know, I used to write riddles on sticky notes and put them in James's lunch box," he said, his eyes bright.

"Really?" I asked, glancing from him to James.

Notes in lunch boxes, a bowling league, singing duets—there was way more to Mr. Bailey than suits and Zoom calls.

We just needed him to see that again.

To remember what mattered most.

James smiled. "He had some good ones. Which is why this will be light work, right, Dad?"

Mr. Bailey gave a quick nod. "Right."

Maybe there was a shred of hope for this guy and our town after all . . .

Jo hopped up on the bench again just as the clock tower finished its quarter-after chime. She held up the megaphone. "You may open your first riddle in three . . . two . . . one! Go!"

The sounds of ripping paper cut through the cold air and were followed by mumbling. Several people immediately ran off in different directions, but James read their riddle aloud a second time. 'I may fret, but I never worry, because I have a neck and no head' . . ."

Mr. Bailey gasped and pointed to the paper. "Look! The *F* in 'fret' and the *N* in 'neck' are capitalized. They must be clues! What's special about a fret and a neck, though?"

James stared off into the night for a moment longer before realization bloomed on his face. "It's a guitar! Oh! Chordcrafters!"

"Nice job!" Mr. Bailey patted his son's back before they bolted across the street together.

It was then that I noticed Mr. Bailey was wearing tennis shoes for the first time since he'd arrived here.

Ha! Someone's not playing around tonight.

Jo, Sam, and I laughed as James teased his dad for running too slow, but then almost took out the decorative snowman in front of Eve's Drop.

Jo turned to Sam and me, and asked, "Can you two take a couple laps around town while this is going on? I need to hang here in case people come by with questions, but if you see anyone who looks lost or someone trying to cheat, text me, okay?"

"On it," Sam said.

On it?

How could he be so casual about it all?

Anytime we were left alone or, God forbid, stood too close together, you could literally cut the tension between us with a broken ornament.

Did he not feel that?

Did he not want to pull on his hair and scream into a pillow because he expected falling for his best friend to be easy and not so freakin' complicated?

Or is it just me?

Sam had always been familiar and predictable.

But lately he had been anything but.

Was it really too much for a little honesty? Put me out of my misery already? At least then, I could have a good cry, eat a pint of Ben & Jerry's ice cream, and move on before literally moving out of Mullings Creek.

And maybe then I could actually hang out with James and not feel so stupidly guilty about it.

I made a face at Jo as Sam turned to leave, but she ignored it and pushed me to go join him.

Sam popped into Eve's Drop and bought us both a hot cocoa as people hurried past me on the sidewalk, mumbling clues and arguing over what they could mean.

"My front and back may matter, but I am nothing without my spine?" Marco read to Nico in the middle of the street. "What the heck does that mean?"

I put my gloved hand over my mouth to cover my chuckle.

"Well, the *F* in 'front,' the *B* in 'back,' the *M* in 'matter,' and the *S* in 'spine' are all capitalized . . ." Nico took the riddle and angled it into the nearest streetlight. "I know this . . . I know this."

"It's a book!" Marco yelled.

Nico smacked him. "I would've figured it out if you gave me like two more seconds."

Marco pushed him and hurried toward the Between the Pages Bookstore. "We don't have two seconds! Come on!"

Sam came outside with the steaming hot cocoa and handed me a cup.

"Thanks," I said, cupping my hands around it to warm them before I took a cautious sip.

We walked slowly down the street, stopping occasionally to let people pass on the way to their next clue, as the sounds of door chimes rang all over Mistletoe Lane.

"This was a great idea." I took another sip, savoring how the cocoa warmed me up all the way to my toes.

"It was," he said, stopping to fix a bow on one of the light pole wreaths. "Did you get some packing done today?"

"Kind of." I kicked a small stone toward him with my boot. "Mostly, I just made some lists."

"Lists are good." He kicked the stone back to me, and the two of us kept at it as we walked toward the end of Mistletoe Lane. It had been years since we'd done this. We used to count how many touches we could get before someone either messed up or ran out of sidewalk.

As we stopped outside of the bookstore, Sam turned to me, and said, "Twelve."

I smiled. "Not our best, but not our worst."

He picked up the stone before we crossed the street and then dropped it back on the sidewalk, where we started our "game" again. A group of middle-school-aged girls passed us on the way to Hal's Hardware.

"'Our silver and gold aren't worth much, but we can help

you nail down your measurements,'" one of them said. "It *has* to be Hal's!"

I hated not being in on the riddle-making, but Jo really did do a great job.

I was just about to text James to see how it was going with his dad when I glimpsed them across the street, coming out of Eve's Drop. Mr. Bailey had four candy canes in his hand, wearing a proud smile on his face.

I pointed toward them. "They're already down to the last riddle!"

"Guess he was right to call it 'light work.'" Sam chuckled. "By the way . . ." He reached into his coat pocket and pulled out a candy cane. "Snagged one for you."

"Thanks!" I tossed my empty cup into the closest trash can and opened the long end of the candy cane, letting it hang out of my mouth. "Remember when we used to pretend these were pipes so we could be like Papa and your grandpa?"

Sam unwrapped his and began to fake smoke it like we used to, making popping sounds with the front of his lips. I copied him and pretended to blow smoke, making him laugh.

"Do you think they're together?" Sam asked as he kicked the stone back to me. "Wherever they are?"

I looked up at the cloudless, starry sky and smiled. "I think so. I think that's why they went together, you know?" I kicked the stone back to him.

"Yeah." He twirled the candy cane back and forth before

speaking again a bit softer. "I miss him . . . especially this time of year."

"Me too." *And Dad.*

Grief was hard that way.

You thought you had moved on, or at least had gotten to the acceptance part.

Like moving the chairs and spots around the table so that no seat was empty, but then you'd spend the entire meal feeling guilty for not leaving a place for the ones who weren't there.

The holidays had a way of bringing it all back to you—the good with the bad.

We stayed quiet for the next block until Sam stopped outside of Phineas's diner and sat down on the bench. A flier for the Mistletoe Masquerade flapped in the breeze on one of the nearby windows. He pointed to it. "So, are you and James going together?"

I sat down next to him, jumping as the cold surface bit through my jeans. "We haven't really talked about it yet."

"But you will probably go with him, right?" Sam kept his attention forward.

"I mean, maybe?" I scuffed my foot back and forth on the sidewalk. "I guess it kinda depends on what happens between now and then . . . if his dad makes a decision early about The Market. I know Jo wants to go." I paused and looked at him. "Do you still want to?"

He shrugged. "I'll go if you're there."

Warmth bloomed across my chest and then crept up to my face.

Oh.

My phone chimed with a text message.

Jo: The Baileys won!

Jo: Round everyone up to meet back at town square in five!

Sam stood and tugged his beanie down further on his head. "How 'bout I go down Elm and Cherry and you stick with Mistletoe Lane?"

"Sure." I got to my feet as he started off. "Um, see you back at the big tree, then."

My stomach in knots, I walked back toward the town square, completely forgetting to tell the families I passed that the scavenger hunt was over, because all I could think about was what Sam had said to me on the bench.

I'll go if you're there.

Just when I thought we were semi back to normal, he had to go and say something like that.

A few minutes later, Jo held up her megaphone and stood next to Mr. Bailey, James, and Victoria, the owner of Glass Works.

"Congratulations to Travis and James Bailey on having the fastest time in our Candy Cane Scavenger Hunt!" she announced.

The crowd cheered and several whistled.

Victoria stepped forward. "Here is your custom ornament from Glass Works. We hope you'll treasure it always."

Mr. Bailey opened the gift bag and pulled out a beautiful clear bauble filled with Christmas-colored confetti and decorated with a frosted image of the Mullings Creek clock tower. "It's stunning," he said, holding it up to the light. "Thank you."

The crowd clapped again until Jo spoke. "Phineas has invited everyone to the diner for half-priced burgers to celebrate! Hope to see you there!"

She lowered the megaphone as Sam and I walked up.

"Congratulations, Mr. Bailey!" I said as I reached out to shake his hand.

"Thank you, Gianna." He beamed and shook mine before checking the time on his watch. "I need to call it an early night. I have a meeting first thing in the morning with some potential buyers for the property, but you guys go along to the diner and enjoy yourselves."

Potential buyers?

The knots in my stomach soured.

He gave James a quick pat on the back and then hurried away toward the B&B.

Jo threw her arms up before dropping them to her side, her shoulders slumping. "Seriously? After all that work . . . nothing?"

Apparently to Mr. Bailey, there was a change.

Just not the one we wanted.

We all looked to James for some kind of explanation, but he just frowned and shoved his hands into his pockets. "I'm sorry, guys. But I'm not ready to give up. Not yet." He smiled, but it seemed far less confident than the ones I had come to know.

Not yet?

What, did he already have some elaborate plan he hadn't yet shared?

Maybe I could get Marco and Nico to steal the salt cod Nona had bought for the seven-fishes dinner and hide them in The Market tonight?

But before I could tell him, James had already jogged away to join his dad.

And with him, what little flicker of optimism I had left got snuffed out.

Chapter Twenty-Four

"I'd hate to see you miss out on something. I'd hate to see you not find what you really want."

—THE FAMILY STONE

I woke up the next morning feeling bloated, from drowning my anxieties in too much Ben & Jerry's Cherry Garcia, and cold because at some point in the night, Jo had decided to take all the blankets for herself.

The sleepover had been her idea. I think she knew I'd probably spiral if I was left alone after hearing about Mr. Bailey's meeting with some fancy-shmancy buyers today. I rolled over and smiled at my best friend sleeping soundly next to me, mouth open as she quietly snored, blond hair spilling around her pillow like sunshine.

The house was uncharacteristically quiet, but then again, there was barely any light outside. I grabbed my phone off its charger on my nightstand.

Ugh. Six forty-five a.m.

It was so hard to sleep in on a Saturday when your brain was auto-programmed on "school time" nine months out of the year.

I quietly rolled out of bed and slid my bare feet into my plush reindeer slippers before shuffling over to my desk. The brochure for the Adventure Italy Academy sat open from where Jo had left it last night. She'd flipped through the glossy pages, reading about the special events, activities, and guided tours, while adding even more to my packing list. I still didn't know how I was going to get everything done while fake dating James and trying to convince his father not to sell The Market to some random person who didn't even know Mullings Creek.

Oh, and how could I forget the ever-so-inconvenient timing that I may, in fact, have had deeper feelings for Sam than I let myself believe?

But sure, let's just flee the country, Gianna.

"You ready for a fun day of shopping?" Jo said from behind me, her voice scratchy. She yawned and sat up, stretching her arms above her head.

I sighed and fell into my desk chair. "Shouldn't we be, I dunno, planning another intervention with Mr. Bailey?"

Jo opened her mouth but was interrupted by the chimes of multiple texts.

She tossed me my phone and then grabbed a pillow to put on her lap.

James: Good morning!

James: Dad's meeting this morning got moved to this afternoon in DC, so we're heading to the train station now. He said we'll be back in a couple of days.

James: He wants to take me to a hockey game and do some shopping.

I read the messages aloud to Jo who lifted her hands in an "I told you so" fashion.

I made a face and then typed a quick couple of messages back to James.

Me: Have fun!

Me: And if you think of another plan for winning him over about The Market, feel free to go rogue!

James: 

I tossed my phone onto my bed and propped my feet up on the Christmas quilt. "Before we go anywhere, I need a shower and coffee."

"Yeah, you do." Jo leaned forward and sniffed the air, laughing as I grabbed a pillow on the floor and chucked it at her.

Northern Virginia may have had some great shopping, but it was the people-watching I loved about it the most. The sounds and stories they all carried on their faces and even in the bags they held as they moved from store to store made me wish I had brought my notepad.

Moving through all of them, though? Not as enjoyable.

I clutched my bags against my chest as we shuffled through the mall for the exit, both of us gulping air when we finally made it to the parking lot.

"It's always worse during the holidays," Jo said, straightening her sweater that got rumpled from brushing by the hordes of shoppers. "There's a reason why so many people prefer online shopping."

"True." I rolled my tight shoulders.

We waited for the line of slow-moving cars to stop before speed-walking through the parking lot toward her car.

Jo tossed our bags into the back seat and then clicked the lock just as my hands moved to open the passenger-side door. "We've got one more stop," she said, twirling her keys in her hand.

"But we literally checked off everything on my Italy lists." I held up the paper with the scratch marks in every column.

"This isn't for Italy." She pointed behind me.

I rubbed the back of my neck as I looked at the boutique store's entrance and someone walking out with a large garment bag. "Jo—"

"Look, whether or not you go with James or Sam or alone, who knows where we'll be next year." She walked around the trunk of her car and faced me. "I'd like to think we'll always come home for

Christmas, but *if*, and I do mean if, The Market is gone by then, the Mistletoe Masquerade will be . . . different."

I sighed.

She was right.

Mullings Creek would always have some form of a dance on Christmas Eve, but I'd be a fool to think it would never change in the years to come—Market or no Market.

She put her arms on my shoulders. "I know we normally blow the dance off for movies and some quiet before the chaos of Christmas, but I'm with Sam. I think this should be the year we finally go."

Screw it. "I'm in."

"Really?" Her eyes widened.

"It's like you said: We don't know what next year will look like." I took a deep breath and then looped my arm through hers as we walked toward the fancy boutique. "*If* The Market is going away—*God, I hate saying that out loud*—then this may be the most important Mistletoe Masquerade that Mullings Creek has ever had. How can we miss it?"

She pulled me into a sideways hug before opening the door to the shop, bringing out deep woodsy and fresh floral scents. After nodding to a salesclerk, Jo and I began meandering through rows upon rows of dresses.

"So, have you thought about which color you're going for?" she asked as she looked back and forth between two long, midnight-blue gowns on the rack behind me.

I held up a stunning emerald-green one that was off-the-shoulder and had a long slit up the side. "Well, I know James loves green."

"True, but when you think about what you want that night to be like on Christmas Eve, what do *you* picture?"

I put the emerald-green dress back on the rack and turned around. "I don't know, Jo—"

"Yes, you do. But you're still too scared to let yourself think it." She briefly touched my shoulder and then went back to browsing through the blues.

Too scared?

Of what?

I ran my hands over the fancy gowns, but the sea of green in front of me now looked drab and uninspiring despite their beads and jewels. The front door opened, and when I looked up toward the entrance, my gaze caught on a circular rack filled with different shades of red garments. A woman called out in the store, and then a little girl crawled out from under the rack with a sneaky smile, winking at me before she hurried away.

And that was when I saw it.

The chiffon dress was floor-length with a black embroidered, beaded lace top that blended ombre-style into a vibrant red toward the bottom. It looked like something out of an old movie, like something Betty would've worn in *White Christmas.* I gasped when I picked it up to get a closer look at the way the bodice laced up in the back.

It was the most beautiful dress I had ever seen.

I moved over to the nearest mirror and held it up in front of me before taking a quick selfie and sending it to my mom.

This was what I pictured when I thought of the Mistletoe Masquerade at The Market. Mom would make me a black-and-red mask to go with it. Bianca would, undoubtedly, want to curl and pin my hair up, and Nona would move around me like a paparazzo, snapping a million pictures until we'd hear a knock on the front door. Leo, of course, would then make it his big responsibility to open the door, and then I'd stare at . . . at . . .

Sam.

Yes, Sam.

In a fancy suit and tie with his floppy but combed red hair and chocolate brown eyes smiling down at me like I was the most beautiful thing he had ever seen.

He would put his suit jacket around my shoulders as we walked out to his truck.

Later, while we danced under the glow of the white twinkle lights dangling from the exposed beams in The Market, I'd stare at the lines of freckles on his face and imagine all the ways I'd like to trace them with my fingers, my lips, until I'd have to lay my head on his chest to hide my blushing cheeks.

He'd rest his chin on the top of my head.

And I'd breathe in his comforting scents of pine and Ivory soap and wonder why we waited so long to do this.

"Oh my gosh," Jo said, appearing behind me as I blinked out of my trance still in front of the mirror. "That dress was one hundred percent made for you, Gianna."

"Too bad it's out of my budget," I said, sighing

My phone buzzed in my pocket. I took it out and smiled.

Mom: Nona said red is definitely your color.

Mom: And that James will love it.

James.

Right.

The person I was actually "dating."

The same person who had made his feelings known, who hadn't held back or hesitated to show me how he felt.

If Sam liked me as more than his best friend, surely he would've told me by now.

You can't go to the dance with a daydream, Gianna.

Guilt slithered through my stomach again until another notification popped up on my phone, but this one was about a deposit that was just made into my Apple Pay.

Wait. What?

Another text message buzzed in, and I swiped it open, smiling as tears filled my eyes.

Nona: Merry Christmas, cara.

Later that evening, back home in Mullings Creek where my dream dress hung in a garment bag in my closet, Jo and I bought roasted chestnuts before climbing the spiral steps up to the clock tower.

"Thank goodness you're not allergic to these," Jo said as she closed the door and zipped up her jacket so it covered her neck.

"Apparently, I could be someday," I said as we walked to our usual spot and sat with our backs against the railing facing Mistletoe Lane. "It's why I have to get blood work done every few years."

Jo cringed. "I hate needles."

"Eh, they don't bother me much anymore." When you got allergy tested annually and had a series of monthly shots, needles became an afterthought.

I took a chestnut out of our shared paper cup and popped it into my mouth. The warm potato-like texture had just the right amount of sweet mixed with nutty, but my favorite part was always the lingering taste of caramel.

"I can't wait to do this someday. Make food that makes people feel good," Jo said before she ate a chestnut and sighed happily. "Something that makes them think about it long after they've finished, so it becomes this like . . . I dunno . . . this memory attached to the taste." She looked up toward the crescent moon.

"You already make food like that," I said. "Everything you

bake is delicious, but what's more is that you can taste the love you put in it." I laid my hand over hers. "Nona always said great food changes hearts more than stomachs. You're already there, and you'll only get better."

"Thanks." She laid her hand on top of mine and nudged me. "Love you."

"Love you back."

I leaned forward as the bells chimed around us. The town square tree sparkled as a group of kids wearing illuminated necklaces wove in and out of the candy cane fence surrounding it. Their parents stood nearby, sharing cups of roasted chestnuts and leaning their heads against one another. Sandy—surprisingly still wearing the red hat Aunt Sofia made for her—padded her way along the sidewalk, stopping outside of the diner where Phineas promptly opened the door and tossed her a treat. Gram and Nona laughed as they walked arm in arm before they ducked into Eve's Drop for their traditional Saturday-night tea-and-gossip session with their "book club." And down the block, Ann locked up her bookstore and adjusted the hat on her snowman, the sleigh bell on the end of her Santa hat jingling as she walked to her car.

I didn't know what the next year would bring or what Christmas would look like if we didn't have The Market anymore, but what I did know was this:

Mullings Creek would keep going.

Because of the people who lived here.

Chapter Twenty-Five

"There's a certain magic that comes with the very first snow."

—FROSTY THE SNOWMAN

Jo, Sam, and I had our Government final Monday afternoon, the last day of the semester. After reviewing and quizzing each other all morning at Eve's Drop, we all felt confident, although the short-answer questions were always a little hard to prepare for. Mr. Bennington stood at the door and gave us each a candy cane on our way out as he wished us a Merry Christmas. I immediately started unwrapping mine before popping the straight end into my mouth when my phone buzzed with an alert.

I stopped in the middle of the hallway and checked it.

James: Just imagine . . . you'll be in front of a building like this next year in NYC!

He attached a selfie of a huge stone building with towers in the center and then sent another couple messages. His father stood off to the side on his phone.

Naturally.

Could the guy seriously not put it away for a few hours with his own son?

James: That's Healy Hall

James: Part of Georgetown University

I called Jo over and took a selfie with both of us and our candy canes hanging out of our mouths and sent it to him.

Me: This is the "History Hallway"—part of Mullings Creek High

Me: Not nearly as pretty though

The conversation bubble popped up immediately before his next message followed.

James: I disagree 😉

Jo made an *oooh* sound behind me before catching up with Sam and Isaiah at the end of the hallway. But while my cheeks definitely warmed at James's comment, I couldn't ignore the cold guilt that had thickened in the back of my throat.

James would come back here in a day or two, and then what? Were we official now?

It definitely felt like it.

So, should I just ask him to the dance?

Or was all of this—the fake-dating-turned-real-dating—a

waste of time, since the Baileys would be leaving soon? Yes, I could see James in the city, but he would still be a senior in high school. Was it really a good idea to start a relationship with someone who was at a different season of their life than me?

And what about Operation Ho Ho Humbug? Were we just dropping it completely? It's not like I should be angry with him if he thought we should, because lately the whole plan felt like we were rolling a snowball up a hill of hot asphalt.

The bell rang for the end of the afternoon exams, jarring me out of my downward spiral, but while everyone around me was cheering and cleaning out their lockers before hurrying out of the doors for the official start of our two-week winter break, I felt glued to the old carpet as Christmas music now blared over the PA system.

Ugh.

Dilemmas like mine were anything but "holly jolly."

Later that night, my entire family plus Sam's gathered at Nona's for my going-away party. Sadly, Jo and her dads couldn't make it. They already had tickets for dinner and a showing of *The Nutcracker* in DC.

The sweet and savory smell of Nona's famous braciole filled her home, making my mouth water the moment Leo, Mom, and I had walked in the door. Sam stood in the kitchen under some red, white, and green balloons with Marco and Nico, all of whom picked at the leftover pine nuts and chunks of pecorino romano that didn't make it into the filling. Leo had immediately run up to Nona for the end piece of the Italian bread she was slicing before she'd warm it in foil in the oven. He knew if he didn't grab it now, one of his cousins would claim it.

"The guest of honor has finally arrived!" Nona shouted, and everyone clapped and cheered.

Mrs. Holt and Gram then went back to chopping fresh herbs from the Holt greenhouse that would garnish the braciole before serving. Nona's small radio, which sat perched on the windowsill above the sink, played music that faded in and out with kitchen conversations and the occasional laughter that drifted in from my aunts and uncles in the living room. I grabbed some olives hidden in the fridge before sinking into one of Nona's old wooden chairs at the end of her table, pretending I couldn't feel Sam staring at me from across the room.

Normally, my feet would just steer me straight over to him, and we'd spend the next several minutes or hours talking about anything and everything.

But tonight, I was too tired to pretend things were normal.

The volume in the kitchen suddenly rose, thanks to Marco and Nico arguing about recent baseball trades and how the Yankees "will never be a dynasty again if they keep sitting on their butts," as I started scrolling through the various Adventure Italy folders in my Google Drive. I wasn't a history buff like my dad, but I still couldn't wait to check out some of the museums, hopefully finding time to see Michelangelo's *David* in person. Nona and Jo had already looked over a couple of the cooking classes with me, both of them envious about the "old grains" and fresh olive oil I'd get to use. I still had a hard time believing that one of my schools would be just a few minutes' walk away from the Colosseum, a place Dad and I had pinned pictures of on my wall when I was a little girl.

The oven timer dinged, and Nona nudged my cousins out of the way as she pulled out the two baking sheets. The braciole bubbled under spoonfuls of homemade sauce. Gram handed her some kitchen shears to cut away the twine, and once she did, everyone in the kitchen applauded. Then Marco and Nico yelled for everyone to grab a plate and get in line.

Again, Nona fussed at them to step back, but this time, it was to let me go first as her "guest of honor." Mrs. Holt and Gram sprinkled the fresh herbs and grated cheese over the top of the dish and Mom pulled out the warmed Italian bread. Then Nona cleared her throat and clanked a butter knife against her glass of Chianti.

"I'd like us all to raise our glasses in a toast," she said as my aunts and uncles and Bianca entered the kitchen. "To Gianna, my smart, beautiful granddaughter, who is going on a great adventure in a couple of weeks to a land that brought my family much joy." Nona paused and looked at me, misty-eyed. "I know her Papa and father would be so proud of her."

My throat turned sore as I blinked back tears and stood, walking closer to the island.

"To Gianna," Mom said next to me, raising her water glass.

"Gianna! Cin cin!" Everyone cheered as I lifted my glass and clinked it against each of theirs. Sam's was the last glass mine touched, and he didn't break eye contact as he brought his to his lips to drink afterward either.

It was the first time I was thankful for Marco stepping in between us to get to his seat.

An hour later, filled to the brim with great food and great conversation, the "kids" went into the living room where Nona had laid out sleeping bags, pillows, and throw blankets between the Christmas tree and fireplace. While we got settled on the floor, Bianca had us all squish together for a selfie as Nona—who still didn't believe in the convenience of streaming—opened her DVD player and put in a disc, winking at me before the menu appeared on the screen.

"*Serendipity*?" Nico asked. "But we always used to watch *Miracle on 34th Street*."

"Nothing wrong with a little change," she said before tossing him the remote. "Right, Gianna?"

I made a face and shook my head. *Sure, Nona*.

"This sleeping bag taken?" Sam asked, standing next to where I sat with a candy cane dangling out of his mouth.

My breath caught as a fluttery feeling started in my stomach before I could tell it to stop. "All yours," I said as casually as possible as I grabbed the nearest pillow and crushed it against me.

Breathe, Gianna.

Sam has sat by you for movies like a million times.

And you're dating James now.

Sort of.

It doesn't matter that the last time you and Sam watched a movie you almost–

"Wedding cookies?" Nico shoved a tin in front of my nose.

"Thanks," I said, grabbing one drizzled with a red glaze before passing the tin off to Sam.

And although our fingers barely grazed each other, energy zipped through mine.

Rookie mistake.

Maybe I should start wearing gloves around him or get comfortable using my elbows?

He smiled, the white lights of the Christmas tree outlining the strands of his hair, and, dang it, a smile like that made you forget your name.

I took a bite of the cookie and groaned. God, I loved the sweet, almost licorice taste of anise.

"So, where's your *boyfriend* tonight, Gianna?" Nico asked.

I coughed up a piece that hadn't quite made it all the way down yet, and Leo reached over and patted my back a few times. "He's in DC with his dad for a couple days," he replied.

Boyfriend. Right.

I guess I had a boyfriend now?

"No doubt making big business deals about our little town, I'm sure," Nico muttered.

"We've still got time, Nico," Sam said, his eyes serious. "I think James may be coming around, and if he is, then who's to say his dad won't, too? Right, Gianna?"

I forced my best fake smile. "Right." *James may be coming around, but not in the way you think.*

Nico hit play, and all of us settled into or on top of our blankets and sleeping bags. I tried to focus on the adorable and quirky John Cusack, but it was impossible to ignore the person on my right.

The nearness of Sam, and how cozy he looked with his hands behind his head, blanket up to his chin.

How easily I'd fit against him, my head on his chest.

My fingers brushing over the collar of his shirt . . .

And how I really shouldn't be thinking about him when I was already with someone.

Around the time of the first ice-skating scene, my eyelids began to get heavy. The last thing I remembered before I drifted off was wondering whether Sam knew his freckles looked like the stars too.

"Gianna," a faraway voice called as something warm touched my shoulder. "*Psst*, Gianna."

I slowly opened my eyes, blinking as the lights from the tree blurred into view. The movie credits rolled on the television, soft voices came from the kitchen where the adults must've still been sitting with their coffee and dessert, and everyone around me was sound asleep except for Sam, who had a giddy look on his face.

"What's going on?" I asked him, quickly wiping the corner of my mouth and praying he didn't see me drooling—not that it wouldn't be the first time, to be honest.

His smile widened as he pointed behind me toward Nona's big bay window.

I turned around and gasped.

Big, fluffy white snowflakes drifted down to the ground, swirling and twirling with the light wind, already settling on the outdoor lights.

"Think they'll fuss at us again if we sneak out there?" Sam whispered.

"Who the heck cares?" I jumped to my feet at the same time he did before the two of us stepped carefully around the sleeping bodies surrounding us.

We slid into our boots, coats, gloves, and hats, shushing each other more than once before I opened the front door for us and took a sharp inhale as the blustery cold air hit me.

I took Sam's hand and tugged him off the front steps. "Come on!"

The freshly fallen snow muffled our footsteps, and it felt like I hopped on clouds as we hurried into the front yard. Nona's lamppost already had snow forming on top, and with its warm, muted glow and the way the powdery snow clung to all of the bare branches of the trees, it was like Sam and I were in our own Narnia.

THWACK!

A snowball shattered against my arm, and Sam pointed and laughed from several yards away as he formed another one in his hands.

I pointed at him. "Don't you dare—"

THWACK!

This time, one hit me in my thigh.

"Oh, you're a dead man, Holt," I said, crouching down quickly to scoop up some snow. But before I could finish packing it in my palms, he barreled into me, knocking me backward into the cold, pillowy ground.

For a minute, neither of us spoke. We stared upward silently as snow continued to fall until finally, the moment broke and our laughter filled the space between us.

I began moving my arms and legs out and in against the snow. "Snow angels!"

Sam copied my movements and then stood, brushing off the backs of his legs before offering me a hand. I took it and slipped, falling forward against his warm chest as he pulled me to my feet.

"Easy now, Mouse," he murmured against my beanie as he helped me step around our creations. "Let's not trample our angels."

"Can't have that," I said, suddenly hyperaware of the fact

that he had both of his hands around my waist and I still had both of mine pressed against his chest.

I looked into his eyes and absentmindedly brushed a snowflake off a curl on his forehead poking out of his hat.

He lifted one of his hands off my waist and held it out for me to take, and when I did, he began to lead me around the front yard in circles, humming "Have Yourself a Merry Little Christmas."

My best friend was dancing with me. In the snow. To my favorite Christmas song.

Someone pinch me, please, since my hands are accounted for.

"I thought you didn't dance," I said.

"Someone's gotta get you ready for that Mistletoe Masquerade." He smiled down at me.

"You're going to go too, though, right?" I asked, blinking a snowflake out of my eye.

He swallowed hard before he spun me out and pulled me back in.

"That . . . depends."

"On what?" My head swirled and twirled more than the snowflakes, making everything from my head to my boots feel fuzzy.

We moved slower now in and out of the warm light from Nona's lamppost before he spoke again, softly. "If I have the right partner with me."

Wait.

What was he saying?

Sam stopped dancing and slowly took my hands, pressing them against his chest, where I could feel his heart beating as eagerly as my own.

"I . . ." He paused and blinked down at me for a moment. "I haven't been honest with you. About how I felt about the fake dating or the dance—"

"So, you're *not* bothered that it's named after a parasitic plant?" I smirked.

He snorted. "No, still not a fan of that, but, well . . ." He stepped back and started pacing in the snow, rubbing his jaw.

I pinched my lips to keep from laughing.

Sam had always been the confident, steady one of our group—even more so than Jo. When stuff hit the fan, Sam was the voice of reason.

Calm. Collected.

So, excuse me if watching him unravel a bit while trying to tell me something made me a bit giddy.

Relieved, even.

Because maybe, maybe all of this wasn't just in my head.

He finally stopped moving, and blurted, "I don't want you to date James."

My breath caught in my throat, but somehow, I managed a small "Why?"

"Because . . ." He closed the space between us, taking my

hands again. "Because *I* want to date you. You're it for me, Gianna. You always have been."

His beautiful words made me feel lighter than air, and I wondered if I'd be up there dancing with the snowflakes if he didn't hold on to me, if he hadn't been my anchor.

Sam had always been that for me.

James was like that burst of excitement you felt when you decided to wander off the trail for a bit, not knowing where you were going or how far you should go before you turned back.

But Sam was my true north.

The steady point of a needle, the guiding light in a star-cluttered sky that I could always count on to bring me home.

The same realization that had bloomed in my heart when we'd nearly kissed in the den at my house, when he had leaned in close during bingo, and countless other times, spread throughout my chest, leaving me dizzy with anticipation.

I smiled and lifted a gloved hand to his cheek. "Sam," I whispered and lifted my chin ever so slightly, waiting.

An invitation.

My invitation.

Please, please accept it.

And he did.

Sam smiled a second before his lips finally, *finally* brushed against mine. Sparks sped through every nerve of my body, wrapping me in a delicious, numbing warmth while the snow continued to fall around us, quietly shushing our racing hearts.

This was what I always imagined a kiss should feel like—charged, intoxicating, giddy, but comfortable. Familiar.

Like we had been doing this all our lives.

His fingertips pressed tighter around my back, and my hands trailed up his chest before looping around his jacket collar, settling in his snow-dampened hair at the nape of his neck. I opened my mouth slightly and sighed as the kiss deepened.

Sam tasted of vanilla and anise and peppermint and . . .

Tears.

Tears?

I pulled back and blinked in confusion, my heart jumping into my throat when I saw the damp streaks on his face. "Sam?"

"I'm sorry. That was . . ." His voice broke as the beautiful blush under his freckles faded just as quickly as it had appeared. "That was a mistake."

A mistake?

"You're with him now." He swallowed hard. "I saw the way he looked at you at the Reindeer Games. The smile on your face when you asked him out in front of your entire family. You two . . . you make it look easy."

Okay, yes, things had changed between James and me.

And yes, maybe it was easy with us.

But what if I don't want "easy"?

What if the best things in life were also the hardest things?

Things you had to fight for over and over because you knew in your heart they were worth it?

Maybe that's why this—us—was so complicated.

I opened my mouth to tell him all this, but he looked skyward as a snowflake fell on his wet lashes.

So I shoved my hands in my pockets and fought the urge to brush it away.

To hold him.

"James is a good guy, Gianna," he said, his voice quiet.

My chin dropped to my chest as a deep sadness panged my heart. *I know.*

"You deserve that."

And without another word, Sam slowly walked away toward the quiet, empty street, the hard edges of his silhouette dissolving into the glittery blur of our magical snow globe while I stood in between our angels, wondering if I had dreamed up the best kiss of my life.

Or if I had just lost one of my best friends forever because of it.

Chapter Twenty-Six

"At Christmas, you tell the truth."

—LOVE ACTUALLY

The next morning, unsteady from a horrible sleep-deprived headache raging behind my eyeballs, I put on my best fake smile for the family over breakfast and prayed that Nona's coffee would kick in sooner rather than later.

I had stood in the swirling snow last night for over an hour, watching and waiting for Sam to come back, but he never did. Eventually, I trudged alone and numb back through the fresh powder over our angels before going back inside to quietly peel off my damp layers. The adults remained chatting in the kitchen and my cousins and Leo still lay fast asleep on the living room floor, like time hadn't moved at all.

It was a gift. For Sam and me. A few free minutes alone during the first magical snow of the season.

Only for it to go horribly wrong in the end.

And it was all my fault.

I should've never gone outside with him.

Encouraged him to kiss me.

It was so completely unfair to him.

And to James.

"Did Sam go home with Mr. and Mrs. Holt?" Bianca asked as she helped herself to a few more slices of bacon from the oven.

I sunk down in my seat and tried to hide behind the steam coming from my large snowman mug.

"No," Nona said while pushing another batch of scrambled eggs around the pan. "He sent them a message that he didn't feel well, and they left soon after."

I sighed.

"Maybe that's who made all those tracks in the snow out front, then." Bianca sat down opposite me, her gaze boring into my face, but I didn't dare look up. She had inherited the same Mancini superpower as Nona: calling someone's bluff just by looking at them.

"A lot of tracks for just one person, especially one who wasn't feeling well," Nona mumbled. "Strano."

Bianca continued to stare at me over her mug. "Strange indeed."

I pushed back my chair, accidentally banging it against the wall. "I gotta go."

"Now?" Mom asked, looking up from today's newspaper.

"Yeah, I, uh, told Eve I'd help get the café ready, since Jo and her dads ended up staying over in DC because of the snow." The second part of that was true, at least.

"Eve won't open on time today, cara," Nona said, stepping

away from the eggs. "Everyone will be shoveling and scraping out their storefronts."

"Exactly! She'll need an extra hand with that, too." I hurried into the front hallway and threw on my coat, hat, and gloves, but before I could slip into my boots, Nona stopped me.

"Are you feeling okay?" She cupped a hand to my cheek. "You look all flushed."

"I'm fine." I stepped back, focusing on the floor.

"Okay." Nona put her hands up and started walking toward the kitchen but then stopped. "Oh, and Gianna?" She looked over her shoulder, a knowing smile playing at the corner of her mouth. "Next time, stomp out your boots, per favore."

Good grief.

Nothing got by that woman.

I took the long way home, savoring the way snow muffled everything after it fell. Jacket zipped up to my chin and hands deep in my pockets, I stepped quietly down the unplowed street, squinting as the sun glistened off the now-sparkling branches. The air tasted damp but clean and fresh, as if some higher power granted all of us a new slate, a new perspective to take into the holidays.

My dad used to say that nature held its breath after a snowstorm so that we could take the time to appreciate it before everything went back to "business as usual."

Dad was good about those kinds of things.

Slowing down.

Savoring small, quiet moments instead of filling them.

Which probably explained how I ended up going to see him first before going home.

The Mullings Creek cemetery was small but beautiful, outlined with tall oaks and birches, which were always filled with birdsong in the spring and summer, a fitting accompaniment to the soft trickling of the creek that ran behind the western end. I had to push the snow away with my boot before I could open the wrought iron gate and enter.

With a mind of their own, my feet carried me down the winding path to Dad's headstone. I wiped the snow off it before running my fingers along the familiar epigraph:

ANTHONY ENZO "POP" MANCINI

BELOVED HUSBAND, FATHER, SON, AND TEACHER

SEMPRE NEI NOSTRI CUORI

"Always in our hearts," I whispered before standing, my throat now tight. "I'm sorry I haven't visited in a while. I'll be better about that." I sniffed. "I got into that Adventure Italy program I told you about before Thanksgiving. Jo and Mom have already helped me pack. I get a certain number of free weekends. You should see the way I've mapped them out." I smiled. "You taught me well, but . . ." I sighed and rubbed my gloved hand against my cheek. "I've gotten myself into a real pickle, Dad."

The wind blew, and snow from the nearest birch twirled in the air before settling onto the ground.

I took a deep breath and told him everything that had happened over the last few weeks. Mr. Paxton's untimely passing. James and Mr. Bailey coming to town. My agreeing to the fake-dating thing with James, how I started having feelings for James, and how crappy the timing of it was because Sam and I could have been finally moving past being just friends.

"I kissed both boys, Dad. *Me.* Crazy, right? And now, James has feelings for me. Maybe Sam does too, even though he won't . . ." I stopped my pacing. "This was not part of the plan. Do I just throw in the towel for Operation Ho Ho Humbug? Did I totally screw up The Market's odds at surviving by getting too close to James?" I sighed and crouched down. "And is it even fair for me to pick someone when it means someone else will be hurt?"

Or what if I do pick someone, but they don't want me?

A cardinal flew by and settled on top of a headstone nearby, its red feathers a stark contrast to the sea of white around us. I loved that certain birds stuck around after the seasons changed. It always reminded me that even though the winter nights were dark and long, spring, a new start, would still eventually come.

I ran my fingers over the grooves of my claddagh ring under my glove and blinked back tears as the answers I needed settled into my heart.

I couldn't throw in the towel for Operation Ho Ho Humbug. Not yet.

My town, my family, were counting on me to give it my all to save The Market, and that's what I would do.

But I had to be honest with both boys.

They deserved that.

I had assumed the arrival of the Baileys was an obstacle, an unexpected knot or a blown bulb, in our predictable holiday strand of traditions.

Maybe the Baileys were always meant to find Mullings Creek.

Maybe some people came into our lives just for a season.

The cardinal chirped before it flew away to a grove of snow-covered trees, its red still visible from a distance.

And maybe others were always meant to stay in our lives during their changes.

After going home to shower and change into warmer clothes, I ventured back out to help as many people as possible shovel out their storefronts. By then, the sounds of laughing, squealing kids filled the air as they took their first sledding trips of the season on the big hill in the park.

Just as I'd finished clearing off the snow from the benches outside Ann's bookstore, a panicked Mayor Moore hurried through the street, slipping and sliding as he went.

"That's never a good sign," Ann mumbled before disappearing into her store where Scout sat at attention, tail twitching.

"Mayor Moore?" I stepped into the street. "You okay?"

He stopped and put a hand on his chest that rapidly rose and fell. "No, Ms. Mancini, I am definitely not okay." He took out a handkerchief from his coat pocket and dabbed his forehead. "Levi has the flu."

"Oh no." I propped an elbow on the handle of the shovel.

He paled and wrung the handkerchief in his hands. "How will we find another photographer for our Breakfast with Santa event that begins in . . ." He stretched his arm through his coat to look at his watch. "One hour?"

"Don't worry. We can fix this." I gently took his arm and had him lead me out into the middle of the street. "What if we sent out a quick text alert and changed it to Selfies with Santa?"

His nose scrunched up in disapproval.

Never mind.

I looked around Mistletoe Lane, hoping something would hold the answers, and that was when I heard Christmas melodies drifting down from Mom's studio. Mom wasn't a photographer, but I'd had a conversation with someone in that studio whose father used to be.

I pulled out my phone and sent a quick text to James.

> Me: Good snowy morning! ❄
>
> Me: Can you and your dad meet me at The Market in like thirty minutes?

The conversation bubble immediately appeared a second before his reply came through.

James: Definitely!

James: Is this a new plan for Operation Ho Ho Humbug?

Me: 😌

Thirty minutes later and with Levi's camera in hand, I stood waiting by Hal, who was fully dressed in a new Santa suit, and I had to admit, he looked perfect.

Maybe even better than Mr. Paxton?

Apparently, he had a special beard made that attached directly to his skin, which his niece had fixed up with makeup to look old and rosy.

James hurried through the main entrance of The Market with his father in tow, wearing the traditional suit jacket/no tie combo he was known for. James's face lit up as he found me, but I immediately flashed back to last night's kiss with Sam. Guilt dropped into my stomach like icy stones.

One thing at a time, Gianna.

"Good morning, Mr. Bailey!" I waved. "Thanks so much for coming."

"He can't wear that," Hal said, suddenly appearing at my side.

"Can't wear what?" Mr. Bailey asked, his stare flitting between the two of us. "What's going on?"

James cleared his throat. "Dad, remember when I told you I took a tour of Gianna's mom's studio?"

"Yes . . ." His voice was wary.

"I *may* have told her you did photography in college." He gave a big "please don't hate me" smile.

Realization dawned on Mr. Bailey's face. "James—"

"Their regular guy who normally takes photos for this event came down with the flu." James put his hand on his dad's arm.

"It's only a two-hour event," I said, cautiously stepping closer. "And as you can see, we already have a line. We could really use your help, sir."

Mr. Bailey's lips pressed together as he rubbed the back of his neck.

"Did I mention the proceeds go toward our high school's choir and band departments?" I smiled and motioned to the space around us. "They set all of this up and do some small performances during the event, too."

While I'd been out shoveling, the local music students had helped set up long tables inside, covering each with new dark green tablecloths dotted with white snowflakes. Local families donated griddles for the made-to-order pancakes, which were set up near the side of Mom's studio. Those students who weren't on pancake duty or performing in the small ensembles helped clear away trash or dressed up as elves to get the children excited. Breakfast with Santa was always one of my favorite events because of the tangible excitement of the children.

Mr. Bailey sighed and shrugged out of his suit jacket before handing it to James. "It's been a while since I've done anything like this, but I'll do my best."

Operation Ho Ho Humbug was back in business!

James clapped his dad on the back. "It'll be just like riding a bike, Dad!"

Mr. Bailey gave his son a look as he took the camera from me. "I broke my wrist the last time I rode a bike, son."

"Then this will be a breeze." James gave him a thumbs-up. "Right, Gianna?"

"Right." I gave him a thumbs-up too and tried not to think about the baby that spit up on Levi last year or the Chihuahua that peed on him the year before that.

A no-leaky-body-fluid breeze.

I hoped.

Hal, aka Santa, stepped forward and held out an elf hat and Levi's homemade red velvet vest, bedazzled in silver and gold poms, sleigh bells, and tiny sequin bows. "Hat or vest, sir?"

"Definitely the vest," James said, taking it before his dad could object.

James and I helped clean up tables during the event, smiling at each other whenever we heard the jingling of Mr. Bailey's vest as he moved for better angles. But despite his occasional scowl, it seemed like James was right. Mr. Bailey's shoulders had relaxed significantly over the last hour, and he looked at ease while he took photos for families, even adjusting the lighting near Santa on more than one occasion.

Did we actually, finally pull something off, here?

Mom came up to me as I finished wiping down a table and handed me a bottle of water. "Is that Travis?" she asked.

I took a sip and then smiled. "Shocking, right?"

Mom pursed her lips as she tilted her head to the side.

"He's been going at it for over an hour now," I said, nudging her. "Maybe you can bring him some coffee?"

"Maybe I will, after Leo sees Santa." She walked away but not before I caught her smoothing her hair and adjusting her sweater.

Leo called out my name and waved from where he stood next in line, his eyes sparkling with excitement. I waved back before dropping my damp dishcloth into a bin near the trash cans. The door to The Market opened, bringing in a flurry of snowflakes on a cold breeze and someone who made my breath catch in my throat.

Sam's eyes found mine in an instant from across the room.

They always did.

Last night's unexpected kiss in the snow, the way his hands felt around my back, the feel of his slightly chapped lips against mine came rushing back, and I had to blink, to look away, just to remember how to breathe.

By the time I willed myself to look his way again, he was gone, and Leo barreled into my side, wrapping his arms around my waist.

"He said he'd do his best to grant my wish!" he said against my sweater, his voice muffled.

"Of course he will, he's Santa!" I said as I rubbed his head.

"Good morning, Gianna," Sam said as he appeared at my other side.

"Good morning." I put a hand against my stomach to try to calm the nerves that did a full Broadway number at his arrival before I patted Leo's back. "Leo, why don't you go grab some pancakes, and I'll sit with you while you eat, okay?"

He zipped away toward one of the open griddle stands, and I took in a deep breath, hoping the right words would come out.

But what are the right words? "Sam—"

"Gianna," he began at the same time.

We laughed, and then he gestured to me. "You go ahead."

Okay. I can do this. "Um, about last night—"

The piercing sound of feedback shrieked through the air before a familiar voice called out over the megaphone. "Gianna Mancini!"

I turned around toward the stage where Santa sat, and my stomach dropped.

Oh, dear God.

James stood with a goofy grin on his face, donning Hal's elf hat, and holding the megaphone in front of his mouth. A second later, he pointed to the small group of brass players who counted off before they started into a rendition of "Jingle Bell

Rock." James began snapping and moving his hips from side to side, and I couldn't help but laugh at his foolishness, or, who was I kidding, his bravery. By now, most of the people inside had their phones out, including all of my cousins, because I mean, why not?

Public humiliation was always an entire-Mancini-family affair.

The band played on until they got to the bridge, and suddenly the megaphone screeched again before James asked me the one question I knew he would and prayed he wouldn't: "Will you go to the Mistletoe Masquerade with me?"

The music abruptly stopped.

The room stilled except for the two dozen or so phones that filmed the entire excruciating moment.

My chest tightened, my hands turned clammy, and the room began to press itself in around me, the exposed beams dropping lower and lower until . . .

The piercing shriek of the fire alarm pierced the air.

Hal, aka Santa, grabbed the megaphone out of James's hand and ordered everyone to stay calm and make their way toward the exits as quickly as possible. I joined the throng through the side door, away from the majority of the crowd.

But not before I caught Nona lowering her hand from the alarm switch.

Chapter Twenty-Seven

"It's never too late. You can always change if you want to."

—SCROOGED

By the time I made it outside, most of The Market folks were already on the street, shielding their eyes from the glare of the sun reflecting off snow. I did the same and found Leo with my mom and most of my family, but Sam had disappeared.

"Hey." A hand appeared on my shoulder. I turned around to find James, a bit flushed but still grinning, standing before me. "I'm sorry. I wasn't sure if you were into grand gestures, but . . . um, I thought I might as well get into the holiday spirit, you know?"

The answer I knew I needed to give, but hated myself for giving, slowly took form. I swallowed over the growing lump in my throat and took one of Leo's deep breaths, then I said, "I can't go with you to the Mistletoe Masquerade."

He slowly took off the elf hat. "Can't, like you've got something else going on? Or like you just can't go with *me* . . ."

Neither? My stomach rolled, souring. "I know I agreed to do this fake-dating thing with you, but . . . um, something has changed."

"I feel the same way." He stepped forward and took my hand in his. "I know it's not what we planned on," he continued. "But—"

Sirens sounded from down the street, and everyone standing in the road hurried onto the closest sidewalk.

I pulled him around the corner and away from the crowd near Cherry Street and swallowed hard. "James, I never expected to start having feelings for you—"

"Me too—"

"Just, hold on. Let me get this out." I took a step back. "It *was* real for me, but . . . it just . . . isn't enough."

I thought finally speaking the truth of my heart would make me feel better, like a weight lifting off my small shoulders, but watching his beautiful smile change to something far worse than sadness like felt the biggest sucker punch to my gut.

I pressed my hand against my stomach. "I'm so—"

"It's all good. Timing was against us, I guess." He pulled his hand away and tucked it into his pants pocket. "Operation Ho Ho Humbug would have to come to a close inevitably, right?"

"Right," I said softly.

So, wait, that was over, then, too?

Of course it's over. You just broke his heart, genius.

Sandy barked and trotted over. James crouched down and rubbed her head for a moment, saying something only she could hear, and then followed her back toward Mistletoe Lane.

The lump in my throat turned to an ache as they disappeared into the crowd.

What a hypocrite I was to think that James's dad would be the Scrooge in this story.

After the fire marshal cleared the building, Breakfast with Santa picked back up, but most people took the alarm as a sign to pack up and go home early. As if my guilt wasn't thick enough, I was now responsible for ruining the band and choir's winter fundraiser.

Humbug indeed.

Thankfully, my family took mercy on me and left me alone while we cleaned up the event and reset market vendor stands so businesses could open midafternoon. When Leo and I were folding our third of the long tablecloths, Mom appeared at the top of the stairs outside her studio door. "Gianna, can you pop in here before you leave, please?"

Womp womp.

"Yikes," Leo said as we finished our final fold. "That was the same face she gave you when you tried painting over the hole we put in the wall."

"You mean the hole *you* put in the wall, you little sneak." I ruffled his hair and then sighed. "Do me a favor, okay? If I'm not out of there in thirty minutes, tell Nona to pull the alarm." *Again.*

Mom stood behind her easel when I arrived in the studio, holding up a finger after I closed the door as she finished whatever she was working on. I walked around her and sat on the windowsill, running my fingers over the leaves of one of her pothos. A couple minutes later, she laid down her brush and wiped her hands on the apron covering her pants.

"All right, Gianna," she said as she walked toward me, stopping at one of the shelves to grab her emergency chocolate stash. "I may not have my mother-in-law's sense for this kind of thing, but I know my own daughter. You've been acting very flighty lately, and I saw the look on your face when James asked you to the dance." She held out the tin of chocolates, and I grabbed a peppermint bark. "That was not the face of someone who is happy in a relationship, or of someone who just picked out a stunning dress for that very event, so . . . out with it."

I took a bite of the bark and sighed as Mom pulled up a stool and took a seat. "I don't even know where to begin, Mom," I said.

"The beginning is always a good place," she said, setting the tin on the windowsill.

So, I started at the beginning and proceeded to unload everything the way I did at the cemetery, omitting the details about mine and Sam's mind-blowing kiss in the snow, because I was pretty sure if I confessed those details to my mother, my face would literally light her studio on fire. I didn't stop talking until I reached my conversation with James on Cherry Street.

And then Mom made a face I hadn't seen before.

It was a combination of stony meets sad, where her mouth

went slack before she slowly shook her head. I didn't think my Grinchy heart could feel any smaller than it did when I rejected James's invitation to the Masquerade, but boy was I wrong.

"How . . ." She stopped and turned her head to the side before she continued. "How could you be so . . . so careless, Gianna?"

"I don't know." My entire body sagged. "I feel awful—"

"As you well should." Mom pressed her hands on her knees. "This isn't one of your Christmas rom-coms, Gianna. These are *real* people, *real* hearts you're playing with so recklessly, and for what?"

"We really thought the fake dating could save The Market," I said, my voice quiet.

"Fake dating doesn't *save* anything." She stood and began to pace. "It only takes and hurts someone, or in your case, two someones."

Tears burned behind my eyes before they spilled onto my cheeks. "I'm sorry—"

"I'm not the one who needs your apology." She stopped pacing and gestured outside. "But you need to fix what you broke."

Do you think I don't already know that?

Or how frustrating it is to be able to fix things for literally everyone else except yourself?

But Mom kept going. "Emotions are not something to play around with. If you're not careful, you may just—"

"Just what?" I stood, accidentally knocking my head into the pothos. "Fall in love? Get hurt? News flash, Mom, I did. And yeah, I feel like crap because I hurt not one but two people in the process, but at least I took chances. At least I put myself out there. When was the last time you did something like that, huh?"

Mom sucked in a sharp breath and stepped back as if she'd been slapped. But before I could try to rephrase or clarify, the door flew open, and Leo hurried in wearing his noise-canceling headphones. "Gianna! Nona said she can't pull the alarm again or the fire marshal will give her a citation, but I swear I smell smoke!" He winked.

I grabbed another piece of chocolate and stormed past my mother before whispering a quick "thank you" to Leo and then hurrying down the stairs and out into the cold midday air.

❄❄❄❄❄

I stayed in my room for the rest of the afternoon. Mom had knocked on my door to ask me if I wanted dinner, but I ignored her. I knew what I had said was hurtful, but she had hurt me too, and I was too emotionally exhausted from the whiplash of the last forty-eight hours to go another round with her or anyone else. Jo and I had texted a few times, but she knew to leave me to my movies and ice cream when I felt like crap.

On my second watch of *The Spirit of Christmas*—*Kate really did have the right idea . . . falling for a ghost is a lot less messy than what I did*—my phone buzzed with an alert.

Auntie Sof: I know you're sulking right now but I need a favor

I groaned and fell back onto my bed, pulling a pillow over my face. The last thing I needed right now was to do an odd job for my aunt. Knowing her, she'd have me go up to that North Pole Suite at the B&B and iron the curtains or launder the sheets while wearing something ridiculous in the hopes of lightening the mood between me and James.

But I also knew that if I didn't do this, she'd probably send Bianca over here, and I definitely didn't want that either.

I sat up and grudgingly texted her back.

Me: What do you need me to do?

She replied instantly.

Auntie Sof: They're shorthanded at Town Hall. The cub scouts couldn't make it in to help put the paper drip protectors on the candles for the caroling.

Auntie Sof: Thank youuuuuu ♥♥♥

After sadly putting on a pair of pants and shoving a hoodie over my head, I slid into my boots and coat and started the long walk to Town Hall. The night air smelled crisp and earthy with a familiar stillness that only happened right before the weather changed. Maybe we would get more snow soon.

Snow.

My heart squeezed at the thought of the last snowfall.

Of who I'd shared it with.

How I had hurt him.

By the time I reached my destination, I wasn't sure I was in the right place. Most of the lights were off, and the building was unusually quiet. I opened the door to the first conference room, where we usually did projects like this, and took a step back.

Mr. Bailey sat at the table with his sleeves rolled up, sliding paper protectors onto small white candles before moving them into a box to the side. He looked up at me and smiled. "Oh, good! I was wondering if I'd have any help."

"Is no one else here?" I stepped cautiously into the room, praying James wasn't waiting around the corner. But the room was empty and quiet except for the instrumental Christmas music playing on Mr. Bailey's phone.

"Nope. Just me." He stopped working and clasped his hands in front of him. "Your aunt told me they needed help, made it sound like a national crisis, actually . . ."

"To her, everything is," I mumbled. Of course she sent him and then asked me.

Those Mancini women truly have no chill.

Mr. Bailey chuckled. "Well, I was beginning to get a bit bored at the B&B anyway, so I didn't mind coming out. I tried to get James to join me, but . . ." He paused and looked away. "He said he wasn't feeling well."

He's not the only one.

I shrugged out of my coat and draped it over the nearest chair. "Well, between the two of us, it won't take long."

He moved his hand over his phone. "I can turn this off if you don't like it."

"Oh, no. Music is great, thanks." I grabbed a pile of bare candles from a box and put them in front of me before doing the same with the paper protectors.

"I find that I need some kind of noise to get work done now." Mr. Bailey went back to sliding the paper shields onto the candles. "I guess the city will do that to you."

"I'm the opposite, actually," I said. "When I sit down to write, I don't want any noise. I think it's because I'm constantly surrounded by it . . . from my family, I mean." I moved the five candles I fixed with protectors into the same box Mr. Bailey used for his.

"James tells me you're going to college in the city next year." Mr. Bailey lowered the volume on the music. "Need a break from small-town life, eh?"

I smiled. "Something like that. But also, I feel like I need to see more of the world if I want to be a better writer, you know?"

"I do." He nodded. "I couldn't wait to break away from home when I was your age, but my situation was, well . . . a bit different than yours."

I didn't ask why, and I didn't offer anything else because

something told me he would keep going, and that this moment, learning about his past, would be an important one.

Mr. Bailey cleared his throat. "My parents fought all the time, and I was an only child, so I had nowhere to hide from it, no one to really talk to. Going home was torturous. So I stayed out late with my camera, taking pictures of other homes and places I wished I could run to."

Oh . . .

True, I'd wanted to hide more than once from my family, but I couldn't imagine what it must've felt like to never want to go home.

"I think James uses music to escape the same way," I finally said.

"Perhaps." He leaned back and clasped his hands over his belly. "This town . . . it gave us both an escape I didn't realize we needed." He paused, and then added, "And you made him smile more than I had seen in a long time."

Doubtful. I scoffed as my chest tightened with guilt. "He seems like someone who is always smiling."

Mr. Bailey moved his head from side to side. "He used to. The, um, divorce between his mother and me changed that."

Changed you too, apparently.

I pushed forward, laying my hands back on the table. "Mr. Bailey, can I ask you a question?"

"Sure."

"Do you like what you do? I mean, your job . . . do you enjoy it?"

He sighed and rubbed a hand down the side of his face, which I just noticed had more of a shadow than usual. "I thought if I became a lawyer that I would help more people, but now . . . I seem to have gotten lost."

I propped my fist under my chin. "My dad's favorite quote was 'Not all those who wander are lost.' "

"*Lord of the Rings*." Mr. Bailey smiled. "He sounds like a smart man."

"He was." I smiled back. "He also used to say that we should never waste the time that we are given. That we should never live to have regrets."

Mr. Bailey sat forward and rested his elbows on the table. "I feel like you're about to give me some advice, Ms. Mancini."

I picked up a candle and twirled it in my hand. "I'd give anything to have one more moment, even if it was only for a minute, heck, half a minute, with my father. Don't waste what little time you have left with James." I sniffed. "You left home because you were neglected and because it wasn't a home for you. Do you want James to do the same someday?"

Mr. Bailey blinked a few times. Then he looked toward the window where the streetlamps illuminated the flurries that now fell gracefully to the ground.

We both went back to work quietly, letting the soft sounds of piano and strings fill the air until he spoke again several minutes later. "I know you're probably a little scared to leave home so soon, but something tells me you'll be just fine, Gianna."

"You think so?" I looked up from my pile of paper protectors.

He nodded. "That family of yours may be a lot at times, but they've raised you well."

I stole a glance at the peaceful snowfall and laughed as Eve, Phineas, and Ann twirled in the street, their arms skyward. "Mullings Creek raised me well, Mr. Bailey," I said.

"A good town will do that."

Chapter Twenty-Eight

"Let's go get the shit kicked out of us by love."

—LOVE ACTUALLY

I woke up on Wednesday morning, December twenty-third, feeling more relaxed than I'd expected to. Working with Mr. Bailey last night didn't exactly make me more confident with the impending outcome of Operation Ho Ho Humbug, but it did leave me with a certain kind of peace. Maybe I couldn't save The Market—maybe I was never meant to—but maybe I *could* save a father and son's relationship.

I rolled over and reached for my phone, but instead, grabbed a small sticky note on its face.

Coffee on the porch? –Mom

Who knew how long she'd been sitting out there in the cold waiting for me, so I got dressed quickly and filled a mug with coffee and creamer before stepping onto the front porch.

Mom sat bundled up in the swing under a large blanket, her coffee still steaming in between her mittens as her snowman earrings dangled from under her knit hat. "Thank goodness. I could use some extra body heat." She flipped the blanket open so I could sit next to her.

After positioning the blanket over both of us, we each took a long sip from our mugs before nearly tripping over each other's words.

"I'm sorry—"

"Mom, I'm sorry."

She laughed and reached a hand up, cupping my cheek. "Me first, okay?"

I nodded.

"I shouldn't have yelled at you like that. You . . . you came to me for comfort and guidance, and I just . . ." She sighed. "I got carried away. Took my own frustrations out on you. And I'm so sorry, Gianna. You're always thinking of others before yourself. You're not careless with hearts, honey."

Psh. I sniffed.

"Hey." She turned my face toward hers. "You can't help what other people feel or don't feel. You can't control everything, no matter how hard you try. That's just not how it works."

I leaned into her hand, breathing in the lingering scent of eucalyptus. "I didn't mean what I said about you not taking chances. I was angry with myself. You take lots of chances, Mom."

"Oh, I don't know about that." She took her hand back and stared at her mug as a light breeze blew snow off our roof, sending glittery sparkles over the front yard. "I used to be much braver." She chuckled. "Heck, I literally left a life that would've been pretty darn successful in the city to move to a small town for the man I fell in love with, and now . . ."

"Now," I said, putting my arm around her shoulder, "you have a very successful small business in that small town, and you've raised two kids mostly by yourself. It takes a brave person to do all that."

"Maybe." She lifted her head and stared off into the trees that lined our property. "But I could be braver . . . with my art and with . . . dating. You know, putting myself out there." She whipped her attention back to me. "But don't tell Nona I said that."

I made a zipper motion across my lips and smiled. "I get it. Letting yourself feel things, dating—even fake dating—is exhausting, Mom."

"Tell me about it."

We both laughed as the clock tower chimed, and then a new thought sparked inside of me.

"Hey, do you want to be a part of my Christmas wish?" I asked her. "You know how I always make one of those instead of a New Year's resolution—"

"Because 'Christmas wishes involve faith and goodwill'?" Mom added, smiling. "Sure, I'd love to. What's your wish this year?"

I turned toward her, tucking one of my legs under the other. "To be hopeful and open for love," I said. "For both of us."

She tucked the blanket a bit tighter around us and then raised her mug. "For love."

I gently clinked my mug against hers. "For love."

The front door opened, and Leo popped his head out, his bed hair sticking up in eighty different directions. "You guys good now? Do I need to set off the smoke alarm?"

"No," we both said before our laughter filled the quiet morning.

Mom stayed home and made sugar cookies with Leo and me while helping do an inventory of everything I had bought so far for Italy. We all ate far too much cookie dough while downing gallons (probably) of hot chocolate, and even though I knew we'd crash hard later, it was still one of the best mornings we'd had in a long time.

After stuffing our faces with a pizza covered in artichokes and meatballs for lunch—a family favorite inspired by Dad—the three of us snuggled under blankets in the den and put on *Santa Claus Is Comin' to Town*. Leo fell asleep within minutes, and Mom followed suit after taking a phone call from Travis Bailey. But as I was enjoying the wedding between Kris and Jessica, a knock sounded from our front door.

I hit pause and carefully peeled back the blanket, sliding my feet into slippers and heading toward the front of the house. A second later, I opened the door and took a sharp inhale.

For one, because despite the partly cloudy sky, the air outside had turned frigid.

And two, because of the person standing in front of me.

"James," I said, blinking a few times to make sure my eyes weren't lying. "What are you doing here?"

"Uh, currently?" He shifted his weight back and forth on his feet. "Freezing, but—"

"Oh my gosh, I'm sorry." I stepped to the side and opened the door wider. "Come in."

"Thanks." He stomped his feet on the mat and stepped inside, taking off his hat. "No offense, but your weather here kinda sucks. I feel like I've seen a few seasons in one day."

I chuckled as I closed the door. "Yeah, that's common."

James pursed his lips as he nodded. "Oh, um, the real reason I came by was to give you something . . ." He unzipped his coat and reached into an inside pocket.

"James, you didn't have to—"

"I *know*, but I came across it in DC and . . ." He pulled out a snow globe and handed it to me. "It had your name written all over it."

I blinked back tears and slowly twirled the globe around.

Inside was the final scene from *It's a Wonderful Life* of the Bailey family in front of their Christmas tree, and the inscription on its base was the quote from Clarence: "No man is a failure who has friends."

"Turn the key on the back," James said.

I cranked it until it couldn't go any further and let go. The closing song from the movie, "Auld Lang Syne," filled the space between us as the tears finally fell down my cheeks.

"It's perfect," I said, looking up at him.

He smiled and stepped forward. "I know we came together as part of a greater plot, and I know I kinda screwed up when I fell for you—"

"James . . ."

"*But* I realized I didn't fail. We didn't fail." He pointed to the inscription. "Because at least I got a friend out of it." He shrugged as his own eyes turned misty. "I don't have many of those."

I sniffed and threw my arms around him, hugging him tightly around his waist. "Well, you've got one now and forever, James Bailey."

He rested his chin on top of my messy hair. "So, what now?"

I stepped back. "What do you mean?"

"Operation Ho Ho Humbug." He crossed his arms. "What's our next move?"

I blinked. "You still want to go through with it?"

"Of course." He cocked his head. "My dad came home last night humming Christmas songs after working on those candle things with you, and then he asked if I wanted to go for a drive to look at lights like we used to. He even left his phone *behind* at the B&B." He raised his eyebrows. "I'd say whatever you're doing is working."

He left his phone behind?

Holy crap. It's a Christmas miracle.

I spun the snow globe a couple times in my hands. "I mean, we really only have two events left: the caroling tomorrow night, and the, um . . . Mistletoe Masquerade the following evening."

"Ouch." James put a hand to his chest. "That's still fresh."

I frowned. "I'm sorry—"

"Stop." He grinned and hit my shoulder. "It's good. Okay? We're good." He straightened himself up and then opened the front door. "I'll see you tomorrow for the caroling, then. And in the meantime, I'll think of something else, too."

"Thank you, James." I held up the globe and leaned on my front door as he stepped onto the porch. "For, um . . . everything."

"Don't thank me yet." He tugged his hat over his head. "We've still got a Market to save."

Chapter Twenty-Nine

"Just like honesty needs a little plus, fate needs a little push."

—WHITE CHRISTMAS

Later that same day as the sun hung low in the sky, I stood nervously on a ladder held by Nico, while stringing up more lights outside of Bud and Bloom. Apparently, he had told his boss, Peggy, that her store was the only one lacking in the "decoration department." One trip to Hal's Hardware later, and she had put Nico to work on fixing the place. He didn't mind, though. Something inside the store had been making him sneeze more than usual, so he preferred being outside anyway.

I stretched and clicked the staple gun against the icicle lights, but no staple came out. "I'm empty," I called down to Nico, handing him the gun.

"I'll go ask Peggy for more. Back in a sec." Nico stepped around the ladder and went inside the shop, the bell sounding on his way in.

A flash of red across the street caught my eye, and my stomach somersaulted as Sam parked his truck outside of the church. He stepped out and waved to someone down the road before pulling on a pair of work gloves, his red hair fluttering in the wind.

My Christmas wish came floating back to me: *Hope for love.*

And before I could talk myself out of it, I stepped down from the ladder and hurried across the street.

Did I know what I was going to say to him?

Nope.

But I had to say something.

He was crouched down in the back of the truck when I arrived and jumped as I put my hands on the open tailgate.

"Hi!" I blurted, almost barking. *Nice one, G.* "Um, what are you doing?"

Sam motioned to the bed of fresh garland around him. "Just dropping these off for Pastor Aaron. He ordered more to go in front of the stained glass windows. I think he's trying to boost spirits however he can."

"Right." I paused and drummed my hands on the tailgate.

Maybe I should've rehearsed before coming over here . . .

"Are you helping Nona out with more caroling stuff?" He came to the tailgate and sat down, his long legs almost reaching the pavement.

I pointed across the street. "No. Just Nico with some Christmas decorations."

"Bit late for that," Sam said, looking at the unfinished job.

"Well, Nico opened his big mouth and guilt-tripped Peggy about her shop needing more Christmas cheer, so . . ."

"Sounds like something Nico would do." Sam chuckled.

"Totally." I laughed, too, and looked down at my thumbs till the words found me. "Sam, about that night, when we—"

"Ate too many Italian wedding cookies and candy canes?" he mused.

I tilted my head. "Actually, you *always* eat too many candy canes."

"I know, and yet . . ." He paused and took one out of his coat pocket, unwrapping some of it before sticking it in his mouth. "I just can't stop."

"Ha ha." I hit his leg. "No, um, I was going to say when we went outside in the snow and . . ."

"Kissed." He took a deep breath in and held it, watching me.

"Right." I swallowed. "I was . . . well, I was wondering if"—*just say it*—"if you meant what you said about me being 'it' for you." I exhaled loudly.

There.

That wasn't so bad.

Other than the fact that my legs are shaking like crazy and I'm regretting that second coffee this morning . . .

Sam took the candy cane out of his mouth and leaned forward, resting his elbows on his knees. "I meant it, but you've got this thing with James—"

"I don't." I swallowed. "I mean, we're still trying to win over his dad, but not by fake dating or, um, real dating."

His eyebrows scrunched together. "What about the Mistletoe Masquerade?"

"I told him I couldn't go with him." I stepped closer to Sam. "That it wouldn't be fair to him." *Because I choose you.*

Sam nodded and looked down like he was deep in thought. "I can't believe I'm asking this, but is he okay? He . . . he's a pretty good guy."

"He is, and yeah, he's okay. We're going to be friends." I smiled. "I think he needs a good one."

Sam smiled, too. "Well, then he's lucky to have you. I know I am."

Something tightened in my throat at those words, and it hurt to swallow over it. "So, we're . . . friends?"

"Of course." He straightened up. "We always will be."

"But—"

"I waited a really long time to tell you all that, Gianna. Too long." Sam hopped off the tailgate. "But—"

"But?" The cold air around me grew still.

He sighed and put his hands into his pockets. "You're going to Italy in a couple weeks, and then college after that, and I'll be here . . ."

My mind scrambled for a response, any response that would help tell him, show him, that it didn't matter where I was going or for how long.

All that mattered was that I wanted to be with him.

But what came out was a very small "Okay."

He took my hand and rubbed his calloused thumb over my claddagh ring. "I just . . . I need some time to think about this."

The soreness in my throat turned thick, but I gave him a small smile, and said, "I understand."

The sun peeked out from behind the clouds as he let go, casting most of the snow-lined street in sparkling light.

I pointed over my shoulder. "I better get back over there before Nico decides he needs a turn on the ladder. Can't have a repeat of three years ago."

Sam laughed. "No. Your Aunt Helen would kill him if he broke another bone."

I gave an awkward half wave and started to make the trek back across the street. And despite feeling a little sad that Sam and I couldn't immediately pick up with where we left off on that snowy night, part of me did feel lighter, even hopeful.

Because Sam didn't regret kissing me.

And he had meant what he said the night that he did.

Sam could honestly take all the time he needed to figure things out.

Because Christmas wishes, unlike New Year's resolutions, didn't have an expiration date.

After dinner at Nona's, I stayed up late, looking at virtual tours and reading food blogs for the best places to go in Rome. I should've been asleep, but I was waiting for Mom to come back from her big date with Mr. Bailey. He'd apparently walked to her studio while I was busy helping Nico and asked her out to dinner. No pushing or scheming from Nona or anyone else in town either.

James had even texted me after his dad had left the B&B for their date that he was "grinning like a fool."

Maybe I wasn't the only one who would get her Christmas wish?

As I stood staring at my old luggage, wondering if I should try to bring an empty duffle for food and souvenirs, the front door opened and closed followed by the familiar *ting* of keys dropping into the tin.

I opened my door and tiptoed in front of Leo's room before I started down the stairs, slowing as the fridge door slammed shut when I neared the bottom.

"What is the matter, Alice?" Nona asked in the kitchen. She had insisted on staying and cooking dinner for Leo and me because "boxed macaroni and cheese is *not* a real meal." Leo had taken great offense to that and quoted *Home Alone*, saying it was "highly nutritious," but Nona waved him away and made us pasta e fagioli.

I rested my hand on the banister and peered around the corner as Mom sank into a chair and groaned, a pint of Ben & Jerry's in hand.

Uh-oh.

It's never a good sign when the pints come out.

"Was it not a nice time?" Nona asked, laying her hand gently on Mom's.

"Actually, it was, at first." Mom scooped out a large spoonful of ice cream. "Travis is surprisingly funny." She took a bite and wedged the spoon back in the pint.

"Is he?" Nona sat back. "Well, that's good to hear."

"Yeah." Mom stared at the spoon as she pushed the end of it back and forth. "We talked about art and photography, and it was going pretty well until . . . his phone rang."

Ugh.

Maybe I could get James to toss that stupid thing into the creek tomorrow?

Nona didn't say anything but just sipped whatever was in her mug and waited for Mom to continue.

"He went to silence it, but not before I saw the name on the caller ID." Mom took another spoonful and spoke, her voice a little muffled by it. "Legacy Construction Group."

Wait.

A construction group?

Nona lowered her mug. "I see."

Mom nodded and leaned back in her chair, crossing her arms over her chest. "I mean, I couldn't pretend I didn't see it, so I asked him about it, and he got all defensive but then let slip that they were coming tomorrow to do a quick survey of the property, but that it didn't mean anything—"

"Scemo," Nona muttered.

Agreed, Nona. He's a total fool.

"And then he said he had other ideas about how to pay off

the back taxes, and, Mom, you should've heard this idea." My mom stood up and began pacing and talking with her hands. "It was ridiculous. I mean, there's just no way it would work."

But Nona perked up. "Now, wait. What was the plan—"

"So, I told him so, and then he had the *audacity* to say that I was just too scared to take risks."

Well . . .

"Me?" Mom stopped and scoffed. "Please. I'm an artist. Every time I put my work on display for the public, I take risks. Right?"

Nona nodded. "Right, but—"

"Anyway, by then the tiramisu came out, but I wasn't hungry anymore, so I told him I had a headache, and I left."

"Well, we both know my tiramisu is better anyway," Nona mused.

"True." Mom chuckled and sank back into her chair before she picked up the ice cream spoon again. "You're wrong, though . . . *I* was the fool in this scenario."

Nona laid her hand back on Mom's. "You took a chance, you went on a date for the first time in . . . what, two years? That makes you the opposite of a fool."

Mom put the spoon back in the pint to wipe her eye. "What do we tell Gianna, the others, about that construction group? It'll completely ruin their Christmas."

Oh, Mom.

Despite having her heart broken on a date, she was still worried about me and everyone else.

Nona took a deep breath and patted Mom's hand before letting go. "We tell them nothing because it may, in fact, be nothing, darling."

Mom sniffed. "But we will need to start looking at other spaces to rent . . . not that there are any, who knows if I'll ever find a place with that kind of light, and The Market—"

"Will be the place it needs to be this Christmas," Nona said, her voice gentle. "And if it's the last Christmas for our beloved Market, well then, we will make it a great one. But for now, I'd like to hear more about this ridicola idea of his." She rose and poured herself more water from the kettle before the two of them went into the den.

I used the railing to creep back up the stairs to my room, my knees too wobbly to walk on their own now as my mind spiraled. I wanted to text James to ask him if he knew what was going on, but I doubted his father confided with anyone.

James had seemed so sure that his dad had changed.

Even I was fooled into believing it.

So, what now?

I thought about texting Jo or Sam, but what then?

How did you tell your best friends that your home and so many lives were about to be changed forever?

I fell onto my bed and pushed my face against one of my pillows as the tears finally came.

So much for Christmas wishes.

Chapter Thirty

"Nothing like Christmas to help a family rediscover its magic."

—A VERY JONAS CHRISTMAS MOVIE

The family group chat buzzed constantly the next day with sightings and "covert photos"—courtesy of Marco—of Mr. Bailey and the new outsiders lurking around town with their clipboards and iPads. Jo said the "suits" even ordered their lattes extra hot, which was not only dangerous for the baristas to make, but it also completely ruined the coffee.

Jerks.

With only one day left till Christmas and just a few short ones till we found out what Mr. Bailey planned to do with the estate of The Market, the entire town seemed on edge. Sure, we sang songs like elves while we worked and continued to get things ready for our final two events of the season, but underneath the holly jolliness of it lingered one of the worst things to have in your heart, especially during Christmas.

Doubt.

Everyone who had a vendor stand in The Market passed the real estate section of the local newspaper back and forth among them, hoping someone would spot a cheap piece of property another person had overlooked. Dana from Creek Gems and Victoria from Glass Works started discussing what their future shared store could look like, but neither had enough money to put down. It was the same for Scott of Whispering Wicks Candles and Ms. Louisa's Cozy Covers businesses. No one in Mullings Creek had realized just how affordable their rent was, how little Mr. Paxton charged them to use the space, until he was gone.

Even Nona's traditional Feast of the Seven Fishes—a meal that was normally pretty tame except for that one time when Nico chased Bianca around with the baccalà till she punched him in the nose—felt different.

Marco didn't make poop piles with chocolate chips near the animals in Nona's nativity.

Aunt Helen forgot to buy the torrone.

And Mom almost burned the panettone.

Sure, several conversations were still happening at once in her kitchen as most of us went back for another helping of the linguine with clam sauce, but they were all about the uncertain future. Mom and Aunt Helen scrolled through property listings while they ate, but nothing had the right kind of light that Mom claimed she needed. Bianca attempted a positive spin, chiming in with different "fun" and "new" stores that could bring in even more business to our town, but Nico shut her down when he mentioned that more business meant more traffic and stoplights—both of which Bianca hated.

When the noise became a bit overwhelming, I joined Leo in front of the living room fireplace. The front door opened and Nona came inside, tucking her phone back in her sweater pocket, my mom following closely behind her.

"Where did you two go?" I asked them as they stepped out of their boots. I didn't even remember them leaving.

"Just outside to take a call and talk about a couple of things." Nona smoothed her hair and walked back toward the kitchen.

"Mrs. Holt needed to run over some details before the caroling tonight." Mom winked at us and then followed Nona.

I took another bite of my lasagna—the melted mozzarella and spinach portions perfect, as usual—and checked the time, frowning.

Hold up.

That couldn't be right.

It was Christmas Eve. Sam's family always went to church before the caroling. And his mom would definitely not take phone calls during church.

My Uncle Gabe popped his head into the living room. "You two up for Spades?"

Leo and I both stood, but I put my hand on his arm. "If it gets too loud in there, just tap my leg with your foot a few times under the table, okay? I'll make an excuse to leave, and you can come with me."

"Next year is going to suck, isn't it?" His bottom lip trembled. "Everything is changing."

I took a breath and swallowed over the ache in my throat. "It'll be great. You're going to try new things, remember? You said you wanted to learn how to play *Magic: The Gathering* with Sam and Nico so you could join the club after school." I took his hand. "Change can be a good thing."

That's rich coming from me.

Leo sniffed.

"Nico told me he's already building you decks." I ruffled his hair. "And you're going to help Mom out with her new location and make sure she remembers that coffee is not a breakfast food and that she has to pack herself a lunch."

Of course, then she will actually have to remember to stop working and eat said lunch.

"But . . . Trent said middle school is horrible, Gianna." He scuffed one of his socked feet back and forth on the floor.

"Screw Trent. It's not that bad." I set my plate on the nearest end table. "You just need to find your people. And you will. You've already signed up for band, and James told me music kids are the best kids."

"He did?" He looked up.

"Mm-hmm." I grinned. "But on the flip side, *if* anyone gives you trouble, it'll only happen once, because we both know Marco and Nico will scare the crap out of them."

He laughed before I gently pulled him in for a hug. "I won't be far, and I promise to come home as often as I can, okay?" I pulled back and held up my pinkie finger, waiting.

He wiped his eyes and looped his pinkie around mine.

An hour later, I was hopelessly losing while Leo did surprisingly well, having successfully gone "low" in the last hand. Nico kept checking Leo's lap under the table, convinced that somehow my eleven-year-old brother was clever enough to cheat an entire table of adults. Nona and Aunt Helen took turns smacking the back of Nico's head to get him to back off while Uncle Gabe hummed "Eh Cumpari"—my Papa's favorite song—on repeat.

I sat back and smiled.

What a chaotic but loveable mess they all were.

Okay, yeah, they were loud and meddlesome.

And yes, they were over-the-top.

But like James had said, they were mine.

And I knew that no matter where I went or what I did, the Mancinis would have my back, and I would have theirs.

Uncle Gabe took a turn shuffling and dealing the next hand, and the noise quieted a bit. Leo drew his feet under him before reaching for another slice of panettone in the middle of the table. "Nona, can you tell us the story about your grandparents immigrating to the United States? The one where they got lost in the city?"

Bianca and I smiled at each other across the table. Then she pushed her chair back to pour herself another cup of coffee. How she could have caffeine this late and not be wired all night was a mystery to me.

"Aren't you tired of that story, cuoricino?" Nona asked, one eyebrow raised higher than the other.

Leo shook his head. "It's tradition."

The kid had a point.

Nona chuckled and then settled back in her seat as Uncle Gabe finished dealing the cards, even though he knew none of us would touch our hands yet. This was a story we had heard every Christmas Eve, but it never got old. My great-grandparents apparently fell in love in a small town north of Rome despite both of them being betrothed to others. They decided to run away to America so they could start a new life together. But when they got off the boat at Ellis Island, the crowds were too big, and they got separated.

According to Nona, her parents spent weeks in New York City trying to find each other, but it wasn't until Christmas Eve that they finally did. Cold and weary, they attended the same small church vigil service on the Hudson River. And the rest was, well, history.

"Anime gemelle," Nona said as she finished her story and picked up her hand.

"Soulmates," Bianca whispered over the top of her coffee cup.

Leo picked up his hand and began to sort his cards. "Nona, can a friend also be a soulmate?"

"Absolutely." Nona looked at me, the corner of her mouth drawing up in the smallest of knowing smiles. I flashed back to the last game of Scrabble that Sam and I had played, to his final word, and to the feelings I hoped he still carried in his heart.

Later that evening, soft snowflakes fell from the dark, moonless sky as I changed into my favorite red cable-knit sweater. My gaze trailed over the piles of notes on my desk and the maps that hung above it.

How was it already Christmas tomorrow?

It seemed only yesterday I was sitting in this very room watching *Meet Me in St. Louis* when the notification came in about my acceptance to the study abroad program. So much had happened over the last month.

We lost Mr. Paxton.

The Baileys came to Mullings Creek.

The fake-dating plan with James that turned to real feelings.

Falling for my best friend.

I trailed my hands down the beaded lacy top of my gown for tomorrow's Mistletoe Masquerade.

It really was the most beautiful dress I had ever seen.

Sam may not have given me an answer about whether or not he'd go.

Or what he'd decide about us.

But maybe the reason Christmas shone so brightly was because of the hope it carried with it.

And maybe, just maybe, Sam would find it in his heart to go.

To come to that dance.

For me.

After all, if Bob could surprise Betty at that dinner club while she wore that freaking incredible dress, maybe it could happen for me?

My entire family walked in silence toward Town Hall, where we'd pick up our candles before congregating with the rest of town at the big Christmas tree. The glow of the lit garland and wreaths now dusted with fresh snow around the light poles lining Mistletoe Lane came into view, and I smiled. I couldn't remember the last time it snowed for the annual caroling, but it sure did make everything more magical.

We all took turns giving hugs and saying hello to neighbors and friends as we picked up our candles and programs.

Standing at the tree, minutes before we were about to begin, I caught Sam walking up with his dad and Gram. Gram's arm was looped through Sam's, and my heart squeezed as he helped her step over the curb to join the group. Like our family, his wore red. The entire town wore either red or green except for the local church choir, who wore white robes.

Our eyes caught across the crowd as Gram whispered something in his ear, and he gave me a small nod, a smile pulling at the corner of his mouth.

I smiled back and lifted my candle in hello before he turned his attention back to Gram.

A moment later, the clock tower chimed, and the crowd

parted for what I assumed was Mayor Moore to get things started. But it was the Baileys who came forward. Both of them wore dark green, and James's signature smile slowly vanished as he caught on to the obvious tension and change of atmosphere at their arrival.

Someone suddenly shouted, "Why are they here?" and a few more voices rose up in agreement, making their frustrations known.

But Nona quickly stepped forward and put her arm through Mr. Bailey's. The crowd immediately hushed at her serious stare.

"Anyone who is in Mullings Creek may go caroling," she called out, her posture straightening. "Tradition is tradition, and these two are a part of ours now."

Some grumbles could be heard throughout the group, but most everyone took her words to heart and stayed quiet.

Mayor Moore then appeared and carefully stepped onto the bench closest to the Christmas tree, clearing his throat. "Ladies and gentlemen, it's hard to believe we've already arrived at our annual caroling on Christmas Eve, but here we are." He paused and lifted his hands. "This has been one of our most eventful and beautiful Christmas seasons yet, and it's because of all of you, of your heart and hard work, and I know I speak for everyone here when I say: Thank you."

Several people clapped but most looked around wistfully, probably wondering the same thing I was.

How different will this be next year?

"So, let's get the evening started, shall we?" Mayor Moore pointed toward Mistletoe Lane where Hal stood waiting. The town counted down from "five," and when we reached "one," all the lights decorating the town went out, plunging the street in darkness except for our candles and the tree.

As was tradition, everyone in Mullings Creek turned off lights in their homes and businesses. Some said it looked eerie, almost ghostly, but I always thought the moving candlelight looked beautiful, angelic, against the dark night.

A moment later, Mrs. Holt played a tuning pitch, signaling the choir to begin their set with the traditional "O Holy Night." Once the choir took their first steps down Mistletoe Lane, the rest of us followed, singing softly and proudly along.

When we rounded Elm Street, passing the B&B, the song changed to "Silent Night" and I tucked my paper away, knowing full well I didn't need the lyrics.

Leo took my pinkie with his free hand and squeezed it as Mom put her arm around my shoulders. "Per tuo padre," she whispered.

My throat tightened.

For your father.

"Silent Night" had been Dad's favorite. In all the years I watched him sing it, he never could make it through without crying.

And now none of us could either.

As the snow picked up a little, and we looped through the park, I snuck a glance over at James and Mr. Bailey. James sang loudly and proudly while Mr. Bailey's mouth moved slower, his voice barely audible.

But he was singing.

After I wiped my cheeks for the tenth time, I caught Sam raising his candle and making a circling motion.

What in the–

His mother, several yards away, repeated the gesture with her candle before stopping and turning around to face the choir. Hands stretched outward, she conducted four counts, and then the choir came in slowly and softly with harmonized *ahhs*.

Oh, right!

Several people near us held their candles closer to their programs, searching for this new song, but I knew they wouldn't find it.

Because it was meant to be a surprise.

As the lyrics of "In the Bleak Midwinter" filled the snow-dappled air around us, Mr. Bailey stepped around the group, entranced, toward Mrs. Holt and the choir, James at his side. Neither of them moved as the choir continued through the song.

By the second verse, everyone had quietly backed away from the Baileys to give them some space.

And when the choir faded out in the final bars to let Mrs.

Holt sing the last phrase alone, no one breathed or moved. Even the falling snow seemed to stand still.

The singing stopped.

But no one applauded.

Like somehow we all knew that this moment was just too precious and reverent for it.

My throat grew thick as Mr. Bailey walked slowly toward Mrs. Holt, his cheeks now damp with tears. He sniffed, and said in a quiet voice, "Thank you."

Mrs. Holt rested a hand on his shoulder and smiled warmly.

I could feel Sam's eyes on me from across the crowd, and I found his in an instant.

"Thank you," I mouthed silently.

He dipped his chin with a single nod.

A little while later, we completed the route and ended up back at the Christmas tree. The mood had audibly changed as the crowd belted "We Wish You a Merry Christmas." When the final notes were sung, everyone clapped and cheered. Mayor Moore thanked everyone for coming, but before the group could disperse, two loud barks echoed through the air. The crowd parted once more, this time for Sandy, still wearing her red crocheted hat. She trotted right up to Mr. Bailey and sat expectantly, something red clutched between her teeth.

I walked toward her just as she lifted a paw toward Mr. Bailey, who smiled and rubbed her head. "Whatcha got there, girl?" he asked.

She lowered her paw and opened her mouth, the red fabric falling into his hand.

Mr. Bailey straightened as he turned the scarf over into his hands, and then he froze. "I . . . I don't understand," he said, his voice soft. "Where did you find this?" He looked down at Sandy, who sat happily panting and wagging her small screwed tail.

"What is it, Dad?" James asked as I moved to stand next to him.

Mr. Bailey put a hand in front of his mouth and blinked several times before he turned the scarf around so James could see. "It . . . This belonged to my father . . . your grandfather."

"That was Granddad's?" James leaned in for a better look. "How did it end up here?"

Mr. Bailey looked up thoughtfully into the snowfall and then softly chuckled. "I had almost forgotten." He brought his focus back to James. "Your grandfather gave it to Mr. Paxton many years ago on one of his visits here. He told me that Mr. Paxton needed it more than he did."

Mr. Bailey smiled and pointed to the golden letters stitched near the fringe as the crowd drew closer. "Do you see the embroidery here? Those are his initials, but it's this phrase here underneath that I don't recognize."

James gently took the scarf and showed it to me as he read aloud. "The Stewards? Who are they?"

And then realization draped itself over me like a warm blanket on a cold night.

Of course.

The framed picture of my and Sam's grandfathers.

The old baseball card of Hal's.

The compass, which I just now remembered belonged to Ann's grandmother, and it used to sit on the counter near Ann's register in the bookstore.

It all made sense now.

I gently took the scarf from James. "They were a group of people from Mullings Creek. They called themselves the Stewards because they felt called to protect our town and swore that they would always make sure that whatever happened here was for the good of all of us." I paused and looked around me at the crowd, several of whom were nodding, having heard this story before. "Many of us had family members in that group a long time ago."

Sandy barked, and I smiled down at her before giving the scarf back to Mr. Bailey. "Mr. Paxton was a Steward. Maybe he hoped you'd come back one day, and that you could be one, too," I said.

James beamed as his father took the scarf and carefully wrapped it around his neck.

"I'm honored you thought of me," he said to Sandy, patting her head before his now misty eyes scanned the quiet crowd around him. "Thank you for allowing us to be a part of this special tradition. This evening was . . ." He laid his hand on his scarf for a moment, swallowing hard. "This evening was one I will always remember." And with that, he turned away and began walking back toward the B&B.

James looked at me wide-eyed and held up his crossed fingers before he followed him.

"Did we just witness a Christmas miracle?" Leo asked, suddenly appearing at my side.

"Maybe, bud." I smiled when the lights on Mistletoe Lane flickered back on, revealing Mr. Bailey with his arm around his son's shoulders, now walking side by side in a swirl of snow flurries.

Maybe we did.

Chapter Thirty-One

"We could be happy anywhere as long as we're together."

—MEET ME IN ST. LOUIS

Normally, I helped decorate and set up for the Mistletoe Masquerade, even though I never went to it, after celebrating Christmas with my family, but this year Jo had ordered me to put my phone on Do Not Disturb so I could actually enjoy my day. And I had. Mom and Nona had surprised me with a new set of luggage that I promptly started to pack, and Leo had spent most of his day finding things he could look at under his new microscope. It was a day filled with laughter and a marathon of Christmas movies before Jo came over to get ready for the dance.

We blasted our favorite playlists in my room while doing our makeup as Bianca did our hair. Jo's gown was stunning, a long-sleeved off-the-shoulder deep midnight-blue sheath dress with a small, glittery belt of snowflakes. Though I didn't think it possible, I loved my dress even more now than when I first saw it. When I spun around in front of my full-length mirror and ran my hands over the chiffon, I did feel as pretty and as powerful as Betty in *White Christmas*.

Mom, Nona, and Jo's dads teared up when we made our grand entrances down the stairs, but before we posed for prom-style pictures, Nona said, "I believe you're missing something, Gianna." She smiled and handed me a small gift bag under the tree, and wrapped delicately inside the tissue paper was the prettiest mask I had ever seen.

Black with red outlines meant to look like lace, it framed my eyes perfectly, but my favorite part was the delicate red-laced poinsettia on the top right corner, which had a tiny pop of green-laced leaves behind it. I hugged Nona tightly before slipping the mask on and standing next to Jo, now donning a mask of her own, dark blue with intricate metalwork meant to resemble lace.

Bianca and the rest of my cousins, aunts, and uncles had already left by the time we stepped outside into the cool, damp air. I lifted my face to the cloudy sky and breathed in the familiar smell of earth mixed with the sharpness of the cold. Maybe we would actually get snow *on* Christmas this year?

The live band could be heard from the street as we pulled up and parked moments later, but while the rest of my family and Jo's seemed anxious to get inside, I lingered at the main entrance of The Market, nerves twisting knots in my stomach.

Would tonight be the night we heard Mr. Bailey's decision?

Would Sam come?

And if he did, would he finally tell me how he felt?

How would he want to leave things between us before I left for Italy?

Nona appeared at my side and pressed her gloved hand against my back. "Coraggio," she whispered to me.

Courage.

Right.

I steeled myself as she stepped forward and opened the barn doors for me, gasping as I entered behind her.

White chiffon curtains draped with dangling fairy lights and topped with fresh garland covered every wall. Two large nutcracker statues framed the stage where a band was playing in front of a new Christmas tree, twice the size of the other two, decorated with red and gold baubles of varying sizes. A few more trees were scattered throughout the room, each with white lights and varying colors of ribboned bows or candied chains. A candy-cane-swirled tablecloth lay draped over each round table, and the surrounding chairs were covered with red velvet tied in the back by a sprig of mistletoe. Every table had a different nutcracker centerpiece, each nestled in a wreath that matched its color scheme.

Aunt Sofia hurried over and held her arms out. "Well? What do you think?"

I shook my head in wonder. "I think it's the most beautiful Mistletoe Masquerade I've ever seen."

A beautiful way to say goodbye to The Market.

If this did end up being a goodbye.

"Oh, good!" She clapped her hands together before she gave me a quick hug. "And you my dear . . ." She stepped back to look at my gown. "Are absolutely stunning. Red is definitely your color."

"Thank you." I ran my hands through the loose curls of my updo, grateful that Bianca didn't go overboard with the hair spray.

With no sign of Sam yet, I decided to drown my sorrows in punch, pouring myself a cup as James walked up. He wore a light gray suit and green tie that matched the green and white checkered mask around his eyes. "Is it spiked?" he asked, pointing to the punch.

"Not yet," I said, taking a sip of the cranberry mix. "But my Uncle Rick has been known to doctor it up in the later hours."

He chuckled before he poured himself a glass. "Noted."

The two of us stood there quietly while watching others work their way out to the dance floor. "By the way," I said, "I've made a list of my favorite Christmas movies."

"Your top ten?" His jaw dropped. "No way."

I nodded. "Yep. I already emailed it to you. Consider it your homework before next Christmas."

He smiled as he sipped his punch. "That sounds like my kind of homework. Did you include *Lord of the Rings*?"

I made a face and hit his shoulder.

He sighed. "Disappointing."

"James . . ." I swallowed over a lump that had formed in my

throat, my chest aching a bit. "I really am sorry for hurting you. If things were different, if—"

"Gianna." He held up a hand and turned to me. "I don't believe in a lot of things, but I do believe things work out exactly the way they're supposed to." He flicked the poinsettia on my mask. "And I consider myself lucky to call you a friend."

I smiled. "It will be nice going to New York next year, knowing that I already have a friend in the city."

"Definitely." He took a sip of his punch. "I'll show you and Jo the best places to get coffee, too. Can't promise it'll be as reasonably priced as Eve's, but I can promise the bagel you get with it will be top-notch."

I was just about to ask him for his favorite spots for breakfast when feedback erupted from the front of the space, startling us. Mr. Bailey, wearing a charcoal-gray suit and an emerald-green tie, now stood center stage, and my heart dropped as he took the microphone out of its stand.

"Good evening, and Merry Christmas!" he said. "I apologize for interrupting this beautiful event. But I know you all are anxious to know the decision regarding The Market."

My mouth turned dry.

Can't he just let us enjoy the night and ruin our New Year's instead?

James gave a quick nod to me before heading to the stage to join his dad as Jo appeared at my side and took my hand.

Mr. Bailey cleared his throat. "First, I'd like to thank all of you for showing me and my son the beauty and real Christmas spirit that comes with a small town such as yours. We loved being a part of your Holly Days and your Reindeer Games." He paused and looked around the room, stopping when he saw me. "But as much as I enjoy good competition, it was in the smaller moments that I realized just how special this place is."

I swallowed and put my free hand on my rolling stomach, reminding myself to breathe.

"I became a lawyer to help people, but somewhere along the way, I had forgotten what that meant . . . what a real community, a real family, looked like." He reached into his back pocket and pulled out the red scarf Sandy had given him yesterday evening.

He still carried it.

Don't get your hopes up yet, G.

It could mean nothing.

"My father believed in this town, in what it stood for, and although he and I didn't agree on much, and although I may not see everything as clearly as he once did, I know now that I don't have to *see* something in order to *believe* in it," he continued.

Wait.

Jo and I exchanged a quick glance.

What is he saying?

"So, I have some good news for you." Mr. Bailey smiled.

"Thanks to a very talented local artist, the back taxes on this Market have been paid off."

My jaw dropped as the crowd gasped in unison, and I searched the room for any sign as to who it may be, but in my heart I knew.

Did she . . . did she actually do it?

"And once that was handled, a very . . . passionate buyer stepped forward and offered a price that the court and I just couldn't refuse," Mr. Bailey added.

So, someone did buy it.

One of those stiff-suit guys?

Mr. Bailey placed the microphone back into its stand and motioned toward the side of the stage where a very familiar figure was making her way up the stairs. "Ladies and gentlemen of Mullings Creek, I'd like to introduce the new owner of The Market, Ms. Silvia Mancini."

Nona?!

Chairs slid back as people jumped up, cheering and whistling wildly. Nona took her spot center stage, giving a small wave while she beamed at all of us. Once she stepped toward the microphone, the applause died down.

"My dear Enzo and I had plans to travel the world, but sometimes plans change, life changes, and we have a choice on whether or not to change with it." She paused and looked down and away for a moment before continuing. "My family is here. My heart is here. And I can think of no better use of that money we had saved than to keep this place, our beloved Market, here too."

More applause and cheers rippled through the crowd, several of whom now wiped their eyes before Nona made her way back down the stairs.

Jo and I turned to each other at the same time.

"Did that really just happen?" I asked her.

She nodded, the feathers on her mask shaking. "You did it, Gianna."

I looked around at everyone in their beautiful formal wear and masks. Phineas stood with Eve near the big punch bowl and was laughing at something she had said. Hal and his son chatted with Sheriff Kingston near the stairs to Mom's studio. And Ann stood with an earbud in next to Levi, who had the other one and was showing her something on his phone. Most of the townspeople who had stands at The Market were now hurrying over to each other's tables, their faces twinkling with hope.

"No," I said to Jo, my eyes filling with tears. "*We* did it."

James convinced his dad to make a gingerbread house and play along with the games.

Jo made an amazing candy cane scavenger hunt.

The Holts donated more trees and poinsettias to small businesses than in years past.

The choir learned a new song to honor the Baileys.

Mullings Creek had shone brighter this Christmas than it ever had before because we were a family.

And families took care of their own.

Mom walked over in her red long-sleeved lace gown, sheepishly grinning before I threw my arms around her, her iris earring cool against my cheek. "I'm so, so proud of you," I whispered.

"I have no idea what you're referring to." She waved me off but then winked. "I'll fill you in later."

Mr. Bailey suddenly appeared at my side and cleared his throat. "Excuse me, Gianna. But would you mind if I asked your mother to dance?"

I smiled at her, and then said, "Not at all, sir."

She took his arm, and then the two of them walked quietly toward the stage, where he spun her around before they danced to "White Christmas."

Looks like Mom just may get her Christmas wish . . .

I peered around the room, my heart shrinking a bit when I still couldn't find Sam.

Guess the jury's still out on me, though.

James came over with a big grin on his face. "Operation Ho Ho Humbug worked!"

I hugged him, my throat tight, and whispered, "Thank you, James."

For a few minutes, the two of us stood side by side quietly watching our parents dance, and I couldn't help but think about how unpredictable this last month had been. This season was always full of surprises and unexpected wonders, and

James Bailey had been just that for me. Experiencing Christmas in Mullings Creek through the Baileys' eyes was one of the best gifts I could ask for myself—especially before I left.

Because maybe when we think we outgrow a place or a person, what we really needed was the opportunity go back and look at it the way we did the first time.

"Did I ever tell you the story about my eighteenth birthday?" Aunt Sofia appeared at my side, cheeks rosy under her mask.

I looped my arm through hers. "Can't say I've heard that one."

"I danced the entire night under the stars with a total stranger who kissed me at midnight . . ." She sighed wistfully. "And then I never saw him again."

"Really?" James asked.

"That sounds like a movie," I said.

"The best moments in our lives always do." She winked.

And that was when I realized the music had stopped, most everyone had backed up off the dance floor and were now turning to look my way.

"What's going on?" I followed Aunt Sofia's and James's stare to the front of the room and felt the ground tip out from under me.

Sam, dressed in a fitted black suit, red shirt, and white tie, his mask all black except for the tiny green leaves and red dots outlining its edges, crossed the stage and whispered something to the lead singer. Then he looked directly at me, beaming. The quiet butterflies in my stomach stirred awake, swirling and twirling as I took in my handsome best friend who now made his way toward me.

"You know, I don't like to admit it when I'm wrong, but it has to be said." James looked from Sam to me. "Red is definitely your color."

I smiled and fixed his tie. "And green is definitely yours."

"I'll see you around, Gianna." He grinned before setting his glass on the table and giving a small bow and a wink while slowly backing away.

I had honestly dreaded that goodbye for weeks, worried that it would make me feel guilty or empty or numb, but surprisingly, it didn't.

I felt strangely okay about it.

At peace.

The band began to play, and hope bubbled up inside of me because it was my favorite Christmas song, "Have Yourself a Merry Little Christmas."

Sam, his brown eyes sparkling under the white lights, held out his hand. "May I have this dance, Mancini?"

"I thought you didn't dance, Holt." My heart pounded wildly as my fingers, humming with electricity, grazed his.

He smiled and led me out to the empty floor before placing his warm hand on my lower back, his fingers twirling around the ribbon of my corset. "Just had to wait for the right partner."

As he gently spun me around, I laid my head against his chest, smiling as I felt the same racing heartbeat to that of my own. More couples joined us, but their movements were mere blurs in myriad colors. Sam was the only one who appeared clearly to me.

He always had.

"Gianna?" he murmured as the song finished.

I lifted my head, feeling a bit dizzy. "Hmm?"

He took off his mask and then slowly lifted mine over my head before he brushed his thumb over my cheek. "Would you come with me somewhere?"

The snow must've started minutes after my family arrived at the dance because by the time Sam and I arrived at his family's farm, the rows upon rows of Christmas trees lining their property were already covered with beautiful, sparkly white powder.

He opened the first greenhouse door for me, and I gasped.

The benches of red and white poinsettias now glowed magically under the twinkle lights zigzagging back and forth under the arched roof. But it was the sparkling snow streaming down the clear film walls that left me completely speechless.

I was inside my very own snow globe.

And it was the most beautiful thing I had ever seen.

Sam cleared his throat, and I turned around.

In his hands was a stunning wooden globe with hand-painted countries on it.

"Sam, it's . . ." My fingers trailed over the cool, delicate surface. "It's incredible."

"*This* was what I was working on in Shop for months. Your mom painted the countries for me, but . . ." He smiled and spun the globe around, revealing tiny red dots over Europe, South America, and Africa. "I added the extra details."

The same dots I had on my maps in my room.

And yet, not the same.

One of them looked much bigger than the others.

I leaned in closer to find not a dot, but a heart painted just shy of Northern Virginia. "Is that—"

"Mullings Creek?" He nodded. "Yeah."

Tears fell down my cheeks.

"You deserve the world, Gianna." Sam's voice had turned thick with emotion. "You should go everywhere your heart leads you. But I want you to remember that no matter where you go, I will always be right here . . ." He pointed to the heart over our town. "Waiting for you."

I rushed forward just as he set the globe down on the closest bench and wrapped my arms tightly around him. "Thank you, Sam," I whispered. "It's perfect."

And it truly was.

Because the boy who had always been my anchor, my home, had just given me the world, and more importantly, a promise that meant more to me than any gift I'd receive this year or in the years to come.

It didn't matter where I went or how far I'd go or how long I'd be away.

I'd always come home to him.

And he would always *be* home to me.

Sam cleared his throat and then looked up, his eyes now misty and playful.

I laughed as I took in the sprig of green hanging perfectly above us. "Sam Holt," I said, amusement in my voice, "don't tell me you're suddenly a fan of mistletoe?"

He brushed a tear off my cheek. "I mean, it *is* invasive."

"Mm-hmm . . ." I slid my hands over his suit jacket, letting them rest on his neck beneath his snow-dampened ginger hair.

"But it does provide a good home for birds and wildlife."

"Homes for birds are very important." The air between us crackled with energy.

"I can admit . . ." Sam slowly lowered his chin. "I *am* starting to see its advantages."

I grinned, stretching forward onto my toes until our lips finally touched, and everything slowed. Heat pooled in my belly before spreading to my fingers and all the way down to my toes as he pulled me closer and lifted me off the ground.

Kissing Sam Holt felt like many things.

Remarkable.

Wondrous.

But mostly . . . it felt like magic.

The kind of magic most people believed only came at Christmas and left in the New Year.

But I knew better.

If your heart was open to it, the magic of Christmas could last all year long.

And for those lucky enough, maybe even a lifetime.

Gianna's Top Ten Christmas Movies

- *Meet Me in St. Louis*
- *White Christmas*
- *It's a Wonderful Life*
- *Holiday Inn*
- *The Santa Clause*
- *Home Alone*
- *A Charlie Brown Christmas*
- *Miracle on 34th Street*
- *Serendipity*
- *National Lampoon's Christmas Vacation*
- Honorable Mention: *The Lord of the Rings*

Acknowledgments

First, I give thanks and glory to God for his abundant blessings, steadfast love, and grace.

To my dear friend and rock-star literary agent, Ann Rose, thank you for your insight and guidance with navigating this roller coaster called publishing and all its unexpected loops.

To my incredible editor, Dana Leydig, you have my sincerest thanks for allowing me to continue working with you. Your feedback and our conversations about all the fun Christmassy elements made this all the more magical for me to write. I am honored to have you and the team at Viking Children's in my corner.

Many thanks to my cover artist, Jessica Jenkins, for your design that perfectly captures the magic of Mullings Creek, and to the powerhouse team at Penguin Young Readers for getting this holiday romance into the ever-capable hands of librarians, readers, and booksellers.

David, Tommy, and Andy: You are all I ever want for Christmas (other than snow, of course). Love you all so much.

Mom and Dad, thank you for always making our Christmases growing up feel special and for giving me a well-rounded Christmas movie-cation.

To the Millers and Hoffs, your excitement, enthusiasm, and encouragement have truly been the loveliest of twinkle lights for me—thank you!

To the Monaco and Sacco families, thank you for inspiring so many of the Mancini holiday traditions. Buon Natale.

My dear #Bookstagrammers and bookish podcasters: You are the tinsel to my tree and the peppermint to my hot cocoa.

Lastly, to the steadfast Kevin McCallisters of books: librarians. You are not alone in the fight, and I consider myself the luckiest woman to know you and to work alongside you

Photo credit: Chelsea Hartman Photography

CASSIE MILLER

lives in Southwest Virginia with her husband and two boys, where she works as an elementary librarian. When she's not writing or reading and recommending books, she's probably outside on a long walk or watching rom-coms with a large mug of tea. Cassie is also the author of *Meet Me Under the Lights*.

You can follow her on Instagram @CassieMillerWrites.